GRIMDARK FANTASY AUTHOR
LIZABETH PHOENIX

THE
GIFTED
KING

THE GIFTED KING

THE ANCHOR KINGDOM TRILOGY

BOOK ONE

LIZABETH PHOENIX

Published by Phoenix Universe Publications, LLC

PO BOX 44

Rowesville, SC 29133 U.S.A.

www.lizabethphoenix.com

Sensitivity Readers: Kaelin Britt at The Abstract Voyager, Samantha Kassé

Developmental Editor: Jean McConnell at The Word Forager

Copy Editor: Aliyah Golden at Metal Rose Editorial Services

Proofreader: Aliyah Golden at Metal Rose Editorial Services

Formatter: Lizabeth Phoenix

Cover and custom title page designed by GetCovers

Interior Artwork: Falling dragon illustration by vishap.art, mountain illustration by vishap.art, custom footer illustration by The Abstract Voyager, custom scene break illustration and custom flying dragon illustration by Lizabeth Phoenix

Map was created with Inkarnate.com and stock images licensed through Canva

Stock images licensed through Canva

Library of Congress Control Number: 2025912774

Hardback ISBN: 979-8-9990901-0-2

Paperback ISBN: 979-8-9990901-1-9

Ebook ISBN: 979-8-9990901-2-6

Originally published in the United States of America by Phoenix Universe Publications, LLC

For the soul who stood by me.
And for Optimus and Megatron,
the best broken brotherhood of them all.

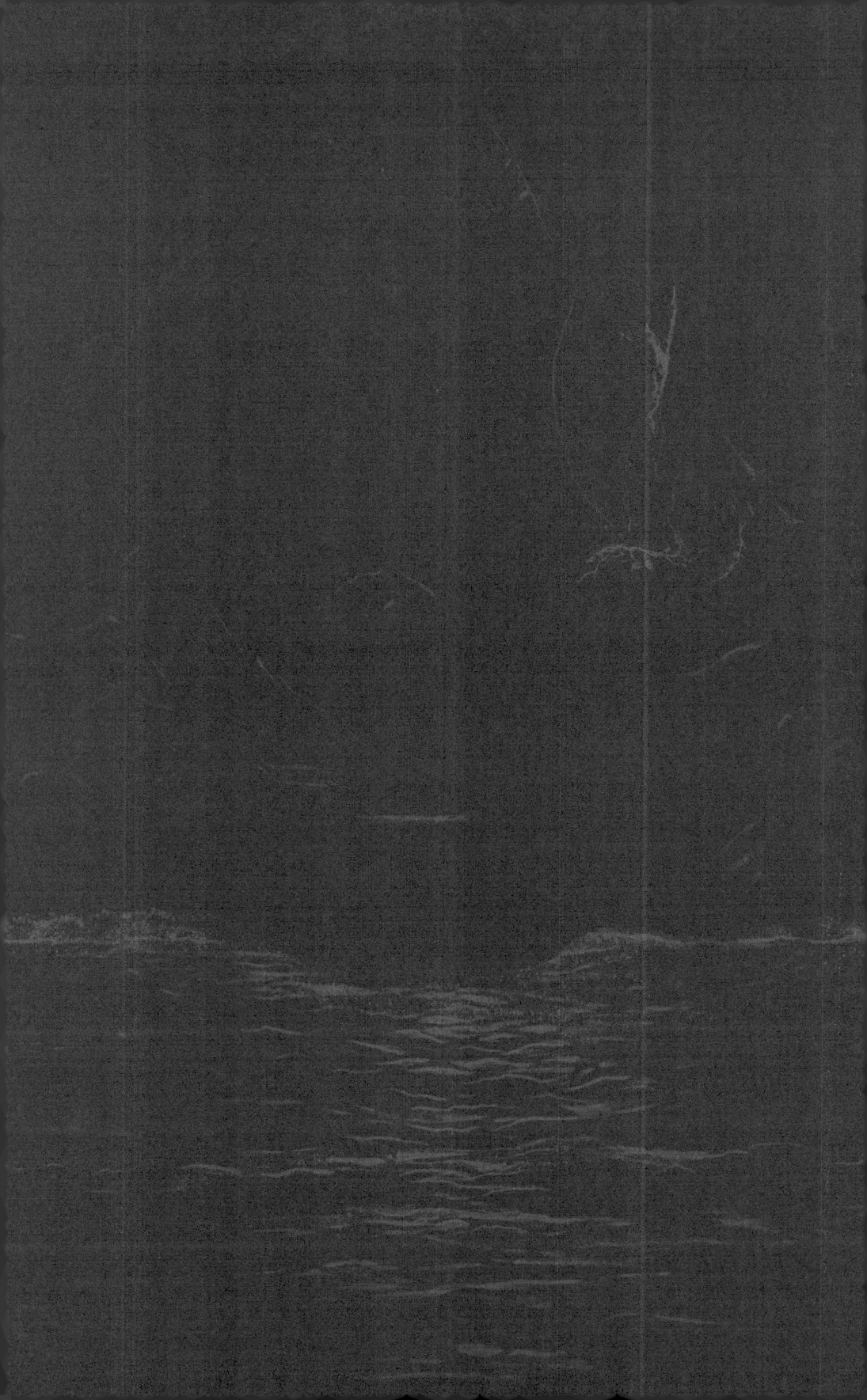

READER'S NOTE

If you are looking for a romantasy,
respectfully, this is not the book for you.

CONTENT WARNINGS

The Gifted King is a tragic grimdark epic high fantasy villain origin story with heavy themes. Reader discretion is advised as this book contains:

Sexual content, graphic violence, gore, adult language, murder, blood, suicidal thoughts, toxic relationships, vague mentions of (off-page) physical and sexual abuse, vague mentions of (off-page) physical and sexual assault, pregnancy, childbirth, emergency cesarean section (C-section) delivery, a traumatic birth experience, terminal illness, death, sudden loss, death of parents, death of a romantic partner/significant other, death of an infant, death of a pregnant woman, animal (bear) attack, killing of an animal (bear), shapeshifting, strong experiences of grief and guilt.

If you experience tokophobia, please note this book features pregnancy and childbirth as major events and ongoing themes.

Please read with care and prioritize your well-being.

SAMIRIA

NIVALIS

SALTSTONE

MARIA

FROSTSPYRE

THE HIGH MOUNTAIN

ANCHORA

CASTLE DAWN

THE VIRIDIAN EMPIRE

PAX ANCHORA
"The Capital"

SOLIS

BLOODFYRE

PRONUNCIATION GUIDE

The Ark - The Ahrk
Invar - Inn-vahr
Tzaddik - TZa-Deek
Rondiel - Ronn-dee-ell
Erembour - Air-emm-bore
Vhogare - Voe-gaire
Elias - Eh-lie-ahs
Alastair - Ah-lah-stair
Aadriek - Ah-drihk
Milan - Mee-lahn
Einar - Eye-nahr
Soleil - So-lay
Maura - Mou-rah
Anchora - Ann-kor-ah
Maria - MAH-ree-uh
Solis - Soul-iss
Viridis - Vihr-ih-dees
Nivalis - Nee-vah-lees
Yigael - Yeeh-gah-ael
Azrail - Azz-rae-ill

POWER TIER

DEITIES
Creation Force: The Ark
Time Keeper: Invar
Spirit & Soul: The Fire Within

THE HORSEMEN
Rondiel | Tzaddik | Erembour
Justice | Judgment | Chaos

COURT OF CELESTIALS
Ryonn | Norindra

GIFT BEARERS
Vhogare

THE DRAGON
VHOGARE

If the world burned, I'd be happy to die with her.

Vhogare smiled as he traced his thumb across Soleil's porcelain cheek, marveling at the softness of his lover's skin. In a sea of faces, he'd somehow found the one soul that matched his own. His violent, storming peace. After years of loving her in secret, Vhogare still could not believe she wished to be his.

Vast swirls of sunlight fell across Soleil's radiant features. Her hair, black to the point it was almost indigo, splayed over her bare shoulders, reminding him of the garden's blue roses at midnight. All the years the earth had turned, all the places in the world that such a fire-hearted woman could be, and Soleil woke up next to *him*. Surely it was some miracle that she chose him, that they lived at the same time and drew breath in the same room.

Noonlight fractured through the stained-glass windows of Vhogare's chambers in the west wing the ruby dragon depicted in the scene painted the stone floor with dancing oranges and reds of fire and blood. Each shard of vivid glass captured the light, illuminating the dust motes floating in the thick summer air.

With a soft moan at his touch, Soleil awoke, pinning Vhogare with a smile brighter than the sun on ice. She pressed against him, naked, under the sheets.

His midnight sun. His mirror.

"You are the wind to my fire, you know that?" Vhogare whispered, still tired from their night before.

The castle hummed, a hive of bees thrumming with preparations for the celebratory hunt. But Soleil had found some time to sneak away again and meet him in his chambers in the middle of the day. To his shame, he'd dozed off after their rendezvous.

"And you are my wild flame." She kissed his cheek. "What woke you?"

He turned to gaze at the canopy above them. Dark silver fabric draped from the ceiling covered his carved four-poster bed in heavy cloth. The castle might as well have been melting; heat and humidity pasted the thin silk sheets to his skin, and he'd let the fire die out. White-hot ash now smoldered in the hearth, sending smoke curling around the two matching chairs in front of the fireplace.

To his left, his stone balcony's curtains billowed, letting in the summer breeze. The thick material rasped against the black granite floor. But it had not been the heat or the dying fire's sweet smoke that woke him, nor the dutiful servants clattering down the halls outside his door.

"I was thinking about. . . ." Before Vhogare could speak of his father's health or Milan's succession, the thoughts turned to ash on his tongue.

Soleil propped herself against his chest and raked her fingers through his straight, black hair. "You shouldn't let Milan trouble you so," she advised, surmising his thoughts.

"Easy for you to say," he scoffed. "Your brother was a saint."

"Hardly." She huffed a sad laugh before gravity stole over her lovely visage. "But my brother died in a ditch before he even made it to serve on your Council. *Yours* is still alive, and you should try to repair this . . . rift between you."

Vhogare sighed and kissed her knuckles. Soleil's brother, Corbyn, had been her guiding light, her mooring in the world. The poor man had died from a horse riding accident mere months before accepting his appointment to the royal council—a move he'd prepared for all his life. Byn's death had been more than three years ago, and Soleil still wept for him some nights.

Since losing him, she spent her days training to be the Crown's head historian. Their current archivist would abdicate the office soon to spend his final days in the countryside, and Soleil, with her penchant for language and art, was a stellar candidate for the role. She attended every Council meeting, often consulting with the king himself on matters of import, and Vhogare never found himself at a loss of pride in her achievements.

Meanwhile, Vhogare's own brother sat in his musty royal study hall most days, reading, and had about as much guiding light to offer as cold ash.

"Do you think he knows he's a disappointment?" Vhogare asked before changing his voice to mimic the announcers at the melees and jousts. "Milan," he announced, waving a hand for dramatic effect. "A steady hand to guide the kingdom, but a vile bastard behind closed doors."

Soleil snickered at his theatrics before sobering. "Has he truly wounded you so terribly?" she pouted.

When Vhogare didn't answer, she trailed a knuckle along the muscle of his neck. "You shouldn't be so harsh toward him." Soleil danced her fingertips over his collarbone, drawing fire across his skin. "We don't keep those we love as long as we hope." She pressed a warm, soft hand over his heart. "Mend things. What trouble can Milan cause us behind all those books?"

"*What trouble?*" Vhogare snorted. "Whenever he deigns to seek human company, he speaks nothing but ill of you. Of us. If anyone's going to let our secret out, it will be him." He ran a hand over his dark beard in irritation, wishing he'd shaved before summer set in.

Soleil rolled her eyes before pressing her lips against his bare chest, inhaling the rich, distinctive scent of the sandalwood cologne he imported just for her. "He wouldn't dare," she whispered against his skin. "Any accusation against you is a stain on the family name, and a coronation is the worst time for a scandal."

"Don't put it past him. Besides, Father has been fighting day and night to secure the succession, even in his fragile condition." Vhogare's stomach churned, and he clenched the silk sheets in his calloused fist. "Yet Milan makes no move to step into his crown unless he's asked. Not a day's gone by that my dear brother hasn't reminded me of his birthright, and now that it's at the door, he lingers to take it."

"So make peace with him *before* he inherits the throne," she sighed, gazing up at him. "Or else he will shut you out. What good is it to be a prince with no real power?"

"I will not bend the knee just for his good graces." He tucked her dark hair behind her ear. "Respect is not begged for. It is earned."

Soleil gave him a fierce smile. "Be that as it may, we get one life, my darling. And it is far too short." She pressed a quick kiss to his lips and sat astride him. Her lilac and lavender scent swept over him, and Vhogare filled his lungs. Pride swelled in his chest at the slight curve of her pregnant belly, and he slid his hands up her sides.

"We can't waste any time," she beamed. "Which is why"—Soleil reached across him, and he kissed her breasts as she retrieved something from the top drawer of his nightstand—"I had your nameday present fashioned early."

Vhogare stiffened. "You know I don't celebrate."

No one in the castle did. His mother had died giving birth to him, and it felt heartless to hold a festival on the day she passed. Not to mention his father had outright forbidden it.

"I know," Soleil said with an exasperated exhale. "But I do." She concealed the gift in her cupped hands and gave him a playful pout. "And you never deny me my happiness."

"Very well." Relenting, he folded his hands behind his head and shut his eyes to await her surprise.

"Don't be silly," she said, "you can look."

Vhogare smirked and cracked open an eye.

Grinning, Soleil unfolded her hands and unveiled his nameday gift: a tiny pewter dragon cast in exquisite detail. The silver beast was rendered in mid-flight, its mighty wings flared wide and its teeth bared as if it breathed fire. In its chest rested a blood-red ruby in the shape of a heart.

Vhogare's throat ached. Ancient dragons were noble creatures, blessed with such wisdom, grace, and strength that all the kings of the earth admired them. The Crown's royal guild must've worked for ages to deliver such a gift.

"Do you like it?" Soleil whispered, anxious. "I overheard King

Ulrich say your mother loved the old dragons, and I studied for days to get every detail right. I think Queen Seonna would be proud to know her son is the very embodiment of their strength."

"It is—" He choked words around the knot in his throat. "I cannot believe you did this for me."

Vhogare's heart seized at her kindness, his eyes stinging as he turned the small statue over in his hand. The beast was majestic, ruthless, and unflinching, powerful in every way. "I've never owned anything so beautiful."

"I'm so happy you like it," Soleil beamed. She waved a hand at the row of paltry presents Milan had gifted him over the years, left to collect dust on the mantle. "Promise me you won't just put it on a shelf somewhere."

"Never." Love burned like a consuming fire in his chest, and Vhogare smudged his tears away with the back of his hand. "I will keep it with me all of my days," he swore, forcing out words as his chin trembled. He pressed the mighty figure against his heart as if he could meld it to his soul. "How did you even get this in here?"

Soleil flashed him a mischievous wink, pleased with herself and her gift. "I do whatever I want, my prince. Whether you're watching or not." She broke into a brilliant smile. "I'm thinking of making the dragon my seal when I become the royal historian." Soleil gestured to a chest by the door. "I've already had my robes made."

His brows shot up. "Shouldn't you keep them at your manor?"

"Don't worry," she chastised, cutting him off. "No one saw me carrying them up here." Soleil gave him a wicked smirk. "I wanted you to see me in them first."

Vhogare clutched the silver dragon to his chest and reached up to tangle his fingers in her hair, pulling her down for a searing kiss. Her soft, dark hair fell around him like a curtain blocking out the world, and Vhogare lost himself in her lavender scent. For a moment, they were the only souls on the face of the earth, and she was heaven in his arms.

He slowed their kiss, and Soleil softened against him, moaning before she broke away to press her forehead against his. A lovely blush flamed across her cheeks. "You don't have to thank me," she whispered, rubbing the tip of her nose against his.

"Don't deny me my happiness," Vhogare growled, and Soleil sank down onto him.

Vhogare's free hand drifted down the smooth skin of her back, and she shivered. Inhaling, he settled his palm on her hip, memorizing every curve. Soleil arched into his touch, and he savored the effect he had on her.

They'd need to be quick. Soon, she'd have to sneak back through the hidden passageway in his suite and make her presence known at the feast before people started asking questions. Hours in Soleil's embrace were not enough, but he wouldn't risk her image at court. It was all she had. All her family had. And she'd been far too careful for him to sully her good name out of selfishness.

Just this once, he could be fast. Vhogare deepened their kiss and melted into her perfect chaos. He wouldn't waste a damned second.

THE CHAPEL
VHOGARE

T he castle's chapel loomed large before Vhogare. Built from black marble, its lofty, vaulted ceiling and ornate goldwork glowed in the light of the thousand candles lining the altars of the sanctuary. Sweet smoke drifted from incense pans and standing braziers, rising through the colossal carved columns depicting the Ark's three celestial horsemen: Rondiel, Tzaddik, and Erembour—Justice, Judgment, and Chaos.

Each horseman stood faceless, their figures shrouded in cloaks and mysteries. Only their weapons set them apart and their sacred metals. Gold for justice, bronze for judgment, and silver for chaos.

Vhogare's footsteps echoed like thunderclaps on the stone floor as he strode down the center aisle. Harun, the head cleric, inclined his head at Vhogare as he made his way to the adjacent scriptorium. The other attending holy souls worked to remove wax from the stone altars and candelabras, the rustle of their long, rich robes whispering in the silence. Halfway through the pews, a strange prickle slid down Vhogare's back like a cold knife. He glanced over his shoulder, unnerved.

The statue of Chaos flickered. Shadows thrown by the candles shifted in an odd pattern across the stone. The difference was nigh imperceptible, but there was something unnatural about the light's movement across the marble—something unsettling that tapped at his senses.

Vhogare suppressed a shiver at the inexplicable perception of being watched and continued his path to the main altar. The faceless horseman seemed to track Vhogare as he knelt beside his father in front of the seventh supporting pillar.

"You always were impatient," King Ulrich growled out of the side of his mouth. He did not look up from his prayers. "Could you not leave me in peace for one hour?"

Vhogare stiffened but pressed his palms over his heart and bowed his head in reverence. "I would never dream of interrupting your communion."

His father snorted, and Vhogare concentrated on his prayers.

The Ark's pillar rose high above him in the beautiful chapel. Carved in the likeness of living flame, it stood, revered, at the front of the worship chamber. No one knew the Creator's face, only that He was the well that all life sprang from, the ship that carried all souls. So in His honor, the kings of the past erected a mighty column of rare marble streaked through with veins of fire, bright and powerful and full of life.

For a heartbeat, Vhogare allowed his shoulders to relax. The chapel always brought him a sense of peace. Safety.

A basin had been carved into the base of the Ark's pillar, a vast well of holy fire, and the heat from the eternal flame within warmed Vhogare as he knelt on the cool stone. Kept by faithful holy clerics, the fire never burnt out, never guttered or dwindled low.

Vhogare wished he could say the same for his father. Forty years ago, the once-mighty king of Anchora had saved the country from a merciless dictator with only his wits and an iron fist. King Ulrich had ascended to the throne with honor—or as much as one could spare with that much blood on his hands. After becoming Anchor King, he'd married a beautiful woman, established a faithful council, and sired two sons late in his days. But Vhogare had killed his mother at birth. He'd turned in the womb, and the holy men had cut him from Queen Seonna's belly and let her bleed out on the sheets.

Twenty-five years had passed, and his father had never let him forget it. Time had worn on, and the Anchor King's sandy hair had grown gray, his full beard patchy, and he groaned every time he moved. The man's limbs—so strong in youth—were withered and thin. Stale, cloying scents of ointments and cloves clung to Ulrich's clothes, and a wracking cough plagued him, waking and sleeping. But no sickness in the world could take the steel out of his father's gray eyes. They were sharp as swords, even as King Ulrich glanced across at him in his vulnerable state.

Vhogare kept his gaze steadfast on the fire. He used to beg the Ark for his father's life—plead that Ulrich's health and strength be restored —but perhaps it was not meant to be. Though it had taken Vhogare years, he'd made peace with the old king's condition. But that did not mean he had time to dawdle.

The sand in his father's hourglass drained fast, and Vhogare needed to ask this final favor while he still could. When the king had finished praying, Vhogare helped him stand and sit in one of the elegant marble pews lining the chamber.

"I'm glad you're here," King Ulrich said before Vhogare could ask the question he'd come for. "Our master of gold was caught stealing from the royal coffers."

The attending clerics stopped their busy work and left to join Harun in the scriptorium, giving Vhogare and his father privacy.

When they had all left, Vhogare snorted. "Midas has had his hands in our affairs for years. Why discipline him now?"

"Because his wife's come to town with their daughter, Maura," King Ulrich answered. He ran a hand over his ornamental silver breastplate, and Vhogare started. His father was not one for showmanship. Most days, he forsook the chains and collars of his high office for practical armor. But today, he wore his black armor and the regal necklace Queen Seonna had given him on their wedding day. The sight of his mother's blue northern sapphire churned Vhogare's heart.

"Zarine has a good mind for numbers," the king continued, noting Vhogare's reaction. "I'm inducting a new keeper of laws and captain of the guard before Milan's coronation. Our current staff has their . . . reservations about your brother's aptitude, and I need to smooth his way."

Vhogare's face flushed. His father was asking for advice. He thought long and hard before giving it. "Make it publicly known that Midas was stealing from the crown, then behead him in front of the city. All the common folk will cheer you; our royal coffers care for them as well as us."

King Ulrich scowled. "His family would not cheer."

Vhogare smirked at the blatant test. Einar, the king's Right Hand and spymaster, had uncovered horrendous things about their master of gold. "His wife and daughter can watch. After all Midas has done to them, they'll thank you for it. But make the new law keeper and captain watch, too. They won't dare cross Milan after that."

His father studied him for a long, long moment. "And what of blood vengeance?"

"Vengeance?" Vhogare scoffed. "Justice. Midas stole from us. We steal from him. His name, his honor, and his life should suffice. Say Milan orders it, and my dear brother won't have to raise a finger to buy the entire country's fear and respect in one move."

"Do you propose a new master of gold?"

Vhogare cracked a lazy smile. "Not master, mistress. Maura has hated her father for years and with good reason. Have Zarine serve as mistress of gold for now and train her daughter to be her apprentice. When Maura comes of age, she can have the position."

To Vhogare's immense pride, his father nodded. "Consider it done. Now, what is it?" King Ulrich rubbed his knees, already aching from his brief time at prayer. "You've got that look about you. Something's gnawing at your mind."

Vhogare had learned long ago not to hesitate when speaking with the king. "Soleil. I've no doubt your spies have told you how I feel about her." Heaven knew his father had not asked about the matter himself. "I've come to ask for her hand in marriage. I know she is not of royal blood, but she comes from Pax Anchora's greatest house and boasts a good bloodline. She is a woman of grace and poise, intelligence, and a strong will, admired amongst ambassadors and scholars alike. Her diligence in preparing for her work as head historian speaks volumes. In two years, when our archivist retires, she will be the first woman in history to hold such an office. And her parents have been nothing but loyal to you—"

"No." King Ulrich looked up at him with the hard gray eyes of a man who had seen far too many battlefields.

Vhogare's heart flattened. He'd held his one dream out to his father, only for the man to smother it beneath his iron fist. Anger rose in Vhogare's throat, but he fought his indignation down. Hooking his thumb on his sword belt, he tried to pretend he wasn't hurt. "I don't understand."

"She is a jewel, aye," his father agreed. "A daughter of such a great house could have sat back and enjoyed the spoils of court, but she joined an esteemed apprenticeship and has worked tirelessly to carve her own name. I could not have made you a better match myself." King Ulrich raised a stiff finger. "But she has a bright future, and I will not have a woman of such intelligence tied to a man like you. You are unworthy of her, and you will leave Soleil out of your path."

Heat spread across Vhogare's neck, running down his back like sharp, prickling-hot knives. "You are on your deathbed," he snapped, dropping all pretense of goodwill between them. "Milan is all but on the throne, and you would deny me this one shred of happiness?"

"My spies have done far more than tell me of your . . . affections." His father broke off in a painful cough before raising his gray-bearded chin. "She lights your fire, and you already have too much to burn."

"She is the water to my—"

"Ah ah, do not play me for a fool, boy." Latching a hand on the pew's marble armrest, King Ulrich struggled to his feet. "I know that flame well. It is unquenchable. You have been the shadow of my sins since the day you were born. The darkest parts of my nature were given to me again as a punishment. And you will make no fit husband."

"Mother loved you well enough," Vhogare spat.

Hatred hardened in King Ulrich's eyes at what Vhogare left unsaid. *Mother loved you, and I do not.*

Smothering a cough, Vhogare's father gave him a mirthless, tight-lipped smile. "Seonna endured me." The way Ulrich said her name made it feel like her ghost was in the room. "If I could've spared your dear mother her pain, kept her from the bloodshed she endured at my side, I would have. Such a faithful woman deserved far better."

Better than me? Vhogare almost roared. But the king didn't need to say it. He'd made his point well enough. So, instead of breaking, cracking apart, and exposing the rawest parts of himself, Vhogare slicked his hair back and stood up straighter.

His father drew himself up, as well, as if preparing to deliver a blow. "You are my blood, son, but I wish you were not," King Ulrich said in a tone colder than a gravestone. "And you are not Milan. You are not made for the throne. Yours is the sword, and I will not give you my blessing to lay her on the blade of your ambition."

Vhogare's mind emptied, his shoulders going slack at his father's words. He opened his mouth to retort, to beg, to demand, but King Ulrich cut him off. "I'll have Midas imprisoned. The castle will be in your charge while we are away on the hunt. See to it that he is executed before I return."

Vhogare gaped at his father. "I am not going?"

"Have I led you to believe that you were?"

"Leave the bloody castellan in charge!" Vhogare shouted.

Harun poked his head around the adjacent doorway and scowled with disapproval. "Your Highness, the chapel is a place of peace."

King Ulrich huffed. The high cleric had never been afraid to speak his mind, but the holy men of the Fire were a law unto themselves, and royal though he was, Vhogare could not rebuke them.

Vhogare waved an apology and lowered his voice. "I *am* your son," he continued to his father when Harun had gone. "A prince of Anchora. I should be there."

King Ulrich did not so much as blink at him. "Your brother will be there."

Vhogare stepped into his father's face. "Elias and Joanna are my closest friends. I will be there to celebrate the birth of their child. If you wish to stop me, you'll have to imprison *me*, and we'll see how well Milan fares on his own."

The king fixed him with a cool, merciless gaze that saw far, far too much. "Very well. But you will behead Midas yourself when we return." Ulrich put his cane against Vhogare's chest and shoved his son back a step to clear the path to the door. "And end things with Soleil. When her studies are complete, she will take her seat on Milan's Council, and I will not have you soiling her integrity."

Vhogare's heart fell out of his chest. He stood rooted to the stone, staring daggers in the king's back as the man limped down the center aisle with defiant dignity. His father's rich silver robes dragged across the bare stone with the sound of the wind cutting through thin trees, and Vhogare suppressed a shiver.

King, he might be, but Ulrich was a ghost with too much blood on his hands and too little battle glory left to outweigh it. Guilt followed around him like a loyal hound. The man's days were hell, and his nights were miserable. Vhogare often woke to the sounds of his father's agony winding through the castle's stone halls, and it broke a part of him to share such hate with the man who gave everything for their kingdom.

Ulrich was cold and vicious but firm and wise in matters of state and war. His prowess over the kingdom was undeniable. Though Vhogare wrestled against his father's strict line and iron fist, his heart still broke over the tragedy of a mighty soldier worn down by time. Failures in fatherhood aside, Ulrich ruled well, and the kingdom would be worse off without him.

But such admirable qualities gave him no right to be such an ass.

Vhogare's mind was still wheeling, trying to decipher some way around his father's warnings, when Milan strode in, freshly shaven and clad head-to-toe in his hunting armor. Vhogare's elder brother's honey-blond hair was braided back, and he gleamed in his steel plate and cloak as if he had stepped out of the sun. Everything from his silver collar to his signet ring shone from polishing. But the burning flame behind Vhogare seemed to dampen when the firstborn prince entered the room.

"So it's a no on Soleil, then?" Milan drawled. Tossing an orange in his hand, he came to stand next to Vhogare and stared into the eternal fire. The blaze shone too bright in his brother's red-rimmed eyes, and Vhogare wondered if Milan had been crying.

Regardless, Vhogare refused his bait. "You heard every word."

"And you should not be surprised, dear brother." Milan poked a few stray hairs back into his half-up braid. "Do you think she'd be with you if you were not a prince?"

A kernel of doubt tickled at Vhogare's mind, bitterness rolling into his chest like a storm at Milan's insinuation. "Soleil is not like that.

Which is more than I can say for the lovers you've courted over the years."

Milan snorted and stripped the peel off the fruit. The sharp scent of citrus erupted into the room, mingling with the warm, cinnamon scent of the eternal fire and tingling Vhogare's nose.

"Perhaps so," Milan agreed, "but spare yourself the pain and put her out of your mind. You delude yourself by thinking you can win his favor this way."

"What of you?" Vhogare snapped, rounding on his brother. Harun peeked around the corner again, frowning, and Vhogare dropped his voice to a respectful level until the cleric returned to his duties. "You're weeks from the crown with no wife," he hissed, "no children. No spies or staff to your name. What merits you his good nature and *favor* besides the blood we both share?"

Any warmth Vhogare's brother had, he saved for their lessers. Alone in the chapel, there was nothing but frigid intelligence in Milan's stormy blue eyes. He tore the flesh from a slice of the orange and glared at Vhogare. "Father may have won this throne with an iron fist, but he's fought forty years to leave his steel behind. A level head for politics and a heart for the people is what will keep our beloved country safe after his death, and that is bought with books and study. Time with the common folk. And *meetings*. You shirked every hour of statecraft to fornicate with the daughter of our richest, most loyal house without their leave. The king noticed."

Cold rage crawled into Vhogare's stomach, tying it in a vicious knot. "Did he ask you? What to do with our master of gold?"

Milan's strong brow knitted together, crinkling his freckles as he popped another slice of orange into his mouth. "Aye."

"What did you say?" Vhogare was tired of this humiliating dance with his father and brother. Tired of living under their mercy. It felt far too good to cut Milan open, even if it was just with words. "What should we do with dear Midas?"

"We should remove him from the Council and send him home." Milan made a dismissive gesture, unconcerned. "Let the stealing bastard buy his bread some other way. He can break his back at labor for all I care."

Vhogare snorted. *A steady hand to lead the kingdom.* Their father always wanted to believe Milan would be strong enough. The crown prince was smart and fair, if not out of the goodness of his heart, than the intelligence of his craft. He was kind to those beneath him and cunning to those above, and he knew where to stick a knife. But when it came down to it, Milan's iron fist shook like a leaf, and he chose paper over steel.

Vhogare curled his lip. "I may have shirked my statecraft, brother, but your level head is useless without a spine."

Milan opened his mouth to retort, but Vhogare brushed past him and exited the chapel, striding toward the castle yard. He was already late, and Elias was waiting for him. Relief sloughed through Vhogare like cool water over a burn. Fresh to knighthood, Elias was the brother he never had, and Vhogare would've traded a thousand Milans for one hour over a tankard with his friend. At least the spymaster's son would not sneer at him or cut him with the blades of the past.

Voices shouting preparations ricocheted off the castle's high walls. The king had summoned all the country's great houses to attend the royal hunt and celebrate the expected birth of Elias's first child. Vhogare plastered a stone smile on his face as he strode beneath the shady fruit trees. *Perhaps Milan will fall off his horse, and Soleil and I can elope while Father mourns his precious, scholarly prince.*

THE GOODBYE

VHOGARE

The walk from the chapel to the castle yard was stunning but sweltering. Vhogare ran his hand along the wall of the formidable keep as he went, his fingers grazing the enormous black granite blocks the fortress was built from. The dark stone seemed to devour the sun and claim the heat as its own. Warmth radiated outward, soothing his frayed nerves. Pax Anchora was a living beast, and her crowning castle thrummed with strength.

A breeze blew through the fragrant fruit trees lining the cobbled path, and red petals drifted across a foreign dignitary lounging on one of the wrought iron benches ahead. The man stood as Vhogare approached, blood-red flowers dancing past him in the wind.

"Good day," the stranger said, stepping into Vhogare's way. Though they were alone, the dignitary did not bow, as all but clerics did to royalty upon first meeting.

"Good day to you as well," Vhogare managed after a moment, trying to puzzle out where their visitor was from to abandon such well-known formalities. He swept his gaze over the man. The stranger's dark armor bore no heraldry or colors belonging to Anchora or her sister kingdoms, and local smiths did not make his distinctive curved blade, but he spoke the continent's common tongue well enough.

"Forgive me," Vhogare hedged, "I don't believe we've met. Have you arrived for the hunt?"

The dignitary's black hair and alabaster skin caught the sunlight as he angled his head. "It so happens I am." He gestured for them to continue walking, and Vhogare fell into step beside him. "Speaking of which," the stranger continued, "what do you think of such a tradition? Rather bloody business if you ask me."

Vhogare shrugged. "Blood buys life. Few things make us appreciate our days more than death."

The man nodded. Small streaks of silver decorated the edges of his hair and beard. "Celebratory hunts are . . . uncommon where I'm from." As they walked, the stranger studied the massive, ancient fruit trees, beautiful with summer's blooms. His gaze stopped and stuck on the fortress's colossal protective walls, seventy feet high and thirty feet thick, with battlements that would make the very mountains envious.

"And where might that be?" Vhogare asked, unnerved by the calculations visible on the man's face. He checked again for any clue as to where the visitor might hail from and found none.

"A land beyond the continent." The dignitary waved a hand in dismissal. "I act as a . . . liaison. An ambassador for powerful individuals. Every so often, I like to dip my toe in the rising nobility to see who I'll be dealing with as things change."

Vhogare's brows knit together. "Well, then. I assure you, my brother is a strong ally to have." Best that anyone poking around assumed Milan was formidable, even if it was a lie.

The man barked a dry laugh. "I'm certain you are more than formidable, as well."

Vhogare stopped walking and folded his arms across his chest. He ironed his features out, adopting the cold, unforgiving tone his father so often used in treacherous negotiations. "I try."

Unfazed, the dignitary paused to take in the rest of the castle. Each watchtower's exquisite dark spire pierced the sky like hands raised in worship. The keep's two beautiful, spiraling towers gave the castle the appearance of a dragon settled against the eastern mountains. A testament to the imagination of the kings of old who'd built such a magnificent stronghold above the glittering loch.

But the way the man studied everything. . . . He examined their defenses like an invading general surveying a battlefield, or a thief scouting a house he intended to sack.

Vhogare's senses itched; he'd seen a similar glint in Milan's eyes when his brother found an opponent's weakness at chess. Gut churning, he reached to clasp the man's wrist. "I did not get your name."

"You did not." The stranger did not take his hand. "But no need to fear, Vhogare." He smirked and prepared to go, his black cloak fluttering in the gusts of wind. "You'll know me soon enough." Walking backward, he sketched a mockery of a bow. "Enjoy the hunt."

"Oh, I will." Vhogare stood rooted in place as he watched the man turn and disappear around the corner of the keep's wall. He lived his life on gut instinct, and it told him something was wrong.

Seeking out the castellan, Vhogare informed the man he was departing for the hunt, as well, and left careful instructions to sweep the castle and ensure no one matching the stranger's description remained behind when they had gone. "And increase the standing guard in our absence," Vhogare commanded. "I want additional patrols manning the wallwalk until we return. Only your most trusted souls, do you understand?"

The castellan nodded, and Vhogare patted him on the shoulder in thanks and walked on.

Perhaps it was a good thing he was going on the hunt, after all. His father, Milan, and Elias would all be in attendance, and no assassin could ask for a better opportunity than a sick man on a horse in the middle of the woods.

Vhogare's temper had cooled somewhat by the time he reached the main yard. Normally quiet and peppered with castle folk going about their daily duties, the green teemed with activity. Every head of Anchora's vassal houses assembled for the royal hunt celebrating the upcoming birth of Elias and Joanna's child, and they'd brought half the kingdom with them. Magnificent horses barded in blues, reds, and purples tossed their heads and pawed at the earth, turning the verdant castle yard into churned mire. Standard bearers held banners aloft, and knights bore heraldry on their shields, the myriad of colors turning the dark castle into a crown of jewels.

The kennel master, however, struggled; the wizened old man fought to contain the hunting hounds that would lead them to the stag scouts sighted days before. Vhogare stopped to pet his two favorite mastiffs; the black and brindle pair had always been particularly fond of him. Leaving the kennel master with a few copper drakes for their care, he made his way through the crowd. The other beasts' frenzied baying added to the ring of armor and shouted orders and the incessant chaos made Vhogare's head throb.

Far worse than the sound was the smell. While Vhogare considered the usual trampled grass and rich soil of the castle yard a fond, pleasant aroma, the crowd had brought a stench. Damp horses and unbathed soldiers combined with the yard's chickens, goats, and dogs crafted a unique and revolting stink.

Holding a hand beneath his nose to ward off the offending smell, Vhogare met Elias, Joanna, and Soleil under the silver royal canopy in the center of the muddy expanse. To his joy, he arrived just in time to overhear Soleil requesting sword-fighting lessons.

"My brother was going to teach me all those years ago," his love explained to their friends, fanning herself with her hand as she spoke. "But he never got the chance, and I'd like to learn in his memory."

"Give me a few months," Joanna told her, pregnant and perspiring in her green gown. "The second I can bend, I'll teach you everything I know. Elias can aid where I'm rusty," she finished, elbowing her husband in the side.

"Of course," Elias laughed, giving Soleil a respectful bow. "I'd be honored."

"I'll be unbeatable after learning from both of you." Beaming brighter than the sun, Soleil clasped Joanna's hands. "Thank you. I'll see you all when we arrive at camp."

Sneaking Vhogare a secret wink, she left to join her noble family at the line of horses preparing to depart. Her father, Raul, glared at Vhogare as she crossed the yard before turning away to help Soleil onto her pale mare.

Vhogare couldn't help but smirk. He had her parents in a vice; he hadn't formally asked for Soleil's hand, so House Corveau didn't dare formally turn him down. But Raul still refused to give her his blessing. The head of their noblest house held Vhogare's gaze with all the unyielding ice of his northern blood, and disapproval bled through the space between them.

"You look like you haven't slept in weeks," Elias jested, distracting Vhogare from Raul's searing judgment.

Vhogare turned his attention back to his friend. Elias's wavy brown hair was limp from humidity and already plastered to his brow the way it used to be when they were boys sparing under the summer sun. Now a man grown and in his lightest armor—simple bronze with the Ark's great fire worked across the breastplate—Elias was still drenched. The sun's heat radiated through the canopy, and Elias had forgone his helmet. Even the cedarwood and pine oils that Joanna's washerfolk used to keep their clothes fresh had long worn off, and his red cloak and linen pants draped with heaviness in the humidity.

Beside him in heavy velvet and brocade, Joanna looked downright miserable.

"Soleil kept me busy," Vhogare confessed, flexing the sore muscles of his shoulders. In truth, while his love had kept him more than occupied, it was worrying over the conversation with his father that kept him up long past the hour of the wolf. He'd been dreading their talk, and King Ulrich had not disappointed.

"But you"—Vhogare turned and swept Joanna a teasing bow—"should not be out in this heat."

She waved him off. "Those stone walls are no cooler. At least out here there's a breeze, even if it smells of shit." Joanna reached up to cup Elias's cheek, running her thumb across his beard. The sun caught in her emerald eyes as she surveyed the growing line of nobles preparing to depart. "I wish I could go."

"Ah, it'll be dull," Elias assured her. "Nothing but trees and horses and dirt for days."

Joanna pouted. "Stop describing heaven when I'm stuck here." She offered him a cheerful smile that dimpled her cheeks. "But at least I get to see my sweet husband off."

"Despite all my protests." Elias turned to kiss the inside of her palm. "Promise me you'll keep out of the sun."

"What, no swordplay?" Joanna teased, giving Elias another wide grin. "All this coddling will drive me mad."

"You haven't seen *coddling* yet," Elias laughed, pressing her knuckles to his lips with a bow as he prepared to depart. "Besides, there'll be time enough for sparring when it's cooler."

Envy constricted Vhogare's chest at the ease they shared. When Elias and Joanna had first announced their engagement, the entire castle had celebrated. Their joyful union had seen its fair and foul weather, but their trials had forged them into a single flame, and it hurt to look too long at their light.

"I swear she's safe with me while we wait," Vhogare teased, shoving his jealousy down. "But it looks like I'll be leaving you, as well," he added to Joanna.

Her mouth fell open in outrage. "You're going, too?"

Vhogare couldn't help but smirk. "Much to Father's chagrin."

"Bastard," she said, swatting him, and Elias chuckled as he left Joanna with Vhogare to bring their horses.

"I can't believe you're both leaving me." Standing at Vhogare's left in the muddy castle yard, Joanna pushed her tumbling blonde waves over her fair shoulder. Her formal gown clung to her legs in the humidity, the burdensome skirt catching in the churned muck at their feet. "Of all things," she groaned. "I used to run these castle walls like a cat, and now I'm about to trip over my own dress." She braced an arm around her belly and tugged at the long skirt, swearing a salty curse as the fabric dragged through the filth.

Vhogare stifled a snort at her language. "We can't have that," he said with a fake pout and reached down to yank the fabric free from the sucking mud. He opened his mouth to offer her some shade and firm ground beneath the smithy or stables, but Milan strode up to them.

Although four years older than Vhogare, the golden crown prince appeared small in the shadow of the castle's dark walls. Reedy and thin, he had a slight stoop to his shoulders from too much time spent over books. They were both fair, but Milan was pale from his hours spent confined indoors studying. Vhogare could not recall the last time Milan bothered to spar in the sun with their master-at-arms.

Even so, Milan never lacked performative confidence. Resplendent as ever, Vhogare's elegant brother straightened his surcoat, humidity pasting loose strands of his straight blond hair to his brow and neck, and offered Joanna a courteous bow. "Good to see you, Lady Joanna. I must say you are positively rapturous even at this miserable hour. How do you manage it?"

"I avoid compliments at all costs," she jested. "It keeps me humble."

Vhogare dipped his head and coughed to hide his laugh.

Milan flashed him a cutting glare. "And humility is an endearing trait for a woman as charming as yourself," he sniped to Joanna before turning to Vhogare. "Certain you don't want to ride at the front, Brother?" As first-born, Milan would travel at their father's right on the road to the king's wood and remain there the entirety of the hunt.

"I prefer the back," Vhogare answered, rising onto his toes to peer over the cramped assembly of knights and nobles from the great houses. *Where is she?*

Across the castle yard, Soleil sat astride her silver mare, the dark blue of her traveling dress swallowing the daylight whole. Joanna waved, and Soleil's rouged lips curved into a secret smirk as she caught Vhogare's gaze.

His heart swelled in his chest. "Besides," Vhogare mused, "Soleil will be far better company than our noble swornguards."

Honorable though they were, the two warriors were poor companionship without Elias around to jest with.

Milan's sharp jaw set like stone. "You should spend what time you can with Father while he's yet for this world. Especially if you insist on defying him."

Ice slid into Vhogare's gut. His brother was right; he should wring every memory from his waking moments with their father, but despite foul tempers, it gnawed at him to see what King Ulrich had become. Anchora's Sword was now mere flesh and jutting bone, a shadow of the fearsome soldier he once was.

The castle had been so humid and depressed of late—Vhogare was ready for the sheer joy of Elias and Joanna's celebration . . . and some time spent alone with Soleil. For this hunt, he wanted to feel nothing but happiness. Yet such joy felt too bright while his father suffered.

"No need to threaten me, dear brother," Vhogare agreed, resentment rising in his chest. As the second-born prince, he fancied himself free from the suffocating sensibility expected of Milan, but occasionally, duty clawed up to remind him of his place. "I'll ride up and join you before we arrive."

He nearly informed Milan about the strange visitor but thought better of it. His brother never took the initiative to give the guards instructions, and the studious prince was a poor swordsman—there was little he could accomplish alone. "See to it Father is well looked after," Vhogare added instead and made a theatrical show of shooing Milan away.

Milan sneered at his dismissal and sauntered, tight-lipped, into the crowd toward his gray charger. The quiet gelding didn't so much as flinch as the prince's squire tightened the girth and assisted his royal highness into the saddle. Milan hadn't even taken the reins before King Ulrich—securely astride a mighty black destrier draped in silver —struck up a conversation.

Vhogare's gut soured, and he sought out Soleil again, hoping to bring himself some peace, but she'd taken her place amongst the column of horses with the aristocracy. Disappointed, he glanced down to find Joanna staring at him, a knowing look in her eyes.

"What now?" he sighed. She was the closest he'd ever get to a blood sister, and she'd long since learned how to scold him into the ground.

"Do you fancy I'm the only one who notices you staring at her?"

"The only one foolish enough to say something about it, yes."

Joanna sucked her teeth. "You should announce your courtship," she whispered, resting a hand on her swollen belly and cutting a concerned glance at Soleil. "Ask for her hand. No more sneaking around the castle. I grow nauseous just thinking I might run into you two."

"You grow nauseous just breathing," Vhogare quipped. "Besides, where's the fun in that? You and Elias had plenty of"—he waved a hand at his friend near the horses, searching for the word—"*trysts* before you married."

How could he tell them his father had said no? He'd loved Soleil since he could call himself a man, and every shred of hope, every dream of a life with her, had been ripped from him because of *ambition*.

Vhogare mopped a hand over his face in frustration, aching

loneliness gnawing at his gut. *She* was his ambition. He had no real designs on the crown or place on the Council if Milan decided he wasn't of use. He was a prince with no power, and all he'd ever wanted was her.

"Our trysts were none of your business," Joanna growled out of the side of her mouth, yanking him from his thoughts. "But Elias, while my prince, was not *a* prince."

As if he'd heard them whispering, Elias paused from checking his saddle and turned to search for Joanna in the crowd of castle staff and servants gathered to see them off. Vhogare snickered as the spymaster's son shoved his hair out of his eyes, aggravated at the clinging humidity. Beside him, Joanna gave her husband a wave to signal she was fine, if not a little overheated from the sun.

"Be serious," Joanna continued, turning to cut Vhogare a warning glare. "Soleil is a faithful friend, and with royals like you afoot, we women look out for each other."

"Royals like me?" he scoffed, only half offended.

"Yes, you." She elbowed him. "I'm sure this . . . secretive romance has been entertaining, but the fantasy needs to become reality. And it doesn't help that you're a terrible liar."

He scoffed. "It's not my fault you're a damn bloodhound when it comes to my business."

"Someone must protect you from 'your business.'" Joanna scowled. "It's not my fault you're reckless."

The criticism punched Vhogare's gut, but he swallowed her words.

She pivoted to face him and shielded her eyes from the sun. "Please, Vhogare. Your courtship is the worst-kept secret of the century, a source of gossip far beyond the castle walls. You need to make an honest woman out of her before things go too far."

A dark chuckle broke out of him. "Things have already gone too far. Besides . . . some good it did you." He braced one hand against his lower back and pressed the other to his brow, imitating her posture, pregnant and sweltering beneath Anchora's summer sun. "The Joanna I knew would've come with us on this hunt."

"The Joanna you knew could see her toes."

"My point, exactly."

"Listen," she sighed, searching the heavens as if praying for patience. Perhaps the Ark granted her such; Joanna kept her tone kind as she whispered, "There are no secrets between the three of us. You know that I know."

Vhogare's stomach launched into his throat. He shifted on his feet in the straw-strewn mud, trying to appear calm, but his heart hammered in his ears with such force he was certain she would hear it.

"And there is no shame in it, but the sand drains down in the hourglass all the same."

"Milan knows, too," he growled. "Though I have no bloody idea how." His brother, though weeks away from being crowned king, had no spies to speak of, and the castle staff usually left him to himself.

Joanna hummed, twisting her golden necklace in thought. The metal caught the light and glinted, a bronze sword with twin wings of gilded flame fashioned for the Ark's celestial horseman Tzaddik, the Fire of Judgment.

"I understand how you feel," she said, keeping her voice neutral, "wanting something to be just for the two of you in this world. But you feel things so deeply; where one man sees a storm, you see the world ending." Her warm, affectionate tone darkened at the edges. "You cannot keep your love a secret forever. Sometimes we lose the things we hold the tightest."

Vhogare massaged the back of his neck, searching for a half-truth. "The second I pull her into this family *officially*, I lay her on the knife's edge. My father is a peaceful man, but his grip on this kingdom weakens, and if one rebel soldier can take the throne, so can another."

Pushing stray strands of hair out of her eyes, Joanna seized his free arm to support some of her weight. "Why is it always all or nothing with you?"

"Because I've seen where nothing gets you." His gaze drifted to where Milan, already their sovereign in all but name, sat astride his gray courser. "And that's why she picked me."

Concern darkened Joanna's strong features. But there was another emotion prowling under it, knitting her bold brows together and wrinkling her freckles. Disappointment? Disapproval? She spoke before he could decipher it, jutting her chin in Soleil's direction. "Fine. Anyone can see she is the wind to your flame. Just . . . take care she does not burn, this time." Joanna took a deep breath, circling a hand over her round belly. "Things come to light before you're ready."

He worked up the nerve to tell her what his father had said, but Elias rode up with Vhogare's mount. The prince's piebald charger tossed his head and chomped at the bit, stamping in the mud like he was born to run.

"Listen," Vhogare said, turning to face Joanna before they had to leave, "I've instructed extra guards to be posted at your door while we're away."

"Is something wrong?" Elias asked from atop his warhorse. "I can stay to look after things."

"No, no." Vhogare waved off his worry. "Father would be devastated by your absence. I'm merely being responsible for a change."

"Aye," Elias countered. "That's what worries me."

"Everything is perfectly fine." Vhogare turned to Joanna. "Just take extra care, considering we'll be off hunting." Forcing a lighthearted grin, he swept her a teasing bow. "I promise to keep Elias safe until we return."

"As you should," she snapped, quick to recover. "Or I'll lock you in the kennels again."

As a child, he fancied he would've been a better kennelmaster than a prince. Joanna agreed and promptly dared him to spend a night shut in with the hunting dogs. He'd walked into the kennels utterly fearless, but a night alone in the dark had changed all that.

"We were ten," he laughed, shirking off the eerie memory. "The hounds and I are good friends now. They'll help me escape."

She pretended to swat his flighty horse on the hindquarters in retaliation, but instead approached Elias in his saddle. Vhogare envied his friend's steady mount; the towering red warhorse was as immovable as a mountain.

His own beast was volatile; young and untried, the horse's blue eyes were wild as a storm at sea. Once astride, Vhogare often held on for dear life.

"Don't be gone long," Joanna half-shouted over the din of the company preparing to depart.

"Nothing could keep me away." Elias bent down to press a kiss to the top of her blonde hair. "If it weren't for damn tradition, I'd be back already."

"Careful," Vhogare jested. "Or my father will hear you."

But the laugh died in his throat; there was no fear King Ulrich might hear them. His father rode at the front of their column with Milan, but the two swornguards on either side were less for protection and more to see that their true sovereign stayed in his saddle. But the Anchor King did not take the throne by sitting idly aside; he lived by steel and blood, and not even a wasting illness could keep him off his horse.

Torn somewhere between a compassionate word and a jesting sneer, Elias shrugged and turned back to his wife. Spymaster's son or not, the man was far from subtle in his affections. "Remember what I said," he whispered to her, just loud enough for Vhogare to overhear.

Joanna's eyes glistened as she gazed up at her knight. His friend was a vision in her green gown, but there was a strange sadness in her eyes. "I've forgotten it already."

Curiosity unsettled in Vhogare's stomach. Had she had another vision? It would not be difficult to believe. Joanna's blurry glimpses came to her during times of great pain or stress.

Once, when they were fourteen, she'd broken a leg and had been incoherent for days. Upon regaining consciousness, she'd driven the entire royal staff mad, babbling about the castle burning down. A fever had swept through the country not three weeks later, culling nearly half the population, including Elias's sweet mother, Aethena. They'd mourned for months, and some of Joanna's maidservants still swore she'd communed with the Ark Himself and the dreams had been a warning.

Her visions had grown few and far between as of late, but that taut, drawn expression had accompanied all of them. Vhogare shook off his concern; Joanna always said she struggled to decipher them, and it did no good to dwell on things they did not understand.

"Stop it, you two," Vhogare chided as their flirtations wore on. He wheeled his nervous charger in a circle to keep the beast from bolting. "Or you'll have him crying like he did on your wedding day."

Disengaging from Joanna, Elias called him the foulest name Vhogare had ever heard. The prince put his heels to his horse to outrun him as they thundered out of the castle.

THE BROTHERS

VHOGARE

Elias won his race and let his warhorse rest by riding near the back of the column with the baggage train, which left Vhogare alone with his father and brother, and the two Marian swornguards who took their jobs far too seriously. The hunting party moved at an insufferable pace, laden with a week's worth of supplies and tents, and the sun beat down on his shoulders with blistering resolve. His poor horse began to lather at the bit and martingale, and his thighs chafed against the saddle leather.

Halfway through the ride, Vhogare gave up trying to make conversation with his kin and sought some relief from his misery. Glancing over his shoulder, he caught Soleil's gaze lingering on him once or twice and winked back.

After hours of small talk and veiled interrogations, they reached the king's wood. The vast expanse of evergreen trees swallowed the hunting party whole, and Vhogare sagged with relief at the shade. Pine, spruce, and fir enveloped them as they rode, casting speckles of sunlight and shadow across the needle-covered ground. Smiling, he hauled in a deep breath of the fresh, woodsy air.

Exhaling, Vhogare lagged as far as he dared until he came up next to Elias. The spymaster's son had spent the day looking for brigands and bandits patrolling the royal road.

"See anything unusual?" Vhogare asked. He scanned the long line of horses and riders ahead of them, but the foreign dignitary from the castle was nowhere to be seen in the stream of pageantry.

Elias shook his head. "Dust and trees and deer." He glanced over at Vhogare. "This wouldn't have anything to do with your worries at the castle, would it?"

Ensuring they were not overheard, Vhogare told Elias of the strange man he'd met before they left. "I'm concerned that an unfamiliar face may be an ill omen."

"I'll let my father know," Elias said when he'd finished. "An assassination attempt, perhaps?"

"I don't think so. The stranger seemed interested in us as allies. But if it is, with my father's condition, I doubt they're after the king." Part of him wished the strange man would hurry up and take Milan off his hands. It would solve many of his problems. But Vhogare beat that part of himself into submission and made plans. "I'll be asking our swornguards to keep a sharp perimeter."

Elias nodded. "I'll stay vigilant, as well."

"With that settled"—Vhogare swigged from his waterskin and passed it to Elias—"help me set up camp when we arrive?"

His friend laughed. "Tired of sitting on your ass all day?"

"Yes, in fact." His seat bones had grown sore from riding, and judging by the thick press of the trees around them, they were nowhere near their destination. Elias's warhorse, Kane, foamed around his saddle. The sooner they reached the clearing and the Ardere River cutting through it, the better.

"Fine," his friend agreed, mopping his face with a damp cloth. "But swear not to tell anyone when I jump in the river."

Vhogare laughed. "I hereby swear. But if Soleil and I get there first, don't stick around."

Elias barked a hearty laugh. "I'd sooner carve out my eyes."

"Oh fuck off," Vhogare jested, and their conversation dissolved into good-humored insults.

Near sunset, the clearing appeared ahead, and Vhogare let out a whoop and raced ahead to tether his horse. They spent the better part of the evening setting up camp. Servants were in attendance, but they were just as exhausted and miserable, so Vhogare and Elias finished his pavilion and volunteered to help raise Milan's and the king's. They tracked all over camp, carrying out their duties, and the dignitary did not appear again to stand in Vhogare's way.

When they finished, the three shimmering silver royal tents gleamed at the center of their company. Various smaller tents belonging to esteemed noble houses spread out in an impressive spiral. Their blues, reds, and purples filled the wide clearing at the center of the king's wood. Each flew their own embroidered banner, the myriad colors of Anchora's nobility fluttering in the wind cutting through the tall evergreens surrounding their camp.

After hours of labor, Vhogare's back ached as if his damned horse had kicked him, but he felt more alive than he had in years. The bright moon beamed through the fabric of the king's pavilion, sweet-smelling beeswax candles refracting firelight off every lingering speck of dust dancing in the air. As the second-born prince, it was customary for Vhogare to accept the gifts presented to the king for hosting the hunt, and with all his father's secret eyes on him, it was not the time to abandon his duties.

Sticky and uncomfortable, he stood in the king's pavilion on the left of the makeshift dais opposite Milan. Alastair, their broad-shouldered and barrel-chested swornguard, made a formidable wall between them and their guests. Vhogare tried not to look at his sovereign seated on the traveling throne behind him —a poor imitation of the massive steel chair back home. The Anchor King was a shade paler than he'd been just weeks ago, and watching him wither felt too much like watching a kingdom die.

So Vhogare kept his eyes ahead and surveyed the crowd of gathered nobles. The strange man did not make another appearance, not even on the fringes. *Perhaps I am wrong, and the threat has passed.* With relief, Vhogare studied the moonlight filtering through the lavish tent and pretended his father was immortal.

Next in line, Elias and his father, Einar, the royal spymaster, stepped forward and presented the king with an ornate breastplate inlaid with rubies and pearls. The jewels and ornaments spread across the face of the armament in the shape of the Ark's great fire of creation.

"To honor your mighty lineage," Einar said with pride, "and thank you for your kindness to House Aldernari over these long years."

"Oh, Father, there's no way it's pure silver," Vhogare quipped, hefting the plate that Einar and Elias offered the king. The flaming jewels inlaid on the steel seemed to burn up at him in the humid night.

His jest had not amused his father. The king sat, stone-faced, glowering at Vhogare until Vhogare's smile fell.

"You accuse me of lying?" Elias joked to save Vhogare from the king's scowl. "I assure you, it is plated in the finest silver the continent can offer. No lesser armament would suffice to thank our good king for his benevolence." He flashed Vhogare a sympathetic glance and hooked his thumbs in his sword belt, smiling in an effort to lighten the mood.

"Of course," Vhogare said, theatrically tilting Elias's ornate gift in the light. Satisfied with his dramatic performance, he buffed the horsehair and dust from his hands off the breastplate and bowed at the waist. "The Crown thanks you for your generosity."

Elias swept a humble bow, the picture of courtesy, before straightening to push his brown waves off his brow. "I am honored my child may come into this world heralded by such splendor."

"The honor is ours," the king answered, smiling and gesturing for Milan to take the breastplate from Vhogare and place it with the countless other gleaming ornaments the Crown received for hosting the ceremonial stag hunt. Shy Maura, dressed in her house's muted purples and matte blacks, looked up at Milan as he deposited it amongst their other gifts. Her distrusting brown eyes flashed before she checked herself and bent back to her tally. Maura's mother, Zarine, their new mistress of gold, did not so much as offer them a glance.

Offering Maura a taunting wink, Milan resumed his place at their father's side, stiff yet ever faithful under his duty as crown prince.

"Your family has been a fixture alongside our house for generations," Milan added to Elias with an ease that toed the line between formal and familiar. "A hunt is the least of our debt to your father and his father before him."

Einar's great house had aided the Anchor King as he took the throne forty years ago and had been loyal ever since. The graybeard stood, armored in the magnificent gilded plate of his office as Right Hand and royal spymaster, and beamed with pride at Elias's side.

Something twinged in Vhogare's chest at the sight. Einar was more of a father than his own had been, and the man's only son was a source of constant comfort. "A grandsire before the week is out," Vhogare congratulated, clasping Einar's rough hand before turning to Elias. "And you—" He had no words for the joy that welled in his heart at his friend's good fortune. "This world will be brighter with more of you in it."

Elias's grin put the damned sun to shame.

Vhogare's throat tightened, and for a moment, he wished they could congratulate Soleil's pregnancy with such public approval. But behind him, the king opened his mouth to say more, and a chest-splitting cough erupted from Ulrich's frail frame.

"Enough with the formalities," Milan said, gesturing toward the tent's exit. "Let's get tomorrow's festivities in order. The sun won't wait for tradition."

The crown prince strode into the waning night heat, chased by their father's wracking illness, and Vhogare followed Elias out so the king might have peace.

On their exit, the second of their two attending swornguards hailed them from the center of the hunting camp.

"Soleil asked for you, my prince, in your absence," Aadriek announced. The Marian warrior's wavy dark hair was braided back as befitting the pageantry of the grand event, his strong jaw freshly shaven, and Vhogare glimpsed the lines of traditional tattoos trailing in intricate designs down the man's neck under his collar. Aadriek's western armor creaked as he straightened, the rough, worn leather worked through with bands of blue. Behind him, the bonfire burned bright against the night.

"Which prince?" Milan jested, slinging an arm over Vhogare's shoulder, leaving it in place, though he tensed.

Aadriek served as Milan's sworn sword, but the crown prince's humor had always been treacherous ground. The warrior glanced between Milan and Vhogare, then raised a brow at Elias.

"I think you're too fair for her taste," Elias interjected, coming to Aadriek's aid. He glanced at where Vhogare's dark-haired beauty sat with the other members of her great house, still preparing the evening feast. "Some prefer midnight to sunrise."

Vhogare's chest swelled. Whereas Milan took after their father, golden and fair, he was proud that his own dark hair and pale skin honored his mother. The north had been strong in Queen Seonna's blood before her passing, and Vhogare would be the winter night to Milan's summer sun till the day he died.

"All the better to be every star in my sky," Vhogare answered.

Pulling Aadriek aside, he informed the swornguard of the strange dignitary and left him with instructions to keep a close eye on both King Ulrich and Milan during the entirety of the hunt. The warrior gave a dutiful bow and departed to pass his orders on to Alastair. With that sorted, Vhogare excused himself to speak with Soleil.

Before he could go even a yard, Einar fell in step beside him. "I have men stationed all over the camp and an extra patrol posted in the trees. Should this stranger try anything, we will be ready." The king's loyal spymaster kept his voice low, ever cautious to maintain appearances as they walked through the dark hunting camp, enjoying the coolness of the night.

"Thank you. I feel safer already just knowing you're aware."

Einar clasped Vhogare's hand, but his kind expression soon faded to one of concern. "On more personal matters, I overheard you speaking with Joanna."

Vhogare's neck heated, and he was grateful the dim light from the flickering torches had hidden his flush. "Do your ears never tire?" he asked as the kind man hooked a heavy arm around his shoulders.

Einar gave him a fatherly smile. "Not where the kingdom's interests are concerned."

"I assure you, I have every intention of speaking with the king."

Einar raised a brow. Did he already know the king had denied Vhogare? Had spies been present when his father stripped him of a lifetime with his love? If Einar knew, he did Vhogare the kindness of not mentioning it.

Vhogare folded his hands behind his back, grateful for the man's subtlety. They passed through the center of camp, pine smoke mingling with the dust of the dry road as they gave a wide berth to the bonfire being built for the night's festivities. "Elias and Joanna take precedence, and then Milan's coronation—"

"That's all good and well," the graybeard interrupted, slowing their pace. "But do not leave your happiness to the last."

"Do you disagree with him on the matter?" Vhogare said, taking a chance.

Einar thought for a long moment. Vhogare didn't mind the strong silence; he always came to Einar with problems that seemed impossible to solve, and the spymaster never failed to come through for him—never left him in the dark the way his father had.

"I do disagree," Einar answered after a time. "You've put Soleil in a delicate situation, and I don't think it wise to leave her to the dogs." He smoothed his wiry beard. "But, while it is precarious to continue your relationship while she holds a seat on the Council, she is a capable woman and can decide for herself what she's willing to risk. You play a waiting game, for now, and I advise you to renew the issue with Milan when it's time."

"You want me to beg him for her?" Vhogare spat. In his soul, he and Soleil were married in all but name. He kicked an overturned stone down the path with far too much force. "I'm tired of playing politics when her heart is hers to give. Why must we ask, but kings take what they please?"

Einar heaved a weighty sigh. "Soleil loves you. And she trusts you to make a way. Sometimes we must humble ourselves to get work done."

"What will humility buy me that strength cannot?" He was a prince, too, dammit, and it grated on him that he had to plead for his brother's leave to make moves.

"Have patience." Einar gave Vhogare's shoulder a heartening squeeze, pulling him close, and Vhogare's chest swelled at the leather-and-smoke scent clinging to Einar's armor.

"There is right, and there is wrong, son," Einar continued, "and we all have to choose—even if it's hard to stomach." He nodded toward where Soleil sat, stunning in her blue gown, a glittering sapphire in a sea of sand. "Do not forsake your sun just because it's out of reach."

Einar's wife had died some years back from the fever, and Vhogare's heart ached to think of what the wise man would give to have Aethena back again, what Elias would give for his mother to be there to see his child come into the world.

"When the opportunity presents itself, I assure you, I will waste no time," Vhogare promised, staggering as the old knight clapped him on the back with a strong, calloused hand. "Of that, you can be certain."

Nodding, the spymaster bowed, his wavy, gray curls fluttering in the wind as he excused himself—but not before offering humorous courtship advice that made Soleil laugh. Vhogare's love stood as he approached, dusting her feather-covered hands on her canvas apron.

"May I speak with you a moment, my lady?" Vhogare asked, offering a half-bow. "Regarding your upcoming appointment."

"Of course, Your Highness." Soleil made her excuses to her mistrustful family, and they walked a short distance down the main road before she followed him past a row of tents for privacy. Her eyes, blue as the northern sky, shone in the distant firelight. Filthy as a scullery maid, yet she was still breathtaking.

"What are you doing plucking chickens?" he demanded. "Aren't there servants for this work?" He took her hands to inspect for any cuts in the flickering torchlight. "No daughter of your house should risk such beauty against a blade." He peppered kisses across her fingertips for emphasis.

"I volunteered"—she rolled her eyes—"much to my dear mother's chagrin." Binding her night-dark hair out of her face, Soleil braced her hands on her hips and glanced toward the woods. "You leave in the morning?"

"Aye." Rolling his stiff shoulders, Vhogare trailed her line of sight to Milan. Orange light danced across his brother's golden hair as he joined Elias by the roaring bonfire.

Soleil's gaze lingered on the crown prince. "How soon will you return?"

"Depends on how the hunt goes." Vhogare battled down the sinking itch at her prolonged attention and forced a smirk to his lips. "But I haven't forgotten."

Her gaze snapped back to him, nervous. "Then you will ask him? Before the hunt is out?"

He dusted a stray feather from her chin, pleased at her eagerness but devastated by his answer. Einar the Spymaster, indeed. "No," Vhogare lied. "The arrangements for Milan's coronation must be made when we return home, but the *second* I have my father's ear—"

Soleil's eyes shadowed, their glacial blue the dark sky before a storm. "We're running out of time." Though she was not yet showing, it wouldn't be long before her loose-fitting dresses failed to conceal their secret.

"You know how he is where my brother is concerned," Vhogare redirected, his heart sinking at his failure. "As soon as the crown is on Milan's precious head, I swear to you, I will ask." *Again.*

"You don't need to swear," Soleil purred and wove her arms around his shoulders. "I know you." She planted a kiss on his nose. "I know you'll do right by our family."

"*Our* family," he whispered. Pulling her close, he ran a hand up the silk of her skin. He ached for her—to say their vows beneath the stars and give her a life that would never bore the wildness of her brazen heart. The woman was terrifying. In a heartbeat, she could take him from roaring anger to on his knees, and he lived for the light in her eyes.

All her previous suitors had been fools; the pathetic saps left off when she announced her apprenticeship and subsequent aim for a seat on the Council. But Vhogare never found her more fascinating than when she relayed her studies, and the fact that she could debate him into the dirt only stoked their flame. His midnight sun had been there for all his darkest hours—for her love, he owed her no less than a crown—his heart on a silver platter.

"Every second you are not mine is a blade carving into my heart," he whispered, "and I'll be damned if someone keeps us apart."

"Just don't make us wait too long." Soleil pressed a soft kiss to the column of his throat. Glancing down between them, she smoothed a hand over the delicate curve of her belly. "I wish for the good king's blessing before he passes."

A stone dropped into Vhogare's stomach. She was his family, and he'd already lied to her. He unwound himself from Soleil, guilt a choking vice around him, and pressed his lips to her knuckles. "You shall have it. I promise."

He would make it happen.

"But tonight"—he flashed her a dangerous smile—"meet me at the river."

THE RIVER
VHOGARE

The moon was high in the star-flecked sky when Vhogare sneaked out of his tent, picked his way past the guards and patrols, and raced through the trees and down the sloping hill to the river. He'd made all the reasonable preparations and left his father and brother in Einar's capable hands. For the night, he could focus on Soleil.

Moonlight glittered across the flowing water, glinting and shining off the moss-covered rocks and the river's undulating ripples. He stripped off his doublet, carefully securing the pewter dragon in its pocket, and padded across the sand. The soothing scents of fresh pine and damp moss drifted past him on a night breeze as he picked his way across the short, decaying wooden dock. Old wood beams creaked and groaned as he walked out onto it before stopping to glance around.

The bank was deserted. The dark woods on either side were dense with shadows. Elias had clearly decided against a dip. *But where is she?*

He'd just begun to wonder if Soleil had been detained by her parents or fallen asleep when she drifted out of the woods.

She was a vision — a cool shadow thrown by a blazing sun. Her long hair flowed in a raven sheet down her lithe shoulders, and the midnight blue velvet of her dress caught and held the moonlight. As she approached, Soleil held his gaze and undid the lacing of her bodice, sultry desire parting her red lips.

She was devastating. Radiant.

My she-wolf in a woman's skin.

Vhogare stepped back as she approached, fighting the urge to fall to his knees before her, and froze as his feet hit the edge of the dock. "You are lovely," he whispered as she stepped up to him and let her dress fall. Though he longed to take in the sight of her, he couldn't strip his gaze from the hunger in her eyes. Smiling, he slid his arms around her waist. "The whole world in my arms."

Soleil made a soft noise, and Vhogare buried his nose in her neck. How could she smell so delicious after a day of riding? Her perspiration mingled with lilac and lavender oils to create an intoxicating aroma, and he trailed his teeth across her collarbone.

"And you," she whispered, voice soft and sensuous, "are too easily distracted."

She launched into him with a laugh and a shriek, tipping them both backward off the dock and into the river. Water sprayed, and Vhogare came up laughing and gasping for breath. After such a long day baking in his armor, the cold shocked away the soreness. Adrenaline sparked through him, and shivers raced up his skin.

Soleil, always a step ahead of him, pounced. The second he gulped down air, she splashed him full across the face. Sputtering, he returned the attack, sending sweeping armfuls of water her way until they were both breathless.

But he was far taller than her and had footing in the deep water where she had none.

Before she could splash him again, he caught her in his arms and spun her in a circle. She threw her arms around his shoulders, kissing him, and he hoisted her legs around his waist.

He had not exaggerated; Soleil was the world. She was life and death, joy and agony, fire and ice. Having her in his arms meant holding the sun. His father was right; she lit his flame, and Vhogare had never been afraid to burn.

His damned father.

The thought—and the small curve of her belly against him—struck him like thunder. Lightning might as well have split apart his chest. Vhogare's eyes flew open, and he broke their kiss, backing away from her to drink down a breath.

"Darling? Darling, what's wrong?" Soleil demanded, swimming over to him and shoving his soaked hair out of his eyes as if it would help him breathe.

He couldn't explain it. Couldn't bring himself to tell her the king had said no. He and Soleil were trapped like this. Suspended in space and time, pretending. Never moving on with their lives without the royal seal of approval. And now his father would rip her from Vhogare's arms forever. Their fate had been decided for them.

Soleil and their child depended on him, and there was nothing he could do.

Panic reared in his gut, indignant rage close on its heels. He staggered back a step, the gritty sediment of the river bottom shifting beneath his bare feet. He was helpless, his whole life at the mercy of another man's crown.

Heat flared in Vhogare's chest. If he even managed to keep his family together, would he one day have to tell his own child to abandon their love for the sake of the kingdom? For the sake of the world?

If they had a boy, would Vhogare be forced to say the same words his father had said?

And if they had a girl, he'd slaughter the man who raked her reputation across the coals as he had Soleil's. He was a hypocrite, a scoundrel, a monster who'd gone too far—

"Talk to me, my darling," Soleil commanded, interrupting his thoughts. "Whatever you're feeling, you don't have to feel it alone."

She'd seen him like this before; ever since his father's illness began, he'd been a mess, more likely to shatter like glass than be the steadfast man she needed. The man she deserved.

Soleil trod water in front of him, fighting the current, waiting for him to speak, but Vhogare's throat closed up as he stood in the cool river. Anger wrapped its fist around him and tightened until he shook, every muscle like a taut wire. His heart thundered against his ribcage, a beast beating against bars, until he was too hot for the cool night. The cold, earthy water almost stung against his flushed skin.

Perhaps his father was right. Perhaps he was no fit husband. Would be no fit father, himself.

"Vhogare," Soleil said, splashing water to break him from his stupor. "You cannot just stand there staring holes into the river." She backed away toward the bank until she could stand on the river bottom. "You have to speak to me."

"I am afraid," he admitted, body shuddering from tension. He swept his arms across the water, stirring up silt. He hoped it would calm him, but it did not. "I am not even supposed to be on this hunt, and Father means to punish me for it—and for a great many other things." He bit his lip. He shouldn't tell her. Shouldn't tell her, but. . . . "I was right to be wary of his blessing."

Concern shadowed Soleil's features. "What did he say?"

An owl cooed somewhere in the trees behind him, and a chill raced up Vhogare's back. There was nowhere he could go where someone—or something—was not watching. Even here, alone in the dark in a river, his failures were not his own. They affected Soleil's entire life, and he couldn't stomach it.

Failing Soleil was worse than death, but he didn't know how to soften the blow. Unable to face her, Vhogare pivoted away to clear the water from his face. "He forbids our marriage," he confessed, searching the deep shadows of the trees lining the opposite bank.

"I am my own woman," Soleil whispered, low but fierce. "A citizen of Anchora. He cannot *forbid* anything. I break no law by loving you."

He turned in time to see her eyes flash, and Vhogare held his hands out in an attempt to explain himself. "No, you break no law. But you have worked for your advisory seat on the Council for years, and our relationship would impact your credibility."

Soleil's mouth fell open. Outrage twisted her features, lending them a feral edge in the moonlight. "I am fully capable of loving you and advising Milan. Does he think I cannot manage both?"

"Oh, he knows you can," Vhogare clarified. "My father is your greatest champion. But he and Einar aside, our council members are smart minds with fickle egos. If you are bound to me, they will question your every idea, and challenge everything you put forth in the name of bias. And when they do, I cannot protect you from their slanders.

"I am afraid I have failed you," he continued, chest heaving as if he were running out of air. "Afraid some days that you're just using me to get to Milan. Mostly, I'm afraid I will be a terrible father."

Soleil opened her mouth to object, but he plowed on.

"You know mine, he's cold. Unforgiving. And I hate him," Vhogare seethed, seizing the water in his fists only for it to trickle through his white-knuckled grip. "I *hate* him, and still he is . . . so small. So fragile in his illness, though in his strength he was a mountain. A bear. A damn thunderstorm." His jaw spasmed from his nervous tremors. "He has never loved me, and I still want to hold him when he dies. To tell him he will be all right and there is no need to be afraid.

"But the world he leaves behind is fit for breaking. He's a poor father, yes, but he is a *good* king. We have known a bloody peace, but peace nonetheless, and Milan will not be able to hold it together. My brother could have the world sitting on his shoulders, and he would ignore it. Father's legacy will crumble to dust in his soft hands."

Vhogare struck the foaming current in a beat of rage. "And I–I will be saddled with all this fear for the rest of my life, from the day my father dies until the day I do. And there is nothing I can do but say yes and bow."

He stepped closer to Soleil, the cool wind biting the buttoned shirt plastered to his chest. The air had become too thin. Heat licked up the back of his neck, and his hands shook beneath the water's surface. He glanced up to find Soleil watching him, her mouth slightly ajar as if she searched for words to say when there were none.

The sadness and uncertainty on her sweet face lit the fire in him.

Soleil bit her lip, and Vhogare waded over to her. He slipped a bit on the algae-covered rocks and growled in frustration at his fight for balance. "I will keep us together," he swore. The water rippled between them, the current trying to pull them apart, but Vhogare slid his arms around her waist. "This, I promise you."

He would find a way. Would make a way.

"But will my child hate me when I am old?" he whispered, as if the words would set the world ablaze. Vhogare cradled her face in his hands. "When I must force them to bend their knees for a kingdom that does not love them? Will they know everything I do is because I love them? Or will they think I am cold, too?"

Exhaling, Vhogare crouched in the water and leaned his cheek against the slight swell of her belly, soothed by her fingers running through his hair.

"Fear is poison," Soleil murmured, threading her nails through his dark strands. "It can paralyze or propel. The difference lies in how we carry it."

He felt her chest swell as she drew in a steadying breath.

"When Byn died," she continued in quiet, measured words, "it took months for my parents to even look at me. He was the light of their life, their precious firstborn, and I lived in the shadow that he cast. But he was my north star, and we never fathomed a world without him. The fear of loss can do unforgivable things to people."

A nightingale sang far off, and Vhogare tightened his embrace, comforting her as her voice cracked. She'd been a changed woman after her brother's death. Even in her sorrow, the fire of her soul seemed to burn brighter somehow, and she never let an opportunity pass her by, never failing to speak her mind.

"But they feel that fear *because* they love me. Because it would hurt them to repeat history. And King Ulrich? He, too, is afraid."

He scoffed. "You need a heart to be afraid. What does he need to fear besides Milan's incompetence?"

Soleil's fingers stilled in his hair. "Mortality. And what his sons will face when he is gone."

Vhogare glanced up at her. "He does not seem to care what happens to me."

She shook her head. "That is not true. The world is cruel, and he knows that more than most. He is afraid you will suffer in this life as he has, and it is hard for him to love you when he hates himself."

Vhogare pulled back, and Soleil knelt until they were eye-level in the water, the current rushing around them. "But if you suffer," she whispered. "I will suffer. And if you thrive, I will thrive."

He smirked, and she held his face in her hands. "I would choose you with or without your royal blood," she promised. "If we were street urchins, or pirates, or thieves, or soldiers, I would still choose you. Your father is a strong king, but he will die one day, and Milan has not the will to keep us apart. We *will* be married. And even if you could never give me a child, I would claim you for the rest of my days. I will sit at the Council and stand proudly beside you as your wife, their fickle opinions be damned."

Vhogare drew in a shuddering breath, and Soleil pressed her brow against his until they shared the same air.

"I love you," she said, "and I fear nothing because I know you will protect those you love—our family—at all costs. Your loyalty is unmatched, and you never turn your back on those who depend on you."

He cupped some water and ran his dripping hand over his face to hide his tears.

"Milan is your brother." Soleil gripped his shoulders. "You must make him see reason. The man is a flicker compared to your blaze; he will come around. And he will see what I see. That you, Vhogare, are a good man. And you don't have to fear what you have not become."

Sniffling, he tucked her dark hair behind her ears. "Will you tell me? If I ever start to become like my father?"

Soleil danced her lips across his, letting him taste all the wind and fire of her spirit. "I promise," she swore, pulling away.

Warmth spread across Vhogare's heart. He smiled as her love wrapped comforting arms around his soul. "Thank you."

"And as for fatherhood"—she pressed a kiss to the top of his head—"do you think Elias is not afraid?"

He huffed a broken laugh. "Elias is not afraid of anything."

"That's what you think." She kissed his nose and stood again, wrapping her arms around him as he rested against her breasts and watched the water bead down her skin in the moonlight. "Joanna knows differently. There are few things more terrifying than bringing life into the world.

"But while I wish you would reconcile with Milan, I understand Elias is your true brother"—Soleil smiled—"in bond if not in blood. And the two of you will make this journey together, as you have made all others. He and Einar and Joanna will help us navigate these new waters, and I promise you"—she ran her hands through his hair—"when you are old and gray, your children will hold you, and you will not be afraid."

He stood, towering over her in the moonlight, and kissed her with a fierceness and devotion he'd never felt before. Warmth and calm poured through him at her touch, like the sunrise over a snowy mountain range. She wove her arms around his neck, holding him, and Vhogare melted into her like obsidian, all his ash washed away by her rain.

"You are my fire, darling," she whispered against his lips. "And I will never give you up."

Soleil led him out of the water, tied up her wet hair, and donned her dry clothes. Vhogare caught his discarded doublet when she tossed it at him. Smirking, Soleil slipped the silver dragon into her bodice and outright dragged him through the trees toward the bonfire's flickering light.

He was soaked and shivering when they sneaked back into camp and slipped inside her private pavilion. The tent was warm and lit with candles, and it smelled like her. Bottles of lilac and lavender oils and expensive lotions stood on her nightstand. He snorted at the lavish, pillowed wooden bed set against one side of the shelter, waving a hand at the assortment of chests and tables against the others. "You travel like a queen," he teased, kicking off his boots beside the bed.

"I travel in comfort, you mean," Soleil countered. "There's a reason we didn't go back to *your* tent. I'm surprised you brought so much as a spare shirt."

"Only because they forced me." Rugs had been thrown over the bare ground, and they muffled his footsteps as he discarded his damp clothes. "A prince must maintain certain appearances."

That earned him a laugh as she flicked his damp hair. "You're failing miserably."

"Aye, that I am." He paused to admire her while she changed, and Soleil flashed a wink over her shoulder before she slipped on her nightgown, leaped into bed, and pulled a heavy historical tome from her nightstand. Sighing, she rested the open book across her face, inhaling the scent of aged parchment and leather.

"You'll be reading our baby ancient history instead of children's books," he jested when she wiggled her toes with joy. Sliding under the sheets, he settled between her legs and pressed his ear to her stomach.

Soleil laughed. "It is never too early to learn about our great land." She tapped him on the head with the spine of her book. "Besides, you'll be reading to them right along with me."

"Every night without fail. Though I doubt you'll approve of my choice in literature." He turned to whisper to her belly with dramatic flair. "Don't tell your mother, but the epics are far more entertaining than her dusty histories."

Vhogare doubted the babe could hear him yet, but he wanted his child to know his voice. He promised himself that they would grow up with a father who loved them, a father who would burn the world to keep them safe. He peeked up to find Soleil scowling down at him, a playful pout on her lips.

"Dusty histories?" she gasped playfully. "The scrolls I'm translating have seen more years than you can count," Soleil boasted, "about phenomena that would put your paltry epics to shame."

Vhogare feigned insult, even as his blood heated at her sharp wit. "I thought we'd established I have no shame." He trailed a light finger down her abdomen, pride welling in his chest at the blush that burned across her cheeks.

"Be that as it may," Soleil countered with a wicked grin and an arch of her hips, "my *dusty histories* win wars." She snuggled farther under the covers—and farther into his arms. "You'll be glad for all my books someday. Besides, I enjoy a good epic every once in a while, too."

"Don't listen to her," he said to the babe in her belly. "It's a trap. The last one I read, she snatched it from me and never gave it back."

"I know exactly where it is," Soleil said, swatting his shoulder. "I'll give it back as soon as we return home since you miss it so much." She laughed as she combed her fingers through his hair. "You should sing something."

Vhogare closed his eyes as she drifted to drawing patterns on his back with her nails, fire trailing in the wake of her touch. "I don't know many songs."

"Liar," she teased. "I've heard you sing a thousand times. You hum when you think no one's listening."

"It's not polite to eavesdrop," Vhogare chided.

Soleil snorted. "Darling. I am anything but polite."

He bit the inside of her thigh. "Don't I know it."

But he scoured his brain for a song from his childhood nonetheless. He'd had no mother, and the nursemaids had been too focused on Milan to show him unnecessary kindness. So he chose a Solan tune he'd heard Joanna sing, one from the water-revering border city where she'd been born.

"Come wind, come rain, come raging fire," he sang,
"Rise up mountains, widen rivers,
Nothing will stand in my way."

He took a breath, kissed Soleil's stomach, and continued,
"Fall snow, burn sun, pour raging fire.
Rise up mountains, widen rivers,
Nothing will stand in my way."

Soleil pulled the sheets closer around them and joined him for the final verse, her soft, high notes melding into his rich timbre.

"When I fear, I remember,
There's nowhere to go but higher.
When I fall, I remember,
I can only climb in one direction.
When I am lost, I remember,
The sky is bigger than the earth."

"Joanna adores that song," Soleil mused, getting comfortable.

He hummed in agreement. "A pity she couldn't come with us on the hunt. She loves these forests."

"Perhaps you can bring her a keepsake."

Vhogare snorted. "Aye, a prize stag if we're blessed."

Soleil's joy fizzled out at the mention of the antlered beast they'd be hunting. "Be safe tomorrow." She settled into the luxurious pillows, one hand holding her book open and the other caressing his bare shoulder. "Come back to us."

Vhogare kissed her belly and her knuckles before drifting off. "I swear."

THE BEAR

VHOGARE

"You make it incredibly difficult to cover for you, you know that?" Elias blustered as he slipped inside Soleil's spacious tent the next morning. Sunlight poured through the linen fabric behind him. "Your squire and I have been all over camp trying to find a prince who wasn't in his tent."

Vhogare groaned as he unwound himself from Soleil and sat. Sumptuous bedding folded across his waist as he dragged his dried, wrinkled shirt over his head. "That's your fault. You should've known to check here first."

"I did." Elias strode to the ornate wooden table nestled against the draping fabric of the pavilion's eastern side and poured himself a drink from the glass water pitcher. "But her parents were right outside. Someone has to maintain appearances." Tipping up his cup, he turned his back for privacy as they got out of bed to dress.

"Are they gone?" Soleil demanded, running her fingers through her hair to straighten her dark, tousled tresses. She leaped behind the woven privacy screen on Vhogare's right and yanked a gown from one of the many chests strewn about the room, dressing herself rather than risk her maidservant's gossip.

Elias stepped to the tent's exit and peeked outside. "You have about ten minutes."

Cursing, Vhogare tugged up his trousers, almost toppling over as he yanked on his boots. They'd just slunk out of the tent unnoticed when Aadriek's brother, Alastair, returned on his powerful gray destrier with news the hounds had been set loose.

Ensuring that no one else was watching, Vhogare gave Soleil a quick kiss and took his leave to join the commanders at their line of horses. "Did I miss anything last night?" he inquired in a whisper.

The hunting camp appeared undisturbed; watery sunlight filtered through the clouds as the muggy morning fog evaporated and revelers milled around smoldering campfires. Plates of food had been left out, a few soldiers had drunk themselves unconscious, and the damp breeze carried notes of bitter tea and roast venison. He hadn't heard about any commotion, but it never hurt to be cautious.

Alastair shook his head and matched his discretion. "No. Neither Einar nor Aadriek and I caught any . . . stragglers . . . skulking around."

"Good." Vhogare's shoulders sagged, but his relief was short-lived. "Will my father still be riding with us?"

"Aye," Alastair answered, glancing across the camp at the royal pavilions. The mountainous swornguard shifted in his saddle, his blue Marian armor groaning. He struggled to hide the troubled scowl darkening his bronze visage. "A man's got to breathe fire to feel alive," he mused, "and your father's been shut up in that castle so long that a day in the sun feels like heaven cracked open. There'll be no keeping him away from this hunt, much to his Council's dismay."

Milan sighed astride his chestnut courser. "You know as well as I that there's no dissuading him."

"I wish he would not endanger himself for my sake," Elias muttered. He glanced around to ensure no unwelcome ears overheard them as he saddled his warhorse.

"What could happen to him surrounded by all these guards?" Vhogare jested, fighting past the lump in his throat. He clamped a hand on his friend's rigid shoulder, ignoring the fact that his father's enemy was not without but within. Assassin or not, there was no outrunning a mortal illness. Even so, he plastered on a brave face. "He wouldn't miss it for the world."

The Arms that carried all would soon hold the old king, and his fire within would join the Ark's eternal flame in the sky. Regardless, the sand was trickling down in their hourglass, and the summer heat did not help.

Elias's glorious red horse startled as he tightened the girth, and Vhogare's unease doubled. It was rare to see Kane unsettled on such a bright day. His own piebald charger snorted, restless as ever, and tossed his head as the prince mounted. To Vhogare's distress, his high-strung horse did not settle as they joined the king and hunting party deep in the shadows of Anchora's southwestern forest.

———— ❧ ————

Hours later, not a stag nor boar graced them with its presence, though the sun baked them in their hunting armor, and they drained their waterskins dry. King Ulrich's heaving coughs echoed off the trees, the old-growth forest doing little to muffle their sovereign's misery.

"There's a bend in the river a few miles west," Vhogare whispered, keeping his voice low so their father would not overhear. Between wheezing breaths, the old king was deep in conversation with Einar, no doubt about some obscure political matter that would dominate the next council meeting. "Perhaps our stag sweats himself to death, too."

"If we find the beast first, we can return to camp faster," Elias agreed.

Milan huffed, uncertain. "Father will have our hides if Elias isn't here to fell the poor creature," he snapped at Vhogare.

"No beast in its right mind will put itself within earshot of this party," Elias countered in Vhogare's defense, gesturing at the hounds baying in the distance. "We stand a better chance of finding the stag alone than with all this noise. No doubt it's in search of water, too."

The crown prince rolled his eyes, unconvinced.

"If we succeed," Vhogare tried, "we'll get Father out of this heat. I know you hear him hacking up a lung. We need to get him out of these godforsaken woods and return him to camp before he worsens his condition, all for naught."

"I advise against this," Alastair interjected, spurring his horse to ride at Elias's side. "Not that you asked." Aadriek had stepped away to relieve himself, entrusting Milan's care to his elder brother in his absence. "At least let me accompany you," their swornguard argued, sharing a noteworthy glance with Elias. "It's the king's wood, and it's my brother's head if the crown prince is harmed."

Vhogare waved a hand at Alastair, gesturing to the commander's considerable height. "Your mountainous absence would be noted. You and Aadriek need to guard my father while we're gone."

"Elias will look after us," Milan joined with a sigh, dismissing the man's concerns. "If anyone asks, you can tell them I ordered you to stay with the king. Besides, I give you both my royal pardon if we're attacked by the trees."

"It's settled then." Vhogare gathered his reins, and his flighty steed threw back its head, ready to run. "Last one there cleans the stables for a week."

⸱—— ▸━◂ ——⸱

They thundered into a small, lush clearing bordering the Ardere River and pulled up short. Last in line, Elias swore and dismounted to walk his heavy warhorse before letting the formidable mount drink from the swollen waters. "The north must be melting," he observed, splashing water on his face as Kane drank deep.

Milan bent to fill his metal flask, but Vhogare snatched it from him before he could down so much as a sip. "Am I to let the crown prince die of a rotten gut two weeks from his coronation?"

"It'd be simpler than putting up with all that fanfare."

"Poor, spoiled heir apparent," Vhogare jeered as he arranged a stone ring for a fire.

With a mocking sneer, the heir thunked himself down against the rotted trunk of a fallen tree and mopped his face. "What, you want all the smoke to scare off the deer?"

Elias tied Kane to the nearest tree and returned with an armful of firewood. "The hounds will have their hunt one way or another. We're not burying you because you shit your brains out from some river water."

"Such a coarse nature," Milan taunted. "To think what Joanna sees in you—"

"Perhaps my sense of humor," Elias countered with a vulgar gesture that sent Vhogare snickering. "And I'll be the perfect father after watching out for you two."

An hour later, the water was boiled and cooled, and the hunting party grew even more distant from their small band. "We ought to catch up with them," Elias said, slapping his knees to stand.

"In a rush to clean the stables?" Milan taunted.

Their comrade gave the coals an overzealous kick, sending dirt onto the crown prince's boots. "A rush to see my wife, yes. For all I know, the babe's been born, and I'm out here in the woods with you sorry excuses for royalty."

"I'm an excellent excuse," Milan countered. "My dear brother, here, is the one who's been bedding Soleil without my father's blessing."

"She is of noble blood," Vhogare snapped.

His brother leaned back against the rotted trunk and folded his arms behind his head. "Oh, yes, a mighty house indeed. I wonder what her leal parents would think about you trading proper courtship for gardens and alleys."

Vhogare flushed crimson, rage sparking in his chest. "Bastard."

"Oof." Milan feigned a mocking wince. "Someone's in a foul mood."

"And you light fires you can't put out." Vhogare got to his feet. "Any chance I find at happiness—at purpose—you never hesitate to strike it down or spoil it with arbitrary standards you forsook long ago. How many women have you courted *properly?*" Vhogare demanded. "Or was it all merely a pretense to deflower them and then call off the arrangement?" His brother preferred hors d'oeuvres to meals, and poor Maura was far from the first.

"When's the wedding?" Milan goaded, sniping back from his seat on the ground. "Or will we be out here on a hunt for your firstborn next week?"

Vhogare stepped toward Milan, only for Elias to put a hand against his chest to hold him back. "Enough. He'll bring it to the king when he's ready, Milan. Two weeks from now, and it'll be you who's concerned about heirs."

Heat flushed up Vhogare's neck, and he swore under his breath.

He needed to tell Elias about King Ulrich's decision. Maybe they could devise some sort of a plan. Some way for Vhogare to wed Soleil without petitioning the Crown for her hand and suffering through whatever miserable price Milan would demand of him for the pleasure.

"Heirs, council meetings, coin—the lot of it." Oblivious, Milan reached for a stick and poked at the dead fire. "We ought to just stay out here and shack up with the mountain folk."

Vhogare and Elias exchanged glances. Shaking his head, Elias finished stomping out the coals, his scowl deepening as he moved to untie Kane. "Still no sound from the hounds."

"They'll find the damn thing sooner than later," Vhogare offered, hoping he was right. No stag was an ill omen for highborn births, and Joanna was too fine a woman to lose to childbearing.

"It's a shame we grace births this way." The sun filtered through the leaves, speckling Elias as he ran a hand down Kane's smooth summer coat. "What joy is there in a hunt when the beast is tied?"

Vhogare shrugged. "It keeps the balance of things. We make room in the world for more."

"It's damn bloody business."

Vhogare strode to his charger, the high-strung horse dancing in place. "Blood is life. And life goes on at any cost."

Elias checked that his bow and sword were secure. "It shouldn't be at this cost. And for what? Prize antlers on the wall, showing I've done something while she labors back home?"

Dread reared its gray head in Vhogare's stomach. His father had been on one such hunt the night he was born. If the castle servants were to be believed, the king had never been the same afterward. Burying his wife had crushed the joy out of Ulrich. All the man's laughter had left with his queen. "She hadn't started when we left. You may be there for it yet—"

Elias threw up a hand as his horse's ears shot up, the whites of Kane's eyes bright in the near dark.

Vhogare reached for his saddle, but Elias held out an arm. *Quiet,* that arm said.

Elias untied Kane with smooth, quiet movements and removed the hunting spear from his saddle.

Vhogare unhitched his black charger as well, swearing. He'd brought a single ornamental dagger for the hunt, trusting the armed guards to keep them safe. But the two swornguards and all their soldiers were protecting the hunting party; he'd hauled the crown prince all the way to the river, and countless trees stood between them and safety.

At his side, Milan went pale.

When Elias crossed back to the fire, Vhogare made out the hulking shadow lumbering toward them through the trees, aiming for the water at their backs. A great bear, dragging Elias's prize stag between its massive legs. The monstrous beast raised its head, its snout covered in gore, and Vhogare's blood burned white-hot in his veins.

"Oh fuck," Milan swore.

Vhogare's elder brother cowered behind him, and Vhogare's heart stopped beating as he found himself between the crown prince and the monster.

Fear blazed through his veins like fire. He was going to die. Soleil would stand at the road into camp and wait for him, and he would never come back. Never hold his child and be the father he'd promised.

"Behind me," Elias said, drawing his blade and stepping in front of Vhogare. Elias's silver sword, Azrail, sang, whistling as he drew it from the ornate scabbard.

Vhogare couldn't move. "Ark above—"

"Behind me," Elias said again, slamming the spear into Vhogare's hands—an order.

Though the spear shook in his grip, Vhogare braced himself and stepped up to Elias's side. A sword was no match for the bear's reach nor strength. Elias's bow was on Kane's saddle, and the horse had run for safety. But perhaps quickness could be their advantage. Thanking the Ark for their hunting armor and Elias's stag spear, Vhogare hauled down a deep breath—one that might be his last—and waited.

"I will give you an opening," Elias growled as the bear dropped the stag and roared at them, saliva dripping in ribbons from its crimson maw. "Go for the throat while his eyes are on me. If I go down, aim for the heart."

Years of unspoken gratitude bubbled up in Vhogare's throat for the brother who shared no blood yet stood in front of him. The friend who offered his life mere days before his child was to be born for a crown prince who quailed behind them. But there were no words in the world that would stop the bloodthirsty beast in front of them, so Vhogare gripped his spear and made ready.

"Go right," Elias ordered, and Vhogare obeyed. He kept Milan behind him, making a wide circle around the bear.

Stepping left, Elias maintained his distance. The monster lunged, swiping, and he punished each slash with a parry, flaying deep gouges in its paws that enraged the beast further. Elias never took his eyes off the creature, dodging back until his heels hit the riverbed and sank.

Elias switched his grip on his sword, and Vhogare swore.

"Elias," he shouted. "Look ou—"

But the man's boot stuck in the mud, and the bear caught him across the chest with a glancing swipe that sheared armor down to flesh. Elias's scream of pain shredded through Vhogare's soul.

Elias crashed into the water, and the bear was on top of him, its massive teeth closing around his shoulder. The monster roared in frustration as Elias, struggling for breath, stabbed his sword into the neck and chest of the creature.

All it earned him was a mauling.

Milan seized the back of Vhogare's shirt in horror.

"Fucking bastard, let go of me!" Vhogare shoved Milan off and his brother stumbled backward, careening into a tree.

Taking his chance, Vhogare lunged, aiming the spear through the beast's neck, but the monster swung around, and his point pierced its shoulder instead.

But it bought Elias time, and that was all that mattered.

Weaponless, Vhogare backed away as the monster turned on him, keeping himself between the beast and Milan, who'd sneaked to hide behind the tree.

"Over here!" Elias shouted to get the bear's attention. Across the small clearing, he hauled himself out of the river, bleeding, and grabbed a river rock off the bank. The beast advanced on Vhogare and roared as a stone struck its face, hurled with all of Elias's brutal strength. *Thank the Ark.*

"That's right," Elias gasped, retrieving his sword. "Come and get me."

The bear changed direction and charged Elias with a bellow that sank Vhogare's stomach, but Elias caught it in the face with another rock. The stone's jagged edge tore open the creature's right eye, flaying skin from bone. Bellowing all its rage and agony, the beast rose onto its hind feet, towering above Elias's hunkered form.

"Now!" Elias gasped, rallying.

Vhogare found his nerve and yanked the spear free from the monster's shoulder. It turned his way for a heartbeat, and Elias used that half-second to stagger to his feet and pierce his sword through the creature's massive heart.

Grunting in pain, the beast gave its mammoth paw a final, weakened swipe. Elias pulled back, his sword slipping free, the rake of paws narrowly missing his eye. A groan of anguish ripped out of the monster as it collapsed atop Elias in the shallows of the river.

Panting, Vhogare sprinted to the carcass, and the sword stuck clean through its skull.

Underwater, Elias had his hands on the beast's shoulders, fighting for breath as he tried to push himself free, but the weight was too much.

"Milan!"

Milan stared at them, his arms wrapped around the tree he hid behind as if it could protect him. Cold fear paled the crown prince's sharp features. The bastard shook like a pine in a thunderstorm, piss running down his trousers. If there'd been a sword in Milan's hand, he would've dropped it.

"Milan, help me!"

Clarity fell back into his brother like a hammer blow, and Milan snapped to attention. Swearing, the crown prince rushed over to them, crashing through the river to heave against the carcass with all his strength. Milan's leather-booted feet slipped on the river rocks, but he held firm. Thin though he was, panic pumped through his veins, lending him unnatural strength. Crying out with strain, Milan lifted the bear's shoulder enough for Vhogare to pull Elias free.

Elias—alive, *alive*—surged out of the water, gasping for breath as he clung to Vhogare's shoulders.

"You're all right!" Vhogare shouted, adrenaline blazing through him. "You're all right."

He hooked his arms beneath Elias's shoulders and dragged him through the mud to shore before collapsing. All the statecraft Vhogare's tutors had taught him, and they'd failed to mention healing. He didn't even have a dry shirt to stop the bleeding.

Fear leached from his muscles, and Vhogare began to shake. He would've given every coin in the Crown's coffers for Soleil to be there. She would've known what to do, how to help.

Cursing his weakness, Vhogare sat to catch his breath and put a hand against the blood oozing from his friend's chest. The shorn steel of Elias's armor cut into his palm, the red fabric of his shredded gambeson squelching beneath Vhogare's fingers.

By the mercy of the Ark above, Elias's life had been spared. Only one claw had made contact with his face as he'd backed away, leaving a slice of flesh hanging free from his cheek. Three deep gouges tore clean through Elias's light hunting armor and flayed some of the muscle of his chest. His right shoulder was dislocated, shredded, and bleeding. But though Vhogare could see Elias's sternum through the initial slice, no organs appeared damaged.

"Can you walk?" Vhogare asked, ready to drag him out of reach should the damned bear reanimate.

Elias nodded, blinking blood and water out of his eyes.

Volleying his thanks past the stars, Vhogare yanked Elias's sword out of the carcass. "Help me get him up," he instructed Milan. "Joanna will burn me alive when she finds out I almost got you killed."

"Home," was all his heartbrother said as they swung him over his horse, and Milan raced ahead for help.

THE BLOOD OATH

VHOGARE

Gossip tore through the camp like wildfire. Every squire, noble, and servant clustered around the healer's pavilion as the attending clerics worked to bind Elias's wounds.

"... covered in all that blood," one young maidservant whispered to another, her dread an adder snaking through Vhogare's mind. "His poor wife'll be devastated."

"Aye, he looked torn right up," an older groom agreed. "Do you think he'll last the day?"

Vhogare put his hands over his ears. Everyone speculated, but no one stepped out of the tent to share news. Their curiosity and Elias's cries of pain chewed at his frayed nerves.

"Where were the swornguards? Aren't they supposed to stop things like this?"

"Why did they depart from the king in the first place?"

"Even nobles can be fools."

Their conversations were unending. Elias could be dying, bleeding out on the inside, and all they cared about was a good story. The prying crowd's constant chatter buzzed like hornets inside his head until Vhogare abandoned his restraint.

"Have you nothing else to do?" he barked at them all. Shoving to his feet, he threw out an arm and pointed to the far side of camp. "If you cannot help, leave!"

They scattered like sheep before a wolf, and Vhogare thunked back down onto his stiff wooden field chair.

He remained outside the white pavilion, bouncing his knees as the clerics mended Elias's wounds as best they could and stanched much of the bleeding. Even Soleil, knowledgeable as she was, lent her skills to the cause. Vhogare waited there, useless, while they worked.

The prince swore under his breath. Elias had offered to stay behind and look after things at the castle, and Vhogare had damn near begged him to join them on the hunt. Guilt sawed through him. He'd brought his dearest friend right into the mouth of the bear.

While Vhogare sat unscathed, Elias had nearly died. Their haunting near-death experience lingered over Vhogare like a ghost, breathing cold mortality down his neck. Elias's scream of agony as the bear tackled him into the river haunted Vhogare's every thought. Death waited for no man, and rather than protect his friend, all Vhogare had done was provide a distraction.

When Soleil emerged from the tent, crimson red and burnt orange seeped across the western horizon, the sunset silhouetting her against the bleeding sky. "He'll live," she reported, giving his hand a light, reassuring squeeze.

All Vhogare registered was the blood on her fingers and arms, smeared across her brow where she'd brushed her hair away during her work.

Blood that bought his life.

Elias won't leave me.

Relief flooded Vhogare, choked by bitter guilt. No one had ever stood between him and danger before—paid guards and sellswords did not count. But Elias had stepped in front of a monster, fully prepared to give his life instead of Vhogare's. He was the only true brother Vhogare had ever known, and Vhogare almost let him drown.

His mouth turned down into a bitter line. *Elias deserves better.*

The crown weighed heavily on Vhogare's family, and though Milan was his kin by blood, any loyalty they shared was pure survival. Milan never hesitated to scratch and claw his way above Vhogare at any opportunity, as if any success Vhogare experienced was a direct threat to his inheritance. And when the bear had come at them, Milan abandoned Vhogare.

Elias, however, did not run.

Vhogare stared down at the small cuts on his palms from Elias's shredded armor. The bear had been no surprise, only confirmation. And Vhogare was not one to wait to be struck twice.

Milan could do without him. Vhogare had so little to offer; he'd barely stood against the beast in the forest. But he would stand for Elias. For the loyalty he'd never known. Reliance was a strange thing for him, but he would not fail again.

Elias's sword weighed heavy across Vhogare's knees, cleaned from the bear's blood, and tucked into its black scabbard. A dark silver beauty, Azrail was nothing like the bright, pearlescent weapon their royal spymaster carried. One day, when Einar passed, Elias would hold Yigael. But Vhogare would never forget the sword that saved his life. The steel that brought down a beast no man hoped to stand against and win.

"Thank you," he told Soleil, seizing her hand and managing his first kind words in hours. "Get Alastair for me?"

She nodded. Placing a gentle kiss on his brow, his love departed to retrieve the esteemed commander. To Alastair's credit, the mountain of a man made haste.

"You sent word." Alastair's leather bracers groaned as he folded his massive arms across his chest, waiting. Worry deepened the sun-etched lines around his brown eyes.

"The bear took down the stag. This disaster can end now."

The swornguard nodded, reserved. "How is he?"

"Alive." Vhogare couldn't breathe around the word. What would life have been like without Elias?

That bear would've ripped his oldest friend from him if anything had gone even a heartbeat differently. And all Milan would've done was watch. Vhogare ran a hand over his face and swatted away the nagging evening bugs. "I'm taking him home."

Milan would just have to die if the mysterious dignitary from the castle were an assassin. Elias needed to be home and safe, where he could heal in peace.

"Tell my father the hunting party can follow us if they wish, but

Elias will not remain in this heat." It would take a day at the least to mobilize the camp, but the flies were already buzzing. "He survived a mauling; I will take no chances with infection."

He wished Soleil could come with him, but she would have to wait and leave with her parents, and he was certain she'd be safe with the loyal guards attending their house.

"Good." Vhogare met the man's eyes, and Alastair extended his tattooed hand. "I took the beast's claws," Alastair told him, dropping seven into Vhogare's palm. They were longer than his bloody fingers. "So everyone will know what he did."

Vhogare's throat closed up as he accepted the gift. "I will not forget this."

Nodding, Alastair excused himself to carry his message to the king, and Vhogare entered Elias's tent. The smell of blood, jarring and mortal, hit his face, stuffed up his nose, and into his heart. For all the noise outside in the bustling camp, the only sound was the rustle of cloth as Elias turned to face him and opened his eyes.

"Give Soleil my thanks," Elias groaned, his voice a hoarse rasp. He gestured to the line of stitches running from the bottom of his nose through his left brow. "Without her here, the healers may have taken out my eye."

Vhogare's heartbrother lay on his back, propped up in a field cot, bloody bandages wrapped around his left shoulder and torso, his face purple and bruised where his cheek was flayed. Bowls of red water were scattered around the pavilion's wooden work tables. Crimson rags, mortars and pestles, sewing thread, and monstrous hooked needles littered the shelves.

"You're a vicious bastard," Vhogare managed, hoping a jest would ease the ache in his chest.

"So much for the stag," Elias husked.

"I'd wager a bear counts for greater." He sat at the foot of the bed and opened his hand, displaying the claws. "Alastair retrieved these for you. Joanna can have your smith add them to your armor, so everyone will know you brought down a damn beast for your child's birth."

"We brought him down."

"The way 'we' brought down the fox that kept raiding the raven lofts?"

Elias's laugh was cut short with a hiss of pain. "Aye. Would that I was as quick as I was back then, I'd have given the bear a proper fight."

Vhogare shook his head. "Don't downplay yourself, Brother. You have a good head for battle. Far better than mine, and I've no shame in it."

"I've seen enough."

He had, too. The odd rebellion stacked up against them, border disputes, jousts and tournaments, and outright combat. But nothing that shredded armor. Nothing that had ever come so close. "Your father taught you well, as mine would have, had he the time."

Elias's mouth tightened, but he held his words.

Vhogare had no such qualms. He placed the claws on the nearest table, covered in bloody towels and bandages, and turned back to face the friend who'd nearly sacrificed everything. "If it had been Milan and me in those woods, I would have died."

Elias pushed himself up in bed. "No one's getting . . . eaten . . . on my watch."

"No." There was no laughter left in him.

Elias angled his head, frowning at the tone of Vhogare's voice.

"Without you, there is no me," Vhogare told him. "No Soleil. No family. No future nor throne nor life save what you bought in that water. I will owe you for this for the rest of my life, and after. I will tell the very Ark Himself what you have done."

Elias held his gaze. "Men go to war for crowns, but they die for brothers."

Tears pricked the back of Vhogare's eyes, but he did not let them fall. Instead, he took a breath to say the words he'd rehearsed while healers cleaned the dirt and gore out of Elias's gashes, the gruesome wounds now wrapped in white cloth. Blood bound souls—lives—together, and Vhogare had nothing else worth giving. Nothing else to prove that he would never stand aside again.

Bracing himself, he took Elias's sword out of its sheath. *Azrail.* Death to man and beast alike.

"I swear you a blood oath on this day," Vhogare said, drawing the blade across his injured palm. "I will fight at your back in battle and stand at your side in peace. I will be the sword to your shield, Brother, and never fail you while I yet live." He held his bloody palm out to the man who'd saved his life. "Should it come to it, and it be my life or yours, I will give mine."

Grimacing, Elias seized Azrail's blade, drawing blood despite all he had lost, and clasped Vhogare's hand, sealing the oath. "I will never drop my shield, Brother. And if it comes to that, you'll have to beat me to it."

"In death and in life," Vhogare promised. The ancient words of honor hummed in the air, weighted with all the blood spilled in their name throughout history.

Elias released Vhogare and pressed his bleeding hand over his heart. "In death and in life."

THE GUARD

ELIAS

Elias's head pounded. Every breath was agony, but it was not as bad as it could have been. Outside, the camp began to pack. Soldiers and servants broke down pavilions and loaded wagons. Inside, the healing tent's white linen canopy let the sun in. Golden light filtered through, beaming on the portable shelves and work tables laden with medicinal herbs and surgical materials. With the smell of his blood dissipated, the dried flowers and fragrant bundles lent the breezy space a pleasant aroma.

Even so, the field cot was uncomfortable. His wounds throbbed, and the heat of high summer did not help. Sweat made his gold ring slide as Elias twirled it around the middle finger of his right hand. If he pressed it against his busted knuckle, he could still read the faded inscription: *Unfailing.*

Promise me, he'd told Joanna before leaving. *Promise me that if I don't return, you will not be alone.* Stag hunts were dangerous; no one could deny the presence of boars and bandits in the king's wood. If anything happened to him, he would've rather seen her looked after than lost.

His wife had bitten her lip, looking for all the world as if she had something she could not say. *I will do no such thing.*

Elias's gut feeling had not been wrong. He'd come far too close to leaving her alone. Far too close to failing. Spymaster's son or not, it was time to settle down.

He studied his bandaged palm for a few moments before noticing his father standing at the entrance to the healer's pavilion. "How much longer?" he called. The carriage ride back to the capital would be insufferable, and he braced himself for the absence of the cool tent. Of stillness.

"Not much." Einar came to stand beside the bed and pressed a calloused hand to Elias's forehead to check for fever. "I have never been prouder of you than I am today."

"It was no more than you would have done."

"And I wish I'd been there instead."

Silence hung heavy in the tent between them.

"You will come to know this soon enough," his sire said, pulling up a chair to sit in his stiff armor. "But a father spends all his life preparing his children for when he is gone. You don't always know if what you have taught will remain behind."

Tears glistened in Einar's blue gaze. Elias straightened the thin sheet over his wounds. He had his mother's brown stare and knew it was sometimes hard for his father to look him in the eye. But after what had happened, Einar did not turn away, even as those tears ran down his cheeks into his beard. "You laid those fears to rest today."

Gratitude welled in Elias's chest, and he reached to pat the old knight's knee, his ribs screaming from the effort. "You've made a good name for our house. I will not see it fall."

"And I pray all His blessings on you for it. But we are shields before we are swords, Son," his father whispered. Glancing over his shoulder, he leaned forward and held Elias's eye. "There are some things worth risking everything for: the belief that good exists and can be saved, that life and peace will win in the end. And there are some things that are not."

He gripped Elias's shoulder in a vice. "I understand your wish to make something of yourself, but you must remember we serve the kingdom, not a king. Protect *yourself* for those you love, or the next time, the bear will get past your guard."

Shoving down the emotion that rose in his throat, Elias recited the vow of House Aldernari. "No war lost, no drop of blood forgotten—"

"—so long as the fire burns in each man's soul." Einar's wooden chair groaned as he sat back and scowled. "That light will never burn out, so long as we fight. But it will be a dark world if all the good soldiers die for silent kings."

Elias opened his mouth to ask what he meant, but his father stood, ruffled Elias's hair, and left before he could find the words. Alastair passed Einar at the tent's entrance, bringing news that Vhogare's carriages and wagons were ready.

While he was speaking, a seamstress slipped past the swornguard's side to pass Elias a hidden note along with fresh clothes. "For your travel," Gabriella said. Brushing her graying curls behind her ear, she flashed him a subtle yet significant look and left so he could change.

"Are you riding in our column?" Elias asked Alastair, sliding the note beneath his pillow as Gabriella disappeared. He at least wanted friends close by if he had to suffer the swaying, bumping carriage ride.

"At the front," the commander answered. "We'll get you home to Joanna in one piece."

"She'll never let me hear the end of this." Elias winced at a spike of pain, the stitched cut on his face pinching. "What of Aadriek?"

"Staying with Milan. The king and his retinue will follow behind, but we set off within the hour. I'm here to help you gather your things."

While Alastair carried his damaged armor and scant belongings to the carriage, Elias retrieved Gabriella's note. *The sand in the hourglass runs down,* her scrawled script read. One of his favorite aspects of his father's most trusted spy was that the woman's handwriting was nigh indecipherable if you weren't familiar with it.

He scowled down at the note. Einar would be busy over the coming weeks; the old king's mysterious illness had worsened. Ulrich's health had become dire, and the transition of power loomed much closer than the rest of the kingdom expected. Elias wondered if Vhogare knew the king was counting his sunrises. For his heartbrother's sake, he hoped there were more than a handful left.

He made a mental note to increase the number of guards present at Milan's coronation. Vhogare's foreign dignitary had not been found, which meant the stranger was either still in the sprawling citadel or on the loose. He prayed and prayed the suspicious man wasn't anywhere near the castle.

Though attending the hunt was his duty, he'd tried and failed to get out of it by offering to stay behind and look after the castle in Vhogare's absence. Leaving Joanna had been a mistake. He'd ensured she was well protected, but it was hell not being with her during such a vulnerable time. Every muscle in his body itched to return to her, and she'd pervaded his every thought since the bear. If he had died, he would've never been able to tell her goodbye.

With he and Einar gone, she was alone. And with strange visitors roaming and the king ailing, they could afford no weaknesses as the crown changed heads. A vulnerable kingdom put them all in danger.

He'd just burnt the note over the nearest candle flame when Alastair returned to assist him to the waiting carriage. "Kane's with them?" Elias rasped. His warhorse had come back for him after the bear. He would not see the magnificent beast left behind.

"Aye, I'll lead him myself."

Grunting his approval, Elias sat, letting out a stream of curses at the pain. The scent of salt and leather clung to Alastair as he helped Elias with his clothes, tugging his new trousers up and the dry shirt down over his head with as much dignity as possible. It was a fight to move with his wounds, and Elias thought Alastair might laugh at his impropriety, but the Marian warrior frowned down at him. "I should have been there. You should not have been out there alone, with the sons of a king."

All Elias could manage was a grateful smile as he caught his breath, battling down the throbbing agony in his chest. He had no time to weigh his friend's sentiments before the big man supported him, limping and swearing, to the waiting carriage.

THE CELESTIAL

VHOGARE

"I f it were me to be king, I'd name you Right Hand the second I took the throne," Vhogare said as their carriage pulled to a stop at a reputable inn on the road back to the capital. "Milan would be wise to do so, as well."

Elias waved him off, pain darkening his brown eyes. "I don't think he's given much thought to the matter, but whoever it is, it better be someone who can sit in a damn council chair." He winced as he pushed himself up onto unsteady feet, and Vhogare caught him before he could hit the floorboards.

"You should rest," Vhogare frowned, "but you won't, will you?"

Elias shook his head, grimacing. "You know I hate carriages. So small and cramped." He shuddered. "I wish I could ride."

"Please." Vhogare snorted. "Kane would take one step, and you'd fall out of your saddle."

Vhogare called for Alastair to help them out of the carriage. With a nod, the swornguard stepped up to the low door and ducked to weave an arm under Elias's shoulder.

"Regardless, it's a long road to the castle," Elias groaned as Vhogare and Alastair supported him down the single step. Dirt swirled around the halted column and sent Elias coughing, doubling him over. "And I'm already tired of pissing in a pot."

There was no arguing it, then.

At least the tavern looked inviting. The sprawling building was well-established, with a thick thatch roof and whitewashed walls. Alastair arranged boarding for their horses in the stables, and he and Vhogare assisted Elias, the stubborn bastard, up the stairs and into the common room. Inside, the smell of travel mingled with the sweet smoke of a fire, and Vhogare hummed a sigh of relief at the busy kitchen. Hard-working cooks meant plenty of food to go around.

They wove through the bustle of rowdy patrons and working folk to find a place to sit. While there wasn't enough space to invite their entire company indoors, Vhogare ensured roast and fresh bread were sent outside to their retainer.

Satisfied, he sank into the booth opposite Elias and rested his head against the rough stone wall at his back. "No wonder Milan is so exhausted all the time."

Elias chuckled, wincing as his wounded chest heaved. "Representing the Crown is tiring work."

"Peacocking is more like it."

"Even so"—Elias raised his cup—"to the Crown."

"To the *Crown.*" Vhogare gave a mocking salute and tipped his cup, draining it. They'd managed to seat Alastair and their remaining commanders and nobility at tables along the inn's southeastern wall, with a clear view of their column out the windows. Vhogare had done his due kindness to his highborn guests but wished he could do more for the dutiful soldiers stuck outside battling the swarming summer flies.

Maybe the campfires will drive the maddening creatures away. It seemed to be doing a good enough job of keeping the pests to a minimum indoors. Despite the heat, a roaring fire burned in the stone hearth built into the far end of the common room, something hearty simmering in a large pot above its flames. A mouthwatering beef stew, if the rich, hearty aroma was any indication.

Past the worn wooden chairs and tables, a couple engaged in a passionate embrace against the wooden wall of the stairs, and Vhogare smirked as weary travelers squeezed past them on their way to the rooms above. His gaze drifted, trailing the hazy smoke swirling and curling up the carved rails of the stairway to the thick oak rafters.

The ceiling was all but invisible, shrouded in small clouds of dancing gray, and Vhogare sensed that many good memories had been made within the tavern's walls. He'd have liked some place like this to call his own if he hadn't been born royal.

Shoving down the dream, Vhogare shouted a bawdy joke at the kissing couple's expense, eliciting a roar of laughter from the half-drunk patrons. When the racket died down, he paid for enough dinner and ale to serve their entire retinue, plus any visiting travelers. The innkeeper labored behind the oak-topped stone counter to deliver their supper. Cooks filed through the narrow workspace to retrieve dishes and supplies from the tidy shelves as the barmaid filled a dozen cups of ale and left Vhogare with the pitcher.

In the booth behind Elias, a cloaked stranger raised his tankard in thanks and emptied it in one go. Elias raised a brow at Vhogare's flagrant spending, but Vhogare shrugged and said, "It's not often a prince comes to town. Best the smallfolk keep good memories of us."

Elias raised a brow, impressed. "My father couldn't have said it better himself."

Vhogare wished the graybeard had come with them. Maybe Einar could've made his son see sense and stay abed. But the loyal Right Hand had remained behind with his king. "Don't seem so surprised. I listen to the old spymaster every once in a while."

"I'm telling him you called him old."

"Then I'm telling him you can't keep secrets. He'll be far more disappointed in you than me, *apprentice.*"

Elias laughed, and Vhogare waved the barmaid over. The ale was passable at best, but he wanted to feel warm inside. "Another round!" When she'd refilled their cups, he thunked his tankard against Elias's and drank deep before slamming it down on the wooden table.

The night carried on with laughter—and almost more toasts to Elias's good health than they could stomach. Vhogare looked on, slowing his drinking to sip at his ale, too busy stewing over Milan's behavior in the woods. He wondered if his blood brother would tell their father the truth about their bear encounter. Knowing Milan, he would, and he'd be worse off for it. Who would respect a king who pissed himself in battle?

But a far darker, more visceral thought gnawed at Vhogare as he pushed his food around in his trencher. He may not be the firstborn, but he was Elias's prince all the same. The son of the oldest king in Anchoran history, and he'd failed to protect his friend. All his training, and he'd proved himself no better than a green soldier, hadn't even thought to bring his own sword into the king's wood.

What if Elias had died?

What if it had been Soleil with him instead? Soon, she and their child would depend on him.

Firstborn or not, it is a prince's job to protect. Einar had taught Vhogare that priceless lesson the year his father first fell ill, and after Vhogare's performance in the woods, their spymaster would've been ashamed.

Shoving his nausea down, Vhogare interrupted their small traveling party with a final toast to Elias's mighty deed. "The whole kingdom will know your name by the time we're home."

Elias waved him off, but the spymaster's son grinned nonetheless as patrons emptied out for the night and the inn grew dark and silent. A peaceful warmth filled the quiet room, and Vhogare exhaled, leaning back in the booth and folding his hands behind his head. Their noble comrades departed to their carriages, but Alastair remained behind to see them out when they'd eaten their fill, and Vhogare slid the man another mug of ale. "Pity we can't make a damn royal progress."

"You should," interrupted the cloaked stranger from the booth behind Elias. "You have quite the tale to tell."

Vhogare went still. The loner had been so silent he'd forgotten the straggler was there. Before he could ask the man's name—or curse his lack of observance, the rogue reached over and put his hand on Elias's shoulder, and his comrade went stiff as steel.

Vhogare's blood froze over as the gash on Elias's cheek healed, blending into his plain flesh and leaving a smooth, clean scar behind. Elias reached up to touch his chest as if the three grotesque gashes there had mended, too.

Sitting at the table's empty far end, Alastair put a hand to the haft of his axe. Vhogare reached for Azrail, the sword at his hip to relieve his heartbrother of its weight, but Elias shook his head and put both hands on the table.

The move of a hostage.

The cloaked stranger kept his grip until all pain was erased from Elias's face. All that remained in its place was brutal, visceral fear. The mortal terror in his friend's steel glare eclipsed anything Vhogare had seen in the woods. But all the visitor offered in explanation was a smile. "I pity the beast."

"Name yourself," Elias demanded, not daring to so much as flinch under that grip.

"I'm an ambassador who wishes to speak to the prince alone. But you may join, if you wish, Elias."

Alastair went for his axe, well and truly at that, but the handle slipped, and the weapon clattered to the floor. Vhogare forced himself to breathe. Alastair had never dropped that weapon in all five years of his service. Whoever the bastard was, something strange was in their midst. No country healer could mend flesh in a heartbeat, nor stop a trained and blooded western warrior from raising their iron.

"Leave us," Vhogare ordered.

Alastair glared at him, incredulous.

"I said, leave us. And take the innkeeper and staff with you. By order of the Crown."

He knew his command was ludicrous. Not two full days had passed since he warned the commander about assassins in their midst. But the bloody stitched gash on Elias's face was a smooth, fresh scar. And anything done could be undone and made worse.

Radiating fury, Alastair did as commanded, and the smoky inn became as empty and still as a crypt. When all the others were gone, the stranger stood and pulled back the hood of his cloak.

The breath emptied from Vhogare's lungs. "I know you."

Elias cut Vhogare a glance. *The stranger from the castle?* he seemed to ask.

Vhogare gave a shallow nod. The foreign dignitary had traded his black cloak for a silver one, but it was without a doubt the same man. Cold adrenaline raced through Vhogare's blood. He'd talked to him, walked with him—this . . . this creature who could lay flesh back onto the bone. At least, if the stranger was there with them, he wasn't back at the castle with Joanna, or anywhere near Soleil.

The dignitary waved a hand at the kitchen doorway that opened into the woods. "Walk with me."

Elias, the bloody idiot, stood to match the man. Vhogare's friend was pale as dry bone and shuddering with fear, but there was not an ounce of pain in his stance as he squared off against whomever—whatever they faced. "Anything you wish to say can be said here. We are alone, as you asked."

Their visitor turned to face him and inhaled. "Joanna sleeps facing the east window so the first rays of sunrise shine on her face."

Elias's hand went to his knife. He didn't make it an inch before his oiled leather belt broke and the blade clattered to the floor.

"My name is Erembour. If you must know. I am a Gift Bearer. Walk with me, or your daughter dies."

Elias staggered back a step.

Daughter.

Vhogare shot to his feet and held a hand toward the door. "After you."

Erembour bade them to walk ahead, out the door, and into the dark forest beyond. Once they were lost in the trees, Vhogare took no more than ten steps before they were back at the riverbank, the bear dead in the water. He spun on his heel, noting the rotting tree trunk Milan had reclined against, the ring of charred stone, and dark ashes from the fire Elias had burnt. Even Kane's hoofprints remained in the soft earth. *This is impossible.*

On Vhogare's right, Elias padded across the forest floor, eyes narrowed with suspicion as he scrutinized their surroundings. But behind them, the stag lay, torn and abandoned. An entire day's travel, reversed in minutes, as if time and space had run past them and the forest folded in on itself.

Somewhere in the trees, a nightjar bird rattled, and Vhogare reached out and broke a branch, crushing the green leaves in his fist. The crisp, woodsy scent of spruce stuffed up his nose. He struggled against the disorientation, battling his senses, but he could not deny the truth. It was impossible—yet the thick king's wood surrounded them, the trees pressing in close. The river roared at his back, and he choked down a gag from the heated stench of the great bear's carcass.

Erembour removed his hood, revealing his ink-black hair and close-cropped beard. At the castle, he'd looked ordinary. Human. But in the dark of the forest, Erembour's alabaster skin was streaked through with silver veins like marble, as if he were carved of living stone. Vicious silver fire curled up his hands and arms beneath the garment's sleeves, raging across his immortal flesh. It twined in ribbons of dancing flame, swirling, but not touching the fabric of his tunic and cloak. The very same silver blaze burned in his eyes.

"As a second-born prince, I assume you are educated," Erembour rumbled, addressing Vhogare in a voice that could've eaten night itself.

Swallowing, Vhogare glanced at Elias and managed a nod. He couldn't shake the sense that they stood in the presence of a predator, and no sword would bring this beast down.

"You know of the Ark of Creation and the three horsemen He has called to maintain balance."

"Justice, Judgment, and Chaos," Vhogare recited, remembering the royal cleric who'd taught him his histories as a boy. He could picture every carved column in the castle's chapel, the three celestials' cloaked statues turned to gaze at the ever-burning flame.

Raw power coursed off Erembour in waves. "I am Chaos, and I come here to make a request."

Chaos.

Vhogare went rigid. The Ark had always made Himself known as loving and kind, a well of unending, unfathomable life holding the world in His arms. But the creature who stood across from them was the darkness of the night sky given flesh and blood, forged from the cold of stars, and the prince felt far too much like prey under his gaze.

"And what request is that?" Elias squared his feet, and Vhogare sent up a prayer of thanks that his friend had been healed in case they had to die fighting.

The horseman strode to the riverside to inspect the bloated carcass. "My two brothers and I serve Invar, part of the Ark's very soul."

Elias curled his hands into fists. "How is that possible? To split one's soul."

He could've sworn Erembour's gaze dampened. "The Ark is creation, as you well know—the very essence of life. There is no end to His soul. If He were to speak with you Himself, He would overmake you in His power." Erembour stood to run a hand across a branch, caressing the summer leaves. New, fresh buds sprouted where his fingers touched. "These lush forests would overrun the crude shelters you call homes, *castles.*" He spat the word as if the colossal structures were pathetic, and perhaps, to a creature like him, they were.

"The great waters would slip their binds and cover your nations," Erembour continued, "every living thing multiplying a thousandfold. Trees would swallow stones, and the earth would swallow you. Such complete *existence* would make it impossible for your flesh to survive."

Vhogare's body betrayed him, and he shuddered. How could mortal man contend with such limitless, unchecked *life?* Struggling to breathe, he clamped his jaw, forcing down air as he fought to stand tall.

Erembour's gaze snapped from Elias to him as if he'd heard Vhogare swallow. "So the Ark took Invar out of his heart, pulling forth a separate being who could commune with you without harm, and set him over time itself. But when He did so, Chaos slipped free. And in his kindness, Invar made that chaos my gift to guard and use as needed." He splayed his hands, silver light flickering across the rushing water. "I was nothing before he made me this, and I intend to do well with it."

"You are a celestial," Elias growled through clamped teeth, fighting against the terrified tremors wracking him as well. "What business have you here, with us?"

With mortals, Vhogare almost said.

"The Ark set Invar in charge of time. But Invar is dying, and your time is running short."

Vhogare's heart fell out of his chest. His hand drifted to the silver dragon hidden in his pocket. *Soleil.* If Invar was dying, Time died, too, and his days with his love grew shorter with every breath.

And against such a fate, the king had denied Vhogare her hand. All she had worked for, all their love, and he could not even marry her before their world ended.

Vhogare swore—*his father.* A good king, a strong man, and a faithful sword, and after all Ulrich had accomplished, his legacy would be stripped from him. Anchora's loyal Sword sat dying of a wasting illness on a steel chair that would remain long after he perished.

Perhaps long after they all were gone, if their time was as short as the celestial said.

"The Ark is eternal," Vhogare demanded, scrambling to form a thought. "How can Invar die?"

Something akin to rage flickered across Erembour's face, but the celestial snuffed it out. "Because he does this for you."

Elias glanced between the two of them, shifting.

"Invar holds your line of time in his hands," Erembour explained with icy patience, "and all others. Your lives are written in his blood—his *life.*" Disgust coiled across the celestial's face. "You *feed* off of his immortality. Invar's blood is the sand in the hourglass of your lives, and it runs down.

"When he dies, this time ends, and all of you end with it. Every world, every heartbeat and breath, is blood-bought. Invar gives all and will take all with him except the Ark Himself when he goes." Erembour squared his broad shoulders. "The longer he holds these worlds together, the longer he bleeds."

"And you?" Elias asked. Demanded. "What of you?"

"I end, as well. Invar's Court of Celestials will die. As will my brothers, Rondiel and Tzaddik, who have not come with me. We will be nothing again. Thus, my request." He held out a hand burning with silver fire. "I ask you to lighten the load of this world. The fewer lives Invar must carry, the longer he will live, and the more time we all will have."

Vhogare's blood frosted over. "You wish to cull the world." Erembour would kill Soleil—their child.

"Part of it." The celestial angled his chin, his coarse beard dark in the night. "A large part of it."

Vhogare could've sworn Elias shook his head, the movement nigh-imperceptible, but he pressed on. "How soon?"

Would Elias's daughter live to see the world? Would his own child even be born?

Or would life itself be ripped out from under them when everything they knew and loved ended? When Time itself ended?

"As soon as I can." Erembour splayed his hands at his sides. "Invar bleeds even now. His very life, given for you."

"Then it is his choice," Elias countered. "And we are grateful for it."

"Grateful." Wrath skittered along the word. "You, who only ask how long you have and forget the reason you have it." Cold scalded the air, and Erembour did nothing to hide his dark fury. "You, who would rather have him bleed."

Guilt slammed into Vhogare. But he studied the scar on Elias's cheek, near-invisible in the moonlit dark. Felt the weight of Soleil's pewter dragon in his pocket. If Erembour took matters into his own hands, would he destroy life impartially? How would he decide who would stay and who would go? Who was worth saving, if anyone, to a celestial who viewed them all as an open wound?

Defiance swelled in Vhogare's chest, desperate and unyielding. "You cannot do this," he said. "If I knew how to stop Invar's pain, I would. But Chaos is a force for good, for change." How many times had he heard that in sermons, in history lessons? "It is a . . . a river of life keeping the world moving. You three horsemen are meant to guide us. You cannot mean to harm us with your gifts."

Erembour's upper lip curled back from his teeth in a vicious snarl. "My brothers and I each occupy two pillars in your chapels. *Two,* for the duality of our nature." He raised his hands, and the ground began to burn around them. "Justice and vengeance. Judgment and wrath. Chaos and death."

Frigid wind buffeted Vhogare, sending him staggering back a step. Silver flame spread out from Erembour in an ever-growing circle, eating the fallen leaves and licking up the trunks of ancient trees. Birds took flight, shrieking from their nests, as dry, icy fire devoured the clearing whole. It consumed all life, reducing everything to dust in a cold blaze unlike any flame Vhogare had ever known.

It blew through the trees like a giant's frozen breath, wreathing the sturdy oaks and vibrant spruce in a tempestuous, dancing blaze. Pines and spruce swayed, fighting to cling to the earth as they were uprooted in the firestorm. Erembour's power blew Vhogare's hair out of his face and hurled him and Elias to the ground as if they were nothing. They raised their arms to shield their faces, hissing as an unearthly, biting cold seared their skin.

Then, like someone had snuffed a candle, the fire ended. Vhogare peeked over his blistered arm as the silver flames raced back into Erembour like water down a drain.

Devastation surrounded them. The dead, shredded stag had been burnt to bones, its flesh piles of ash on the forest floor. Trees lay as uprooted husks, their trunks and branches charred black. A strange, acrid smell clung to the air, like a sword held too long above a flame.

And the bear. . . . The bear had been left untouched, bloated, and half-submerged in the river, exactly the way Elias had left it.

A show of not just power, but control.

Erembour glared at them as they gaped at the ruined clearing.

Fear struck Vhogare full in the chest like a warhorse at an all-out gallop and shredded him down to his very core. He quaked as if he stood before the bear again, staring down a beast with only a spear in his shaking hand. But where most men would've found silence, shock, or reverence in the face of such power, all Vhogare unearthed was rage.

"How dare you," he heard himself say, staggering as he struggled to his feet. Hurt and disbelief cycloned through him, nausea churning his gut at his blistered arm, but only wrath and indignation clawed out of his throat. "We trusted you!"

Erembour angled his head, a bitter, conflicted smile ghosting over his lips.

"You were meant to look after us!" Vhogare shouted. "You're *made* to protect us. Chaos is endless chance. Beautiful, boundless opportunity. Not endings. Not darkness." His chest heaved, his breath coming too fast. "You represent hope in the face of oblivion."

Sharp pain split Vhogare's ribs, and he clenched his hands into fists as rage clawed up his back at the scathing betrayal. "We rely on you to lead and guide us like kings do their kingdoms, and you come down here and throw us to the wolves because you are scared to die?"

Elias stood and gaped at him, slack-jawed, but Vhogare couldn't stop. Couldn't justify his anger. But he'd spent his life against a wall, locked between the crown and the sword, always at another man's mercy—and this bastard meant to peel everything he loved out of his dead, ashen hands.

Wrath roared through his blood like lightning, turning his skin to fire and his heart to a beating drum. "This is not justice," Vhogare growled. "This is not good judgment. You mean to take their lives away, their world. They do not even get to decide."

"No. They do not," Erembour said, as if their fate had already been determined and nothing more needed to be said.

As if it were already over.

"What of mercy?" Vhogare demanded, unable to fathom the depthless, heartbreaking cold in Erembour's onyx eyes.

Erembour's brow furrowed as if he did not understand. "Mercy? There is no room for mercy when your god dies."

All thoughts emptied from Vhogare's head. Sound itself seemed to cease, the world around him falling away in his consuming anger. "No," Vhogare said again, his voice broken and harsh in defiance. "You cannot take away our happiness, our lives, just because he's dying. I do not care if you die with him, you have no right—"

Erembour lunged.

Elias made to move between them, but the celestial clamped his flaming hand over Vhogare's mouth—and then . . . and then the world burned.

***

Great columns of flame surrounded his home, devouring it. Their dark, beautiful castle roared with fire. Towers fell, and his father's bones sat on the throne. The crown fell from King Ulrich's broken skull and cracked the stone floor. Anchora herself burned, chaos and anarchy a living force in her midst.

Vhogare stood in the square, gaping, as Soleil ran to him through a burning city. Her dark hair streamed, smoldering, behind her, his favorite blue gown torn to shreds. Entire rows of homes and roads went up in silver fire as she raced past the city's great houses, their waving banners dissolving into fluttering cinders. Her dress was bloody, and she held their child in her arms, weeping as she wailed Vhogare's name.

He caught her as she barreled into him, the scent of singed lilac and lavender stuffing up his nose through the smoke. Their baby cried. Tears streaked through the ash clinging to Soleil's face as she looked up at him and opened her mouth to speak, to warn him, but no words came out—only a scream as she withered to bone dust in his arms.

"Soleil—"

Vhogare reached, scrabbling, to catch their child before it fell, but the babe was ash in his hands—small piles of embers in his palms. He never even got to see his baby's face.

There was nothing human in the scream that tore out of his chest at that loss. Vhogare's wail of torment was so loud and hopeless that his voice shredded and splintered, breaking until no more sound came out, only breath.

"YOU CANNOT DO THIS," he roared, heaving, falling to his knees on the cobbled street and clutching their ashes against his heart. Despite the fire, the world had gone cold. Colder than the north in the dead of winter. Colder than life without the sun. "You cannot take them from me."

Vhogare shut his eyes against the consuming terror and folded his arms against his chest as if he could still hold Soleil. Could still keep their family together. But they were gone, and his arms, his heart, were empty. In the dreamscape, he did not even have the silver dragon to clutch for strength. Gasping for breath around back-breaking sobs, he blinked the ash out of his eyes only to find himself out of the city's streets and inside the castle.

Vhogare knelt with his back to his father's throne. Behind him, the entire rear wall of the throne room had been torn out. A gaping hole yawned open where the three floor-to-ceiling windows should have been. Their wondrous, pale stained glass lay in shattered shards on the floor. Half of the columns supporting the ceiling had crumbled and broken.

And yet Elias stood in the center of the colossal throne room, shield raised, as the world shook to her bones.

There was no Soleil.

No Joanna.

No little girl at Elias's side or in his arms.

Somehow, in his soul, Vhogare knew they were gone. Pax Anchora was ruined, flattened, torn apart.

His heartbrother was alone.

And still, Elias stood, bleeding and broken, Vhogare's castle coming down around him. Still, he held that shield like his life depended on it.

Like all their lives depended on it.

Vhogare rocked on his knees, holding ashes against his chest, sucking down air like a drowning man. There was nothing he could do. . . .

Erembour appeared in the vision, clad in his dark ethereal armor. He strode through the fire and blood to stand in front of Vhogare and grabbed his chin, forcing him to watch as the blood ran down Elias's side and flame curled around his heartbrother's shield.

"If you do this for me," the celestial said, "you can keep him. Joanna. Soleil. Your heart."

His grip on Vhogare's chin tightened to the point of pain. "But if you refuse, I will take them all."

The ceiling above splintered, broke, and fell, enormous beams and boulders tumbling down to crush Elias to a bloody ruin upon the stones. Vhogare shut his eyes as the world blew apart, peeling open in a great canopy with bones of flame.

He opened his mouth and screamed, and fire—silver fire—ate the world.

Erembour let go of Vhogare's face, and Vhogare found himself on his knees on the bloody riverside, his throat raw and torn from screaming, and his jaw wet with tears. The sides of his face ached from the force of the celestial's grip. He crumpled, gasping, into the dirt, unable to get air down fast enough.

Above him, Elias stood staring, pale as white stone.

Hunched over, Vhogare wretched. He couldn't get Soleil's ashes out of his nose, his mouth. The scent of burnt lavender seemed to cling to his face. He heaved until his stomach was empty and only bile leaked from his lips. Still choking down air, Vhogare wiped his face and braced himself against the solid ground as his world spun.

A cool wind blew across his face, and with it came clarity. For a heartbeat, Vhogare stared down at his hands. His arms shook, his skin cold and clammy, but there was no ash beneath his fingernails. No bone dust on the back of his palms. Panicking, he searched every pocket until he found the pewter dragon Soleil had given him. Fresh tears spilled as he clutched her gift against his heaving chest.

It wasn't real. It had been some dream, a trick.

But the celestial of chaos still stood in front of him, as solid and immovable as the rocks and the ground. His jaw throbbed where the horseman had gripped his face.

And what he'd seen *had been* real. He felt it in his soul, far beyond mere flesh and blood. Vhogare labored over a breath. It had not been a dream but a vision, a warning, and after all those years, Vhogare knew what Joanna meant when she said she couldn't understand; she just *knew*.

When he managed to command his voice again, Vhogare sank back on his knees and stared up at the celestial that had come to rip them apart. "You came to us," he managed, his throat dry.

Erembour scowled and laid a hand on the curved blade at his hip. "I know a scythe when I see one."

A reaping blade. Perhaps it was unavoidable, but if there was a chance he could save those he loved, he had to take it.

"You know how to stop Invar's pain," the celestial said, squaring his stance. "I've told you. And now I hold you accountable."

Vhogare swallowed the bitterness in his mouth and forced himself to consider. "The few for the many?"

"And the many for the few."

Soleil and his baby would live. Elias and Joanna could meet their daughter. The day-old slice on his palm itched, and Vhogare staggered to his feet. He held out his hand. "Swear that we will choose who to cull and who to save."

Erembour nodded. "So long as the weight is lightened, it makes no difference to me."

"Vhogare—" Elias started, but Erembour held up a hand, and Elias froze, his hand clutching his heart in sudden pain.

"Stop," Vhogare snarled. Panic flared in his chest as he stepped between Elias and the celestial. "You'll have what you want from me."

"Cut them down yourself," the celestial finished, stepping back and releasing Elias, who crashed to the ground, wheezing but otherwise unharmed. "Or I will return. And if you fail, on my gift, you will pay dearly for the time you stole."

"How?" Vhogare rasped. Air ghosted over his lips, all his voice gone. His life was worth nothing without theirs. *How can I stop it?*

That silver fire erupted from Erembour's palm, pouring out to dance in a wild flame above his fingers. Around them, the forest seemed to rise from the dead. Trees righted themselves. The stag's flesh mended back onto its bones. Vhogare stared in shock as the blisters on his and Elias's arms healed as if they had never happened. The clearing sped through each season, leaves blooming and dying and blooming again, as the forest molted once again into its original summer-kissed state.

Erembour smiled at Vhogare's fear. *Chaos.* The celestial's very eyes lit with it. "Name your weapon, and it will be yours."

Vhogare clutched the tiny dragon to his chest with a trembling fist. He opened his mouth to answer, but Elias stepped in front of him, panting like he'd been in battle.

"I know the Ark," Elias grated, straightening. "I know of Invar and his three horsemen. But there has never been any history, no prophecy—spoken or otherwise—claiming what you say about Invar is true."

Erembour frowned. "Why would they tell you your world was ending?"

"If there are three of you," Elias growled, "there may very well be more. If this Court of Celestials exists, let us speak with them. See if they corroborate what you claim."

"You wish me to call down the Fire of Judgment upon your head?" The celestial trailed his burning gaze from Elias to Vhogare. "Do you want to know what Heaven's Justice would say about you?"

Vhogare froze under that dare, that fire—beautiful and fearsome as life and death—dancing above their heads.

Elias didn't back down. "We make no choice until we know you speak true."

With the forest healed, Erembour's silver fire banked out, leaving a dark onyx glare in its wake. "Every second you spend deciding bleeds him more. I owe Invar too much to stand aside and let you waste his life. Choose, Vhogare. I will see your work begin in three days, or I will have blood."

Strange letters began to glow across the celestial's face as if a book had opened beneath his skin. Words in an archaic language that Vhogare did not understand, had never seen, traced lines down Erembour's neck and arms until they began to meld together, like rivers of living silver in his blood. Time and space ran past them once more, pulled inward in a vast, blinding vortex. Erembour vanished into the swirl of light, stepping out of existence as if he'd never set foot on the mortal plane.

Behind Elias stood the inn again. The tavern's whitewashed walls seemed to glow in the moonlight, the thatched eaves casting long shadows across the grassy yard. Vhogare shook uncontrollably. One of the innkeeper's black-and-white goats approached them. All he could do was stand there and watch the thing as it chewed on the end of his surcoat. Tears sliced down his cheeks, too cold against the warm night.

Elias fared no better. Vhogare's heartbrother retched onto the grass until his gut was empty. Wiping his mouth, Elias staggered across the dark lawn to the well and splashed water on his face as if he hoped to wake from a nightmare. Alastair's powerful, resonant voice shouted search orders somewhere by the road. When the swornguard found them, Vhogare had no words to explain their absence.

One look at the pallor of their faces and Elias's healed wounds, and Alastair swore. "What happened?" he demanded, gripping Vhogare's shoulder. The commander had been in the inn and seen Erembour's healing take place. "The stranger—"

"Was a foreign dignitary in truth," Elias cut in, "sent here to negotiate. There are . . . political games afoot. Dangerous games."

Alastair searched his face. The man knew Elias was lying, but they had no other options. Who would believe them? Until he knew more, it was best to keep it between them.

"Have you sent word ahead of my injuries?" Elias demanded, thinking for both of them as Vhogare stood stiff and unblinking. Frozen, just as he'd been against the damned bear.

Alastair nodded. "To Joanna. The castle will know."

"Then we will say it was not as bad as first believed. The camp healers did a wonderful job." Elias straightened, though his hands still shook. "The rest, I will speak with my father about."

Einar's son, through and through.

Alastair squared his shoulders. "Very well. I am sworn to serve."

Forcing himself back to his senses, Vhogare held the warrior's iron gaze. "So serve." He did not know if it was a plea or a threat, but he stood on a knife's edge, and they needed secrecy. The faithful swornguard brothers never failed them.

Alastair studied him for a moment as if weighing the raw terror in Vhogare's eyes against the command in his voice, but eventually relented. "Everyone waits for you at the carriages. I will recall the search party once they see you are both safe." Alastair pinned Elias with a warrior's scowl. "Until then, I suggest you still act injured."

Elias glanced at Vhogare. *Can you do this?* his friend's eyes seemed to ask. *Can you pretend until we reach somewhere safe?*

But there was nowhere safe. There was no running. No escaping a fire that could eat the world.

Summoning all his determination, Vhogare swung Elias's arm over his shoulder, pretending to support his friend's weight as he had upon first entering the inn. "We need to get home."

With a nod, Alastair led the way back to the road.

THE GARDEN

ELIAS

I n all their years, Vhogare had never screamed. Not since he was
a child.

A shout of pain, a battle cry, but never the gut-rending
agony that had shredded his heartbrother's throat as Erembour
gripped Vhogare's jaw. That sound had been pure anguish, pure loss.
Elias had not even known such a heartbroken wail could tear from a
human chest. It etched into his memory, burrowed so deep there was
no forgetting the sheer pain.

Three heartbeats had passed between Vhogare and the celestial,
but it had been enough to break something in the man.

Nothing had ever horrified Elias more.

The remaining carriage ride to the castle was dead quiet. Vhogare
stared at his boots the entire time, turning the silver dragon in his
hands and refusing to meet Elias's eyes. Elias couldn't bring himself to
break that silence. Erembour's vicious voice kept ringing in his head.

Walk with me, or your daughter dies.

Daughter.

How could he have known? How could *anyone* in the world be
certain until the babe was born? Midwives had their methods, but
there was no certainty until birth.

Still, some part of him—a part that terrified Elias beyond his bones—believed the stranger. Erembour had come not to assassinate the king but the world. Elias unwrapped his bandaged hand and gazed down at the healed scar crossing his palm. *In death and in life.*

In the span of a day, the two had become the same. Invar bled so the world could live, and now Erembour would slaughter them all so he could survive.

Unless Erembour had lied.

Elias spent every second of the rumbling ride begging the Ark that he had not jeopardized his child's chances by standing against the celestial. Prayed Joanna had not yet gone into labor.

He'd left her. He'd left her alone at the castle, and he hated himself for it.

If something happened, and he had not been there with her. . . .

The carriage wheels creaked as they crossed the ornate, arched granite bridge spanning the Delys River, marking their entrance to the capital. Elias's heart beat in his throat as the draft horses' shod hooves drummed against the gray cobblestone streets. Outside their small, curtained window, Pax Anchora was radiant. The city's arborists had been hard at work; each street's flowering trees bloomed with white, orange, and red in the height of summer.

His home was glorious; after four decades, there was no trace of King Ulrich's brutal war, and the builders had surpassed themselves in revitalizing the destroyed capital. But the close-built stone townhouses had never felt more suffocating. As they drew closer to the city center, humble terraced homes gave way to ornate granite and black slate architecture, each street and shop guarded by decorative wrought iron fences.

The city was dark yet beautiful as the sun glinted brightly off the inky tiled roofs. Opulent fountains bubbled in every square, hemmed in by blooming rose bushes, their myriad colors radiant as fire against the ironwork. Ruby rows of flameflower lined the roadside, and verdant fruit trees leaned over the roads, but no summer birdsong could brighten Elias's mind.

His mood was as dark and foreboding as the fortress nestled against the lush eastern mountain. The sun began to set, its last rays illuminating the castle's west wing, and the imposing walls seemed to shadow Elias's dread. Each sharp, gothic tower stared down at him until the carriage wheels could not turn fast enough. He bounced his knee, anxious, as they thundered across the lowered drawbridge and under the portcullis, pulling up to the dominating keep looming like a curled beast against the evening light.

The moment they stopped inside the castle walls, he leaped from the carriage. Vhogare swore a string of colorful curses as he vaulted out behind Elias and sprinted to offer support, struggling to keep up and maintain Elias's charade of injury. Servants and castle staff muttered as the two of them staggered past, but Elias ignored them, moving as swiftly as he could while maintaining his cover. Alastair would spin his tale, and the speculation would pass. Joanna could not wait.

Elias shuffled and limped as fast as he could through the elaborate main hall, turning right at the throne room's huge doors and climbing the sweeping staircase to the east wing. Every heartbeat was torture as he took the steps two and three at a time. The additional guards saluted as he drew near to his quarters, and though no screams ricocheted down the stone walls, he could not be certain that did not mean the worst.

Vhogare left him at the entrance to his suite, and Elias nearly took the door off the hinges as he burst in to find Joanna standing by the eastern window in her nightgown. Their four-poster bed was a mess, the green sheets tossed about, and maidservants fluttered around the room, lighting candles and stoking the fire against the oncoming night.

Joanna spun to face him as he stumbled in, her honey-blonde waves cascading over her shoulder. A hand went to the swell of her belly before she recognized her husband. His friend since he was four-and-ten, his constant companion—the woman he'd cherished and supported and fought for—was safe. Elias nearly fell to his knees.

But she'd been crying. Her eyes were red and swollen, her jaw quivering. The freckles dusting her nose and cheeks stood out against her flushed skin as she took in his presence and the look on his face. No words passed between them as he crossed their room and held her to him with as much strength as he dared.

Joanna threw her arms around his shoulders and buried her face in his neck. "The raven said—"

He cut her off with a kiss. "Are you all right?" he asked before kneeling to put both hands on her belly, feeling for the child within. A tiny push greeted him, pressing up against his palm. Elias choked on a sob and laid his brow against the soft fabric of her nightgown.

Joanna brushed his hair out of his eyes. "The pains are coming quicker, but my water hasn't broken. The midwives have been pestering me day and night."

He stood to kiss her again. "I will be right here. Pestering you far more."

Her laughter died at the tears running down his face. She reached up to wipe them away, tracing the pale line of the scar that had not been there when he'd left. "What happened?"

How could he tell her? How could he not? "I promise we will speak of it when she's in our arms."

Joanna's brow quirked. "She?"

Elias stood behind her, wrapping his arms around her chest. He stroked a thumb over the linen of Joanna's nightgown as they gazed out the eastern window at the mountains and the glittering loch below. Stars had begun to appear in the orange sky. "One can hope."

He held his ground with Joanna, refusing to share more for fear of making her labor difficult, but he did not leave her side until she fell into a fitful sleep, doubtless the last she'd get until the babe was born. Vhogare creaked open the door in the hour of the wolf. Glancing to ensure Joanna slept, he gestured for Elias to leave the room.

Putting away the history book he'd been poring over by candlelight, Elias stood from his wooden chair by her bedside, tucked the sheet back over Joanna's bare leg, and stepped out, shutting the door behind him. He pinned Vhogare with a steel glare. "Whatever you say," he growled, "speak it quietly. We will not risk her for this."

"I should've taken the gift Erembour offered. Made that . . . creature our ally." Vhogare slid down the wall opposite. "Why did you stop me?" he demanded, sitting with his head in his trembling hands. "Do you have any idea what he could do?"

"Do *you?*" The prince was about to answer, but Elias cut him off. "We require more information before we start a massacre."

Vhogare held up both hands to shush him, cutting a glance at Joanna's room. "I have no desire to lose our people to his fear. But I've given it much thought," he confessed in the dark hall. "And I see no way out but through."

"So you'll put yourself in league with a nightmare brandishing a trick of the light?"

Vhogare got to his feet, dark fury on his face. "In *league* with him? I'm trying to buy us time to think of something to use against him. And that was no trick of light. You saw what he did to trees far older and far stronger than you or me," Vhogare growled, raw terror prowling the ice of his eyes. "Hold your wife again, with a shoulder that got ripped from the socket." He struck Elias on the sternum with a finger. "Against a chest that was torn to shreds right in front of me."

"How do we know it will even happen in our lifetimes? In hers?"

"Is that all you care about?" Vhogare demanded, throwing an arm in the direction of Joanna's door. "What about your daughter's children and her children's children? *My* children? Soleil——" Vhogare's voice broke. "He will kill them all, Elias. And they will die in pain. Would you not do anything to stop that from happening?"

"You know I would!" Elias thundered before catching himself. "But we must be wise about this."

"Wise? We must be fast. Strike quickly. They will know life," Vhogare swore in a vicious whisper. "Even if I must die to see it through."

"Perhaps Erembour speaks true." Elias had interrogated his fair share, but this celestial was a foreign entity; there was no telling what he could conceal.

They fell quiet as a group of servants approached with an armful of wood and tinder, gossiping on their way to refresh the hearth fire in Einar's solar upstairs.

Elias lowered his voice as the attendants turned the corner and disappeared up the steps. "Perhaps Invar is dying. Perhaps he is not. Perhaps this rogue celestial is not all that he claims."

"Perhaps tomorrow we will all wake up dead," Vhogare muttered before raising his voice to a whisper. "Regardless, I will have a say in what happens to my country."

"Yes, but if he gives you pruning shears, which of us will be the flowers, and which will be the weeds?"

Vhogare had no answer for that. He leaned against the sill of the hall's eastern window, the moonlight illuminating his face as he searched for words.

Elias paced the humid corridor. He raked his gaze across the ancient reliefs carved into the stone walls as he listened, checking for more servants or his father's prying eyes. For the moment, they were alone, and his mind cycloned.

He'd trained for such a time as this—for this very hour. Perhaps not against celestials, but spycraft was his trade by birth, his game. His father was the royal spymaster, advisor, and Right Hand to the oldest king in Anchoran history, and he was nothing if not his father's son. He could outmaneuver this somehow.

"I agree we need time. If—and I do mean *if*—Erembour speaks true, we need a hand on the reins."

It was Einar's first rule. Control the board.

And Joanna and Soleil were in play if they failed.

"Besides, there is no proof the Ark Himself even sent Erembour." All they had was one celestial's word, and for all Elias knew, the bastard lied. "One horseman is better odds than three."

And he would never dare challenge the One who put Joanna in his life, who brought their child this far. The Ark was creation, not destruction. That great Love would never take Elias's child from him. His daughter would not fall to some star creature who could very well be a rogue scythe sweeping clear the world.

But they needed more information before they could fight.

Vhogare tracked him as he paced. The prince's visage was ghost-pale in the night.

"Erembour said Invar's death is inevitable," Elias began, pausing with his hands braced on his new sword belt. "The longer he holds us, the more he bleeds. If Invar gave Erembour power and made him what he is, it stands to reason that Erembour wants to lighten the load to prolong his *own* life. He is the bear all over again, protecting his heart." He ran a hand through his hair, scowling as he tried to force the pieces together. "But Invar chose this. His blood is his gift."

"This is not a stag hunt, Elias," Vhogare snapped before silencing himself back to a whisper. "It is not a blessing but a price. Look at your face, your chest." He paused at a rustling sound, continuing when he was certain the hall was clear. "I count myself more fortunate than most. I've seen nigh every corner of this country, every set of the sun across its face. Soleil's face." Panic edged Vhogare's words, no doubt at the thought of his lover burning along with the rest of them.

"My father lived and bled for this kingdom," the prince continued, "and my mother died so he could cement his damn legacy. Gave her life for *me*. I will not let her pain be in vain. Her memory will not be bathed in blood because of one weak link—"

Elias seized his collar. "Keep your mind, soldier," he growled. "We will not lose this. We cannot."

Vhogare shoved him back. "He will reap our world whether we choose it or not."

"But if he were to give us the sword. . . ."

Elias did not need to say the rest; Vhogare understood. An ember sparked in the prince's frost-blue eyes.

Something red-hot and lethal welled up in Elias's chest at the thought. This moment could change the trajectory of their lives forever. If they went down this road, nothing would ever be the same again.

"If we make no choice, he will cull us all," Elias reasoned. "But it does not need to be that way." He glanced at the door, his heart beating for the woman behind it. "It is a price, aye. But not at this cost," he vowed. "We take the sword. Protect our world. And turn the gift on the giver when he comes to collect."

Vhogare chewed his lip, considering. "If there are two other celestials, there may be more to take Erembour's place."

"And if he was bluffing?"

"Bluffing?" Vhogare gasped, incredulous. "Will not the Ark strike us down if we disobey?"

"Your father has suffered his fair share of traitors. How many of them spoke as if they had the king's mouth?"

Vhogare's brow ironed out.

"Invar is a piece of the Ark's soul, above all three of their horsemen. If he bleeds for us, he will never cut us down. We are sons of Anchora," Elias rasped. "Charged with her safety. We do no rogue bastard's bidding." He snatched Vhogare's bandaged hand from his side. "You bled. Would you cut me down?"

"Never."

"Then I see no reason to let this traitor live. Erembour's fear will not claim our kingdom." *Our world.* "And we can save Invar the trouble of killing him."

Vhogare swallowed. "Then the only question is who should claim the gift."

"I will stand in your place. In case this is some trick." Elias forced his thundering heart to slow. Tried not to think about Joanna and all he'd be giving up if things went wrong. She was everything, his very sunrise, and she deserved whatever chance he could give her. "Some things are worth giving everything for."

Vhogare glanced at the scar on Elias's face and curled his fist. "You will do no such thing."

Elias opened his mouth to reason with him, but Vhogare cut him off. "You are my sworn sword. And as your prince, I order you to stand aside."

"You choose tonight of all nights to pull rank?"

"I did not make my vow lightly." A fierce and biting cold stole over Vhogare's sharp features. "You speak true. I am a prince of Anchora, my father's son, and I bend no knee. You and yours, me and mine, against him and his. When the celestial returns, he will be sorry he ever threatened the Crown."

Elias's blood boiled. But when Erembour returned, they would stand a far better chance against him with the chaos gift in hand. Vhogare could end this before it started if the sword—the gift—was theirs. Better the brother of his heart bear the gift than a stranger— better Vhogare than running the risk of losing Joanna.

Fire burned in Elias's soul, but a sliver of ice shot through it. This choice was irreversible. If he was wrong—if Erembour was not a traitor and was instead some loyal son—they were going to trick a celestial. Steal the gift of chaos itself. And try to kill one of the Ark's horsemen with the very silver fire Erembour handed them.

No. Elias was certain his reasoning was sound. The Ark loved them. Invar bled for them. Erembour was a traitor. And they were keeping a knife out of Invar's back with this choice.

A chill trickled down Elias's spine. They were mere mortals playing a celestial game. Would Vhogare be enough? Would *he* be enough? To go up against death himself and win?

"We can do this," Vhogare said, reading the fear plain on his face. "You told me once that you wish to do something with this life." The prince straightened, glancing over Elias's shoulder to ensure they were still alone. "You are the brother of my soul, and I am grateful you stand at my side. Let me do this thing for you. Let me spare you this blood, however much of it needs to be spilled to carve out a weapon that will take down this beast."

Elias's heart thundered, a hammer against a glowing anvil in his chest.

"Soleil and my child will live." Vhogare thrust a finger at Elias's door. "Joanna and your daughter will be safe. But her father's hands should be clean. We will make the world safe for them so they can grow old. I will do everything in my power, at all costs, to see them survive."

"We will get one chance," Elias cautioned. If they made this choice, there would be no going back. No retreat or forgiveness if they were wrong. "He may already know what we've planned." If Erembour knew of Joanna's window, would he not know of this?

"He does not know my heart." A war grin split the prince's face. "Any price for any chance." Vhogare held out his hand. "We buy them time."

Elia shook on it, scar to scar. "I will not leave you to do it alone."

"No fire shall touch them so long as we live."

THE FLOWERS

ELIAS

Elias woke to Joanna tearing his shirt open at the chest. Buttons flew across the room, and he started, his neck aching from sleeping in the wooden chair. Wincing, he found her standing above him, studying the healed scars crossing his chest.

"I have stood by your side for ten years," his wife panted, her face twisting in pain. "Through every injury and rebellion and sleepless night. I bear your child." Joanna's gaze hardened, the summer sky before lightning struck. "You tell me what happened," she groaned, staggering back to grip the nightstand as pain seized her. "And you tell me now."

"We will speak of this—"

"We speak of it now. And you will give me no shit—" She broke off to breathe through a contraction, humming against the pressure. "No shit about gardens, either. You killed a bear, and you climbed the tower stairs the day after."

Elias opened his mouth to respond, but Joanna held up a hand and cut him off, swaying on her feet. Her eyes—always green as a forest before a thunderstorm—appeared to lighten to a pale gray, and sweat ran down her neck and chest. She pressed a hand to her forehead, panting.

"Are you seeing something?" he whispered, stepping forward in case her knees buckled and he needed to catch her.

"It's the pain," she growled, gripping his hand for stability. "I keep slipping in and out. That world and this one. They blur together. A distant voice I can barely hear."

Concern locked a fist around Elias's chest. "You should sit," he suggested, his throat tight.

Joanna shook her head, frantic. Shuddering, she blinked up at him, refocusing. "You speak with Vhogare about celestials and swords in the dead of night. Unless you have rekindled your interest in poetry, something . . . has happened."

"I'm afraid you will think me mad," he confessed, bracing her.

"I have told you things that any other man would've disowned me for. Worlds and creatures and riddles I cannot begin to understand. Do you think me mad?"

Elias shook his head. "Never. And if you were, I would love you all the same." Just months ago, Joanna had gone into false labor. When the pains had subsided, she whispered to him about a man with eyes like the sun sailing on a pirate ship, and when he cut his hands, he bled gold. Not three weeks later, Einar caught Midas with his fingers in the royal coffers.

"Whatever happened to you," she bit, stabbing a finger at the deep scars on his chest, "is not enough to break us. Tell me, Elias. While I can still hear you."

And so Elias did.

When he finished, Joanna trembled with dread, a hand on her swollen belly. She could not ask him any questions not answered by the three lines across his chest. "How long?"

He should have known she wouldn't question him. All the things she'd told him, everything she'd seen in those blurry glimpses . . . such a fierce woman would not blink an eye at a horseman arriving on earth.

"I don't know." He reached for her, and she let him embrace her. Perspiration from her exertion plastered his shirt to his chest, and her breath trembled. Elias pressed a kiss to her brow and steeled his heart. "But I will not let this happen."

Joanna shuddered again, and Elias held her all the tighter. Man versus immortal, he may be, but it would take every shattered star in the sky to break his shield. "Our daughter will live," he promised. "I swear it."

Joanna rested her cheek against his shoulder. "Does Soleil know?"

Elias shook his head. "She traveled back with her parents. Vhogare had no chance to tell her."

"I want to be there when he does. She will be . . . beside herself. I'll try to explain more of how I see . . . in my visions so she knows he's not lying. Perhaps something in her studies can help us." Joanna stepped back to gulp down cooler air. The sun had risen, the castle sweltering at the height of summer, and there were no drafts to stir the stillness.

"Do you trust him?" she demanded.

Elias frowned. "Erembour?"

"Vhogare." Joanna shook her head, her jaw clamped. "He always plays with fire, and it always burns him. If he gets you hurt—"

"I trust him with my life."

"Do not give it." She clutched his sleeve for support as she buckled at the knees and spoke through clenched teeth. "You know as well as I that he is reckless and impulsive on his best days, and dangerous at his worst. Do not leave us alone if that creature speaks true."

He was about to promise—to comfort her—when Joanna froze, gasping, and Elias glanced to find blood staining her nightgown.

THE SWORD

VHOGARE

oanna's screams ripped the castle apart. Vhogare waited outside the door as long as he could. Waited for the babe to be born, confirming or denying what Erembour said.

To the prince's knowledge, Elias had no chance to speak with their spymaster about the celestial. Einar had arrived from the hunt just that morning—two days after almost losing his son—to receive the grave news that his gooddaughter had gone into labor, and things were not progressing well. Vhogare had ordered a cushioned chair to be brought up to the eastern hall for him, and the graybeard sat straight-backed. Only Einar's white-knuckled fists betrayed the spymaster's fear.

Vhogare wished he could say something to comfort the man, but he had no hope to pull from. His father had been taken straight to his royal apartments and could not rise from his bed.

Soleil rushed in and out of Elias's suite. The most educated woman in the castle, she'd volunteered her healing knowledge, and her face grew tighter and more bloodless with each passing.

"How much longer?" he asked as she pushed past him, hurrying for fresh linens.

"The child is turned," she panted, smudging her cheek with a soiled hand. "The midwives and I are doing all we can." Her chin began to tremble, and whatever was left of Vhogare's heart broke open.

He seized Soleil's shoulders and made her look at him. "Joanna is a strong woman. She will survive this."

His love fought back tears as she gripped the stained linens with desperate strength. "But she is in so much pain."

"And you have a gift for this," Vhogare reminded her, pressing a searing kiss to her brow. "Are there any records, any histories, of a woman surviving a child being cut from their womb?" Soleil was the most well-read mind he'd ever met; if anyone would know, she would.

Her eyes snapped to his. "No," she gasped, horrified. "There is no way to stop the bleeding."

"What about cauterization? If someone could apply heat fast enough—"

"I suppose." Soleil's brow furrowed, the wheels of thought turning as she explained what such a figurative process would entail. "It would have to be done very quickly," she cautioned when she'd finished. "And with extreme precision. But we don't have the tools. The risk is far too great to even consider."

"But it would not be impossible if you had those things?"

"Well, not impossible, but—"

Vhogare kissed her. "I will be back before morning. Do not leave her."

"Where are you going?"

With a final inhale of her lilac scent, he stormed down the corridor, the smell of fear chasing him through the sweltering stone halls. And under it crawled the sweet stench of death.

There is right, and there is wrong, Einar had told him before the bear nearly mauled Elias to death. *And we all must choose.*

When Vhogare reached the main hall, he searched for the nearest commander. With Aadriek and Alastair keeping Elias company upstairs, the prince settled for a lesser-known man. "Bring Midas to the yard," he told a cold-eyed, obedient knight named Banan, who'd been lounging in a chair by one of the many fireplaces. "And tell Maura her father's time has come."

He needed an excuse, a reason he could leave the castle unattended and without question. If the entire staff thought he was grappling with guilt over beheading the traitor, he'd have some time to himself.

By the time Vhogare reached the muddy castle yard, the sky was dark with the promise of a storm. Lightning crisscrossed the clouds, and the scent of rain weighed heavily in the air as two guards dragged Midas out of prison. They hauled him, begging and pleading, across the sodden grass to the block at Vhogare's feet.

Vhogare had told his father they should kill the man in front of the city and let the whole world know what happened when someone stole from the Crown. But Maura and her mother would have to suffice as witnesses. With their soon-to-be mistress of gold's clever gossip, the entire city would hear of it by morning.

To be sure, he called for the marshal, kennel master, and castle servants to gather around in hopes that word would spread farther and faster. Perhaps even Erembour himself was watching.

Good, Vhogare reasoned. *Let him know I am not afraid to spill blood.*

Grimacing, Vhogare drew Azrail. The silver sword sang as it whistled across the steel scabbard, and he could've sworn Maura smirked in grim satisfaction. For a heartbeat, vicious pride welled in Vhogare's chest. He was her vengeance delivered; her father was a heartless beast, and Vhogare meant to make his death count.

"Midas," he bellowed, loud enough to be heard over the thunder. The milling castle yard fell silent, and all the servants gathered went still as death as they waited for his next words.

"You are found guilty of treason." Vhogare tightened his grip on the sword. "You have stolen from my father and taken from the royal coffers that our realm relies on for security and sustenance. You abused your position and, more importantly, your family."

The man bent his neck, weeping tears that would buy him no mercy.

"Your daughter, your wife, and every soul in Anchora trusted you to protect them," Vhogare thundered. "Trusted you to keep their best interests at heart, and you have failed them. Betrayed them. And for that, you must die."

Midas opened his mouth to speak, to beg, blubber, plead, or promise everything he could not deliver. Saliva drooled from the man's quivering lips, his eyes too wide in his terror-stricken face, but Vhogare had no time to parley with traitors. He swung Azrail in a smooth, high arc and took off the man's head before he could say a word.

Midas's widow Zarine, the new mistress of gold, put a hand over her mouth at the raw red stump where her husband's head had once been. Maura, however, began to clap.

Every pair of eyes in the castle yard turned to gape at her audacity.

Maura did not seem to care. She struck her hands together in a slow, sharp staccato. The unforgiving sound echoed across the quiet castle yard, ricocheting off the high, dark walls of the keep. A cruel sneer split her thin lips as she watched her father's head roll, his mouth open in a final plea for the compassion he'd never once shown her.

"Thank you," Maura told Vhogare, her husky voice strong enough that everyone in attendance heard. Dark justice lit her brown eyes as she tucked her spiraling curls behind her ears and curtseyed. Above them, a thunderhead rolled in.

Vhogare slung the gore off his sword. Humid sea wind whipped his hair across his face as he sheathed Azrail. "You're welcome."

Shaking with nerves, he kicked Midas's head across the mud for good measure and turned to go. Guards made to follow him, but he waved them off with a sharp command. "Bury the man, or feed him to the dogs," he ordered. "I do not care."

Word would reach the ailing king, and Vhogare's father would know that he'd done his job. And until then, Vhogare would be granted peace. Time to be alone for just long enough to get this done.

In the stables, Vhogare's black charger met him with a frightened toss of his head, as if the creature could sense his thoughts. The hunting hounds bayed and howled behind him, their anxious cries shredding the dark, and Vhogare couldn't shake the sense that someone was watching him. He put a hand to his horse's white blaze, but the beast's blue eyes would not quiet.

Vhogare had no more mastery over his own heart. He'd hoped to ride out into the woods beyond the city, but his hands were too unsteady to get the saddle buckled. Frustrated, he left it and raced on foot for the southern gate set deep in the castle's ancient walls.

The winding sea stair beyond yawned up at him. Seaspray misted the beach five hundred feet below, the drop on either side sheer and fatal. There was no railing; each wide step was carved deep into the mountain's stone side. Servants, laborers, and sailors frequented the sea stairs during daylight hours, tracking up and down from the docks below. The rough stone was worn smooth with their steps, but even as a child, Vhogare had never dared the descent alone.

Loch Orianna's ocean wind beat into him as if in warning, its invisible, mighty hands shoving him away. But he had done so little against the damned bear. He would not be a mere distraction again. Stomaching his hatred of heights, Vhogare took the stone steps as fast as he dared.

Joanna had labored all day; the sun was setting as his boots sank into the beach's white sand far below. Gulping down breaths, the prince strode across the shore toward the water. The castle stood in stark silhouette behind him, up the sheer cliffside. At its back, the eastern mountains rose, slumbering beasts resting in defiance of the dark. So far down, the torches lighting Elias's quarters in the east wing were smaller than sparks. Beyond those immense walls stood all the beauty in the world, all that he could not lose or let down.

To hear his father tell it, Vhogare all but murdered his mother when he came into the world. Soleil loved him, and he had not even sworn her his wedding oaths. Elias had damned near died for him in those woods, and Joanna lay on what very well might be her deathbed, laboring over a child that might live just long enough to see their world burn.

Vhogare steeled himself. Carved out every ounce of steel in his soul. He would not fail them. He would not lose Soleil. She would mourn no death today, and Elias would bury no wife and child.

This one thing. This *one thing*, he could do.

The castle cast a great shadow over the beach, the cliffside shrouded in mist thrown by the roaring waterfall in the distance. And though Vhogare longed to have the fortress walls around him, he walked to the edge of the water and ensured he was alone. At the inn, Erembour had wanted no prying eyes nor listening ears. In the yard and the stables, someone had been watching him. Perhaps the celestial would make himself known there on the desolate, white-sand beach.

"I have your answer," he shouted into the waves and the wind, wiping the salt spray from his face. Loch Orianna tossed tumultuously as ever, her summer swell rising around his ankles and knees. Vhogare's black hair whipped around him, plastering to his pallid skin. The storm rolled in at the loch's maw, casting the twin watchtowers in shadow. Lightning struck far off, the sky meeting the water in a blaze of light.

"Where is your brother?"

Vhogare turned to face Erembour behind him on the beach. Glowing letters receded up the celestial's arms and neck. The bastard did not mean Milan.

"Save Soleil. Save Elias and Joanna, and their daughter. And I will burn this world to the ground."

They would not die because he had failed. So he had sworn.

Erembour's brows dipped into a frown. "I cannot save Joanna."

Vhogare's heart might as well have fallen out of his chest onto the sand. "In the woods, you put the flesh back onto that stag's bones," he shouted over the wind. "The trees bloomed right in front of me. And you mean to tell me you cannot save a woman who is not even dead?"

"Did the stag get up and walk?" Erembour demanded, his voice a thunderclap in the near-dark. "Did the bear draw breath? I force change, not life. If I could give life, do you think I would be here and not at Invar's side?"

At Vhogare's silence, an ageless, consuming sadness crept into Erembour's gaze, so stark against the immortal stone of his alabaster skin. "I am chance, choice, not raw creation." He bent to scoop a handful of sand and let it fall through his fingers. "Not life. That is the Ark's power, not mine."

The sand turned to glass before it hit the beach. "And even if I could"—he looked from the shimmering droplets, bright as fresh rain, to Vhogare—"I wouldn't. I came to bury this planet, not breathe life into it."

Vhogare clenched his trembling fists at his sides. "Surely you can do *something.*"

All he needed was some information. Information that Elias would know how to use. Together, they could figure this out.

"I can end you all now and spare you the trouble of watching."

Vhogare swore under his breath. The bastard would call his bluff.

The celestial sighed. "I cannot give all. Give time. If I could, I would not need to do this." He spread out his arms like he held Vhogare's kingdom. The world.

Vhogare summoned all his nerve and stared the Gift Bearer down. There was a way. And if there wasn't, he would make one. "But you are not powerless," he said, baiting.

Erembour missed no tell. "No, I am not," he answered, giving Vhogare no quarter, no room to pry or maneuver. "Even so, I have brothers, too." Vhogare bristled as the celestial turned to gaze up at the castle high above. "You would give anything for him. I would give anything for them. There is no end to what I will do to save them, and my anything is your world."

Erembour squared off to him, and the sand rippled like waves around the celestial's feet. "I am not offering you a bargain. I will not trade. You do it, or I do it myself. Your choice, or mine."

Vhogare staggered as the weight of those words hit him. Sunk into him and latched their teeth around his throat. "If I do it, I would choose who lives?"

"You may have a few."

"A *few?* What of Soleil's family? Einar and Alastair?" Why did he always have to beg to keep the people he loved?

"Even Chaos has rules." Erembour ignored Vhogare's distress and laid his hand on the ethereal scythe at his hip. "This is all I can do. Invar bleeds, and the sand in the hourglass runs down. I need my hands washed clean of this earth."

"Why not just do it yourself?"

The celestial stiffened. "Because I already broke His heart, but there is no choice. I would keep as much blood off my name as possible." He studied Vhogare the way one would a commissioned blade. "You will do well enough. Perhaps He will thank us both, in the end."

Vhogare was no spymaster, but he knew a confession when he heard it. Invar did not send this monster. Erembour had betrayed the Ark, his very Maker. The celestial viewed this ruthlessness as a mercy, and any soul so desperate would see no reason—no way out save the way he had decided. There was nothing else, nothing left that Vhogare could barter with to buy their lives.

He looked around, desperate, searching for anything he could do.

Panic seared through Vhogare's blood like wildfire until he felt like he floated above the beach, above the world. All that anchored him was the tiny pewter dragon weighing down his pocket. He reached and closed his fist around the gift, Soleil's love for him given form.

Your mother loved the ancient dragons, she'd whispered just days ago. *Seonna would be proud to know her son is the very embodiment of their strength.*

Something vicious was uncovered in Vhogare's chest, and he extended his hand. "Then give me your word—on your gift—that nothing I saw will come to pass. Spare me these five. And give me fire." Ruthless, efficient. And if they cut the babe out of Joanna, perhaps he could sear her shut. "I will do it."

Fire would fight fire well enough.

The celestial might not save Joanna, but he could.

He could save them all.

Erembour searched his gaze as if he felt the trick, but nodded all the same. "You have it, from one traitorous son to another." The celestial glanced at Vhogare's clothes and furrowed his brow. "You will want to remove those. This will hurt, and you need to maintain your mortal appearance. To some degree."

"You both shame and threaten me?" Vhogare growled, aghast. "First, you demand death, then my dignity?"

Erembour's eyes narrowed. "You have no shame." He angled his head, the movement inhuman, and the air around them seemed to crackle and hum. "Would you not give all for your world? Your pride is a small price to pay for the power you seek."

Hate and indignation roiled in Vhogare's gut, but he stripped and set his clothes aside in the sand. The tiny pewter dragon tumbled from his pocket, and he snatched it up to clutch it in his fist. Heat crawled across his back and neck as he straightened, his heart hammering like a war drum against the bones of his chest, but he would take this risk. Claim the fire and turn it on the one who meant to shear their world down to its bones. He was his father's son, the next sword of Anchora, and he never ran from his odds.

Fighting down his frightening vulnerability, Vhogare squared his shoulders and stood naked on the beach.

For Soleil, he reminded himself, setting his jaw. She was worth the risk. Worth every risk. Soleil loved their kingdom and had spent years studying the world's hidden, ancient secrets. His midnight sun would not go dark for this monster. *For Elias and Joanna. And our children.*

"Your humiliation is not my purpose," the celestial said as he approached, the beach undulating beneath his feet. "I am no mortal man; I care not whether you wear armor or skin."

Something quailed in Vhogare at those words. It would not matter how well he was armed against such a creature. He could wear all the steel in the world, and it would be paper to the thing that stood before him.

Vhogare shuddered with dread. He was but flesh and bone, about to accept a gift from one of the Ark's horsemen; he may not even survive.

But there was no choice.

Erembour gave him no time to consider. He took Vhogare's arm, wrist to wrist. "This is not the thing you should fear."

The celestial's skin was cool, unforgiving stone. Silver fire seared Vhogare's flesh at Erembour's callous touch.

"Are you ready," the creature asked, "to divest yourself of this world to save that which you love?"

White-cold, scorching tendrils lanced into Vhogare's bone, but he ground his teeth and raised his chin. *Divest myself.* He did not know what bravery seized him, but he tightened his grip on the horseman's muscled arm. "So it is true, then," he whispered. "Invar does not know you're here."

Something ancient and deadly devoured whatever emotion Erembour had dared show. Frigid wrath sliced over his sharp features. "He knows what I've done. And that I do it for him. That is enough." The silver fire began to trail down his arms, and Vhogare fought the urge to step back—to run.

A strange, ethereal, charged scent ate the air, like a blade held above a blazing fire. Fighting to steady his breath, Vhogare clutched Soleil's silver dragon in his free hand. He tightened his fist around her gift until its wings pierced the raw gash of his blood oath, and he bled around the silver. He could do this. For her. For them.

The flames reached Vhogare's skin, and Elias's scream erupted inside his skull.

A roar of loss, of breaking.

Of ending.

The vision brought him to his knees. "You will not," he growled at the creature of chaos and chance, choice and change. Spittle flew through his clamped teeth as visceral pain lanced through every muscle, fiber, and splintered bone.

Against the agony, rage stoked like a furnace in his soul.

Vhogare held onto Soleil's gift as if it could anchor him to the world. The sand danced around them on the beach, jumping like raindrops striking water, but he trained his mind on Soleil's silver dragon until it was all he knew. His father had been right; he was a sword. *Her* sword. And he would strike true.

Light ignited within Vhogare, and he tilted his head back in an anguished roar. The silver fire shone through his ribcage from within, silhouetting his beating heart like a beacon in the night. A cry of torment ripped out of his throat; the air had become flame in his lungs, searing and sizzling from the inside out. Tearing his gaze off the sky, Vhogare pinned Erembour with a glare so vicious the celestial's lips curled back into a grin.

"You will *not* take them from me," Vhogare growled. He rose up on his knees, teeth clamped against the inferno surging through his soul.

There would be no world without Elias and Joanna, without Soleil. He'd once been willing to burn with her. But mortal or not, he would raze this creature to the ground if it meant keeping her safe.

This gift would be his sword, and with it, he would save them all.

"My brother, Tzaddik, has a heart of steel and fire," Erembour rumbled, releasing Vhogare's arm and staring down at him as the prince fought for breath against the scorching anguish. "And Rondiel is Justice himself. I do not punish a man for having a spine." He glanced past Vhogare at the storm rolling in, impatient. "But I will tolerate no soft-hearted soldiers."

The prince stood, wrath in his eyes. "I am no traitor. I gave you my word."

A sadness washed over the celestial's face. "Love is a lodestone. The heart breaks all. It is the thing that destroys us in the end."

"You do not know my kingdom. All that it is worth."

Erembour's onyx gaze shuttered as he glanced back at the castle.

"Perhaps not. But you have your brothers, and I have mine." He turned to pin Vhogare with a merciless stare, both eyes blazing brighter than white suns. "And I will do far worse to see them through. Do not force my hand."

Vhogare ground his teeth as the gift roared through his veins. Cold, raw fire thundered into his soul. If Invar was a part of the Ark, Chaos was, too. What had Erembour done to it to make such beautiful power hurt this way?

"What are you?" Vhogare managed, his voice gravel from the splintering torture. Icy heat shredded him, rent him, tore him apart. "Truly."

"The heart of a star." In front of him, the celestial drew the hood of his cloak back up over his dark hair, his right arm still silver from imparting the gift. "And I am willing to do what needs to be done."

Vhogare forced a grim smile. "As am I."

Erembour meant to take everything he loved, and the bastard was sorely mistaken.

Ripples lapped at Vhogare's ankles like the very waves of the loch knew what power he'd been given. He couldn't help but feel them whisper, *Run.* But he ignored their pleas, mastering himself as his stomach heaved. He would not vomit, despite his skin pulling too tight.

No. He raised his face and found comfort in the warmth of the sun setting behind the castle. Its last rays beamed down upon the mountain it crowned and on his blood brother, Milan, safe in his royal apartments. The heir to the throne was no doubt sleeping, though Elias stood at Joanna's side. Their childhood friend, ripping apart from the inside.

Unearthly rage crawled through Vhogare, and he contorted, scales sliding out of his skin. "Does our world's end have no hour?" he rasped around teeth that lengthened.

Vhogare clutched Soleil's dragon until he could hold on no longer. Until bones shredded and spines tore their way out of his back. He dropped the pewter statue onto the sand as great dark wings flowed out of his flesh.

Tremors sluiced down his massive arms at the stranger's presence, the power's nearness. "Speak it to me," he rumbled, his voice no longer his own. "Tell me what you want done. I will ensure it comes to pass."

Nausea coursed through him, and saliva ran into his mouth. His world was inverting, flipping on its head, and falling apart. Vhogare bent onto all fours, claws digging into the spiraling, swirling sand, and he fixed his gaze on that beautiful silver dragon.

Soleil, he repeated over and over again in his heart. *Elias. Joanna.*

They were his anchor, the ground beneath his feet, and the sky above his head.

He could do this for them.

Vhogare heaved for breath through scaled nostrils and felt his lungs expand with heat like a smith's bellows. If he could just get some information out of the monster, Elias had trained for years as a spymaster. He would know what to do, how to maneuver or leverage the celestial's plan for their benefit.

"You're no leal soldier, Vhogare. You wouldn't follow orders." His coal-eyed benefactor smirked, turning to go. "Be creative. I'll return to measure your success, Gift Bearer." Erembour's smile fell. "Remember what hangs in the balance."

Vhogare struggled to master the fire in his bones. Cruel, merciless chance carved its way through him. Chaos itself, waiting for a command. "The few for the many," he rumbled around teeth sharper than swords.

Erembour smirked at him. "Years for eternity," he answered and left Vhogare alone on the beach.

THE HEAT

VHOGARE

A dragon. He'd heard of such creatures from distant lands, written into the bygone eras of the world. But, though Soleil had gifted him a pewter likeness of one of the ancient beasts, he had never seen one in his lifetime.

And now Vhogare's chest burned with dragonflame, his boiling heart a crucible of determination, and his soul a river of silver fire. He growled at the heaviness of his monstrous new form, and the sound rolled across the mountainside, forced from massive lungs. No longer a man, the dark dragon took up more than half the beach, taloned feet sinking deep into the white sand. Silver scales thicker than armor rippled and flexed along Vhogare's chest, their bright shine stark against his frame's glittering black.

Jagged gray bone spurs spiked down his spine. Panic, raw and gut-rending, flared through Vhogare as he stared down at his enormous, scaled forelegs and clawed paws. He was so heavy that he sank past his ankles in the sand.

Even as a dragon, Vhogare's right arm was scarred silver with Erembour's gift. The jagged mark lanced like lightning across his flesh, a permanent reminder of his choice.

What have I done?

Had he lost his humanity? Vhogare's heart thundered against his cavernous ribcage. Would he ever hold Soleil in his arms again? When his work was done, would he be able to forsake this fire and scale for flesh and bone? Or was he stuck like this, forever? A monster with the heart of a man.

Flame rose like bile in his throat.

Vhogare shook his head, spines rattling. He clutched his heart as he stumbled backward into the waves. *No. No, no, no.* He'd asked for fire. Not to be this . . . this *beast.*

Vhogare had always revered the ancient dragons, but to be one was another matter. His new form was unnatural, monstrous. Vhogare's massive form sent waves rolling outward as he crashed into the loch like a horse backing away from the bit.

Lightning flashed, striking one of the twin watchtowers in the distance, and thunder boomed above his head.

Even if it was a spark, he carried the flame of Chaos inside him, and it ached like forcing a wildfire inside a jar. Erembour's fear had twisted the gift, but Vhogare could still sense the light deep down, brighter than any fire tower guiding ships to shore—a beautiful, brilliant tether anchoring him to the vast Heart of creation. Vhogare's fire within flared at the gift's presence, fierce, relentless, and uncontainable, like a blaze fed by a southern wind. He would not have believed it possible if he had not been lit from the inside out, able to see and count every bone in his body.

But everything about the last two days had been impossible. Vhogare clamped his enormous jaw, dagger-sharp teeth sliding into place. He'd asked for this. He had not died yet. And he was tired of being afraid.

If he did right by this, Invar would forgive him.

He and Elias would deal with the aftermath later. For now, all that mattered was that he had the gift. The sword was in his hand, and he could cut the traitorous celestial down when the time came.

Raising his head, Vhogare flared his dark wings, the shining silver membranes catching the moonlight shimmering along their veins. He'd always despised heights, but with this new fire in his chest, he itched to fly, to be one with the storm and the thunder, and experience the depth of this new power.

But Vhogare refused himself. That was not what he had done this for.

Chaos could change things. Fix things.

All was not lost. Vhogare's gaze fell on his discarded clothes and Soleil's tiny silver dragon, where it had fallen in the sand. The celestial had made him lay aside his clothes for a reason. Maybe that meant he could use them again. He wasn't stuck like this.

Closing his eyes, Vhogare braced his colossal feet in the sand. *This will hurt*, Erembour had said, *and you need to maintain your mortal appearance.*

His mortal appearance. Perhaps he had not lost his humanity entirely. Perhaps the man was still somewhere, hidden inside. Snarling, Vhogare searched for it. He peeled through the power, hunting through every inch of his soul, seeking his mortal form.

His fire within warred against the chaos, twin flames doing battle. At last, the power seemed to reconcile with its new vessel. The gift stopped railing against the bars of his soul and turned to listen.

I want to be a man again, he pleaded. *Give me my body back.*

The chaos paused, pulsating. It hovered, burning in his soul like the sun inside the sea. There was a sentience to it that Vhogare did not understand. Something ancient, foreign, and as far from a mortal mind as any living thing could get, and it did not like him.

Locked in his soul, Chaos was his to command for now, but not his to own.

Please, he begged. *Joanna is dying. Soleil needs me.*

In answer, the gift softened. It gave up its form in his spirit and twisted, flooding him like flaming oil spread across the top of the water. Vhogare coughed out a breath in relief. Though reluctant, Chaos understood his wishes as if it were some living, breathing thing that nodded when he asked for its favor.

The unbearable heat subsided, and Vhogare willed himself back into his human skin. He struggled to force the change, his skin shrinking and compressing into a body that felt too small and weak, too stagnant, too powerless.

The moon had well risen by the time Vhogare regained his man's legs. As soon as his hands were his own again, he knelt and dug his palms into the beach, anchoring himself. Erembour had turned the sand to glass; the tiny baubles of glimmering light remained, not three yards from him. They caught the moon's brilliance, shimmering like tiny stars fallen to earth. If he could do the same, he would have the precision to save Joanna.

His first try proved disastrous. Uncontained, silver fire shot forth from his palms as he raised them, aiming far away from the stairs. The sheer force of the blast sent him tumbling backward onto his ass. His blaze scorched the cliffside, devouring massive chunks of the stone.

There was no controlling it. The gift raged, a beast leashed in his bones. Vhogare stood and tried again, only to stumble back from the strength of the firestorm pouring out of him and fall into the water. Waves wove around him, cooling his scalding skin.

Stop, the water seemed to say.

But there was no calm to be found. Vhogare's mind blazed with the gift. The chaos ate any silence inside his skull, a constant hum prowling at the edges of his thoughts. Crawling out of the loch, he bent over his knees and continued.

"For Soleil," he whispered to himself as he struggled. "For Elias and Joanna, I can do this. I *will* do this." He had no choice.

Vhogare ground his teeth, crying out with strain as he focused and worked the gift down from a mighty blaze to a flickering flame. But it did not burn hot enough.

Vhogare swore.

He would need more force.

The gift was wild. Beautiful and relentless and alive. It raged against his mortality as if the very power itself knew it was meant for far greater than mortal bones. The silver fire danced in his heart like a phoenix locked in a cage.

He adjusted his approach. Chaos was no wild horse to be tamed but a love to be embraced, and Soleil had prepared him for this very hour. His love's tempestuous nature had been everything he needed and more, and he had learned to love the fire.

Vhogare relented. He opened the door to the cage of his soul and let the silver flame burn through him. He let it eat up his heart, everything he held dear. He fed it his pain, his fear, his heartbreak. The gift recoiled, at first, at the crushing dread it found inside him, but all Vhogare wanted was to save them—and this fire was the only way he could.

The thought seemed to settle something between him and the power. He exhaled as the beast in his bones stopped fighting and decided to stay, as if the chaos coursing through his blood accepted it was chained inside him and waited to see what he would do.

For that moment, all he wanted was control.

Vhogare drew upon every story he'd heard of his birth, every cleric who'd mentioned the medical work behind his lovely mother's death and his tragic delivery, and whittled the mighty blaze down. Begged it to work alongside him rather than rebel against him.

Exertion ate at him, and hours had worn by before he managed to maintain a stream of fire thin enough and strong enough to turn small strips of sand into glass. Thin slivers of the new material glittered across the beach, lined up like countless throwing knives from his practice. The last one still glowed with heat, hot enough to cauterize and thin enough to heal.

Confident he could do it, Vhogare retrieved Soleil's silver dragon and donned his sandy clothing. Clutching her gift in his fist, he scaled the winding switchback stairs to the castle proper, practicing all the way. Thrice he almost fell to his death, but the wind seemed to push him back against the stones.

Perhaps the celestial had seen right through him. Perhaps this endeavor would tear him apart, but he would do as he promised. He would buy them time.

A line of scorched stone trailed him up the staircase, left by the lit fire blazing from his palm.

My sword.

Maybe Invar would thank him for fighting against the traitorous horseman and putting a stop to the bloodletting done in his name.

More than half the night was gone when he reached the top of the thousand stairs and staggered, breathless, across the vacant yard into the castle's keep. Forcing his aching legs to carry him farther, he climbed the spiral staircase to the east wing, clutching the wall to force his cramping thighs to conquer each step. He had to crawl up the last flight, but he made it.

Soleil met him at the start of the hall, weariness dragging at her delicate features. "Vhogare!" she cried as she found him on his hands and knees on the stone floor. "Are you all right?"

Swallowing, he nodded, waving off her concern. "I'm fine. I was . . . on the beach."

She sank to her knees in front of him. "Why? You hate that path. I would've gone with you—"

"I needed air," he snapped, cutting her off. "And you are needed here." Hurt flashed across her features, and he relented. "I'm sorry, darling. The storm caught me on the stairs." He got a knee under himself and prepared to stand. "Tell me what's happened."

Scowling, Soleil grunted as she heaved him to his feet. "We're attempting to get the child into position," his love reported.

Vhogare leaned against the wall, panting. His heart caved in at the exhaustion purpling the skin under her eyes. "Are *you* all right?"

Soleil wove her hair back into her loose braid. "It is arduous work, but Joanna's still fighting." She stood on her toes to press a kiss to his cheek. "The Council has called a meeting. I have to go, but Elias is down the hall. Send my page if anything happens, I—" Her voice broke. "I will be there if we have to tell her goodbye."

"There will be no goodbyes," Vhogare promised, wiping the tears from her eyes.

Soleil did not seem convinced. Squeezing Vhogare's hand, she departed, and he staggered, alone, down the hall to the birthing room.

Another of Joanna's broken cries swallowed up his thanks to the Ark. Her voice had grown hoarse and damaged, and the sound cracked against his skull. The stone hall passed in a blur, every servant a ghost, as he opened the door and was met by a scene from his nightmares.

Stained bedclothes littered the floor. Joanna had lost so much blood. . . . Not enough to kill her, thank the Ark, but enough to leave her weak. Bowls and tools lay everywhere, and she rested on the floor on all fours, a midwife encouraging her attempt to turn the child.

Elias shot to his feet. Swearing, he shoved Vhogare back out the door into the hall. "You forget yourself," Elias thundered, flushed red. "You cannot just barge in! Where have you been?"

"I'm sorry," Vhogare rasped. "I. . . ." He trailed off at the state of his friend.

Elias's hands shook, and he mopped a hand over his bloodshot eyes. Fearless before the bear, and yet the man couldn't get a breath down at whatever happened behind that door. They were running out of time.

"You were right." Vhogare glanced to the far end of the hall by the eastern window, out of the immediate earshot of those waiting, and Elias followed him there. Panic—raw and desperate—rolled off the man in waves, and Vhogare almost wept at the scent. "Erembour betrayed the Ark, betrayed us all."

Elias's eyes flashed. "You met with him? Without me?"

Vhogare nodded, displaying his trembling right hand. Burn scars covered his skin, trailing up his arm to his shoulder and chest beneath his sandy shirt. "He commands Chaos itself. *Chance* itself. I thought—I thought if I—"

"That you would get more than you were given?" Elias demanded, understanding all that hung in the air between them. "He offered you a weapon, Vhogare, not a remedy."

"Any price for any chance." He could not lose Soleil to that monster.

Elias's face softened, and he gripped Vhogare's shoulder. "There is hope yet."

He'd just finished his sentence when King Ulrich's royal page ran up, breathless and red-faced. "Your father," the boy gasped to Vhogare, panting from the stairs. He struggled to bring his voice to a whisper. "The king is dead."

THE DROUGHT

VHOGARE

Aching dread dropped like a stone into Vhogare's gut. "Dead?" Surely not. Just three days ago, King Ulrich had been on his horse, talking Einar's ear off about some boring matters of state. The king had accepted celebratory gifts and had given orders, demanded Midas's damned execution for heaven's sake. He could not be dead.

The boy nodded and shifted on his feet. "A few hours ago."

"*HOURS?*" Vhogare thundered.

The poor page shrank away from him. "Prince Milan did not wish to worry you with Lady Joanna in this . . . state."

Elias put a hand on Vhogare's shoulder, a silent reminder to leash himself. But his father was dead, and Joanna was dying, and all the fire in his soul wanted to do was save them all. It was his duty as prince to attend his father's deathbed, but he couldn't bear leaving Elias alone, and he could not be at both places at once.

Swearing, Vhogare weighed his options. He would handle this business and return in time to see that Joanna lived.

"My apologies," Vhogare whispered to the boy. His knees felt like water, like he stood in shifting sand. But he slicked his damp hair out of his face and tried to breathe. "Please inform Milan that I'm on my way."

He dismissed the page, promising to follow, and seized Elias's arm. Vhogare would not ask him to leave Joanna's side, but Erembour's information could not wait.

"Chaos is both a creative power and a destructive one," he told Elias once the boy had gone. "And we—this country, continent, the whole bloody *world*—are pawns in his game of time."

Elias stiffened at the new information. "You kept your vow?"

"Aye." There was no time to feel the cutting insult hidden in that small grain of doubt. "How can you fight someone with all that strength if you don't have a shred of it yourself? And yet it is still a whisper compared to what he is." Terror slid into Vhogare's gut like oil. "A shred in the tapestry of his power. I will do all I can to save us, but we will need everyone to stand against him." He tightened his grip. "Whatever it takes."

Elias set his jaw. "Whatever it takes."

Inside their suite, Joanna groaned in pain, the sound full of such agony and despair that Vhogare's heart split open. "Get your father's cleric," he ordered. "Jesse delivered me. We can save Joanna and your daughter."

Elias paled. "Your mother died."

"She bled out because they couldn't sew her up fast enough." Vhogare focused, letting the tiniest amount of the heat that now coursed through him flare through his fingers. Elias drew back, hissing, to find five small holes singed into the arm of his shirt.

All the blood drained from Elias's face. "You would . . . burn her shut?"

"Soleil believes that with enough precision, it may be possible. I see no other way."

Elias stepped back, staring out the eastern window as if searching for the sun in the night sky. "If this kills her. . . ."

Vhogare steadied himself and willed all his strength through his eyes as he said, "If Joanna dies, you can rip my heart out of my chest. But she will not. Ask her." He flung an arm toward Joanna's door. "Ask her if she wants to die tonight or take a chance and live. I know what my mother would say."

Silent tears ran down his heartbrother's trembling jaw.

Vhogare seized Elias by the back of his neck, bringing their brows together. "You will lose no wife and child tonight. This I swear." His gift surged inside him, a phoenix beating against iron bars. *Save,* it whispered. *Save, save.* "I will do everything I can."

"She must agree," Elias growled, pulling back to pound a fist against Vhogare's aching chest. "There are no more secrets between us three."

Vhogare nodded. "Get the cleric, then get me, and I will do the rest."

Leaving Elias to it, he stumbled down the hall after the page, exhausted and unsteady. Every step made his knees quake, and bile rose in the back of his throat. What was the last thing he had said to his father, face to face? *Mother loved you.*

But did *he?* Did he love his own father? Vhogare wasn't sure. Ulrich was hard and fair, but he was not kind or compassionate. An iron fist had no need for padding. Softness was not a king's purpose.

His father had seen Anchora through her most tumultuous time, established a reliable, just rule, and held the country steady the way a sailor would steer their ship in a summer storm. And with the wind in the mast, there was no room for hesitation or weak knees.

But affectionate father or not, King Ulrich had died sick in his bed, and Vhogare had not been there to say goodbye. He would never know his father's last words. Never know if the steel-souled man was afraid when he left for the life beyond. Would he have gripped Vhogare's hand? Held his shoulder and given him some wisdom to carry him through the oncoming days? Heaven knew Vhogare needed it.

And now, such wisdom would never come. He and his father would never mend the divide between them, and the gap between life and death had become a chasm. A sob choked Vhogare, and he pressed the back of his hand to his lips, pausing to catch his breath. His father's quarters were far below—a veritable vault of rooms built for times of siege—and Vhogare was breathless and far too near fainting by the time he reached them.

He stood outside the stone doors, carved with reliefs of Anchora's bloody history, and stared at the seam between the rock. Sweat ran down his neck in rivulets, racing along his spine. *Why did you leave me?*

They were always leaving. His mother. Milan with the bear. And now his father had gone, too. No one was ever coming back for him.

But he would not leave Soleil. She, Elias, and Joanna needed him. Vhogare wasn't going anywhere. In this one thing, he refused to be Ulrich's son.

Summoning all his strength, Vhogare shoved open the heavy doors. Milan caught him as he staggered through and sat him in a chair as his legs gave out at the sight of his father.

King Ulrich lay stiff in his bed, all color gone from his lined face. Blood speckled his gray beard, though Harun and the other royal clerics and failed healers were attempting to wipe it away. Vhogare's father had been frail and withered, but he had grown smaller somehow in death. All the might he'd once commanded couldn't hold a blade against the end. Vhogare prayed Ulrich was a soldier again in the Ark's arms, as fierce and strong as he had been when he wrested the kingdom from a tyrant's grip and set his blood-bought legacy on the throne.

"He had no last wishes," Milan muttered, trailing Vhogare's stare. "But he was never one to mince words, was he?"

"You were . . . here with him?" All the fire in Vhogare's soul banked out, leaving nothing but ash. "He called you first?"

Milan sighed. "I sent for you as soon as I could."

"As soon as you could. . . ." Air had become water, and Vhogare was drowning. Where was Soleil when he needed her? If his love had been there, he could've held her, leaned on her warmth to steady himself. But his brilliant historian was with the Council, steering a kingdom that needed her far more.

One of the attending servants had left the nearest window open to the summer thunderhead. The wind gusted in, and a candle flared on the table beside Vhogare before it blew out in a counter-draft. The weaker part of him wished he could leave with the smoke, but he stamped down his sadness. There were wars to fight.

"Did he not ask for me?" Vhogare demanded, his cracking voice betraying him. "When he left our life for the next."

His brother's mouth drew into a thin, hard line, and Vhogare swore.

"You were always shit at card games," he seethed. Milan had too many tells and never knew when to bluff. "Tell me when my father died."

The crown prince sighed. "The hour of the wolf."

Then, Vhogare had still been on the beach. Fighting for time that had already been taken from his father. He leaned back in his chair and set his jaw. "Was he brave?"

Milan's chin trembled, and he sank into the cushioned armchair next to Vhogare. "The Ark will be proud."

"May He carry him," Vhogare prayed, unable to take his eyes off the pallor of the Anchor King's face, the gray cast of his skin. The chest that had heaved a thousand dry laughs now lay empty and still. Arms that had not held Vhogare in long years folded over his frail chest in eternal peace. *Whatever peace can be found by a man who never failed to raise the sword.*

"May He carry him," Milan repeated. His brother leaned on his knees, squeezing his brow, but it did little to hide his tears. "I wish he had stayed longer."

Revulsion coiled in Vhogare's throat. "You wish he had suffered?"

"I wish he had fought!" Milan shouted, standing. "I wish . . . I wish he had not left me"—he wiped a hand across his tear-damp face, sobbing through his teeth—"with a kingdom on my shoulders I do not want."

The truth shattered against the carved walls like glass. *A kingdom he does not want.*

Fury swelled in Vhogare's chest. "Leave us," he growled, and Harun ushered the royal clerics and hushed servants from the room in a flurry of medicines and tools.

"You have trained for this all your life," Vhogare snarled into the stunned silence. "Father prepared you for the throne since the day you drew breath, and yet you shirk it in his dying hour?"

"Aye," Milan barked. "He made sure I could sit on the throne but never asked me if I should. Do you think the king he killed to get there loved this kingdom any less? We are a new line. He bought that steel with blood and asked me to bathe in more to keep it."

Milan raised his shaking hands as if Vhogare could see the terror in them. "Have I not been suffocated by this life since birth? I do not want to die alone and tired in a castle that drained me dry."

Some small part of Vhogare knew he should put an arm around his elder brother's shoulders and comfort him in their hour of grief. But where Vhogare searched for compassion, bitterness answered. "Then why work so hard for it?" he demanded. *Why cast me aside for something you hated that I would have loved?*

"A good king cannot be a fool. But the more I read, the more I studied and learned about the world, the less I wanted to be here. I wanted to sail beneath the sea arches to the west, climb the eastern mountains, and see the desert cats and winding ocean serpents of the south. But the throne is a lodestone; I could never escape it, and I have been crushed beneath its weight all my life. Now," Milan cast a hand at their father's corpse, "he has wrapped it around my neck and let the deep swallow me whole. Tomorrow, the fish will feed on my corpse."

Vhogare gaped at Milan, at the smoothness of his pale skin and the fineness of his clothes. This had been the man his father wanted at his bedside at his passing hour. A spoiled princeling who spent every waking hour enjoying the luxury of his station and never using his power to make a choice.

Revulsion crawled through Vhogare, pulling at the corners of his mouth and tightening his fists. The golden son had always stood at their father's side when the king sat in judgment. Their citizens brought their petitions, their disputes, and injustices, to the throne in search of aid. And yet while Milan gave ear to their struggles, he chose the long-suffering, patient solutions rather than get his hands dirty and *serve*. Instead of fixing things with finality, he spent his time studying and making Maura's life hell. And if Vhogare's father had taught him anything, it was that taking your time meant people died.

Milan had been granted every gift and opportunity, yet he was the best at nothing.

Wanted nothing.

And now the crown prince of Anchora was nothing but a coward who had stood behind Elias and wet himself. Vhogare had once thought Milan a truth-teller, even when it didn't serve him. But standing there, witnessing the weakness in his brother's eyes, he would've bet all the breath in his body Milan didn't even tell their sire what he'd done—how he'd run from the bear and hid behind a damned tree when he should have fought.

Vhogare's thoughts roared, deafening inside his skull. He clamped his fist around Soleil's silver dragon as he fought for reason, for mercy. "This throne—this burden—is your birthright."

Milan shook his head. "Some of us wish for a softer life, brother. Not everyone was meant to live by blood and steel."

But blood and steel are the only way we'll win. Hurt and wrath curled inside Vhogare's soul, latched scorched fingers around his heart. The river that washed Milan's shame away had more mercy than Vhogare.

Heat rose, boiling, beneath Vhogare's skin. Talons itched to tear free of his fingertips. "We all must make sacrifices," he managed, curling his fists but keeping his voice clear. "And you must be strong. Your coronation has advanced."

Milan gaped at him. "Strong? I have feared this day all my life." His confession fell like a blade between them. "I hoped Father would live forever, but kings are mortal men." The heir apparent glanced over at the sovereign who'd taken the steel throne forty years ago and held it with an iron fist ever since. "Much to my despair."

A vice clamped around Vhogare's heart. "Despite your *despair,*" he rasped, forcing himself to stand, "we must discuss it."

He swayed on his feet. Bracing himself against the wall, Vhogare fought the nausea down. "Let us give our father peace and leave the clerics to their work. I will meet you in your chamber to lay plans."

Taking his leave, Vhogare shouldered through the scraping stone doors to find Maura waiting outside. "What do you want?"

"Milan wanted me here." She waved a hand at the doors behind Vhogare. "But he shooed me away as he always does." Their mistress of gold's daughter wrung her hands and glanced both ways down the hall before she approached him.

"Did he tell you?" the girl whispered, keeping her dark eyes on the far doorways lest they be interrupted.

Cold sank into Vhogare's gut. "Tell me what?"

Maura pinched her thin lips into a line, the sharp planes of her young face tightening. "King Ulrich was beside himself when he died. He begged for you so he could ask your forgiveness, but Milan would not let the guards leave to retrieve you."

Vhogare's heart sank. "For what?"

The girl chewed her lip as if debating whether or not she should say.

He seized her shoulder, leaning his weight on her in his exhaustion. "Out with it, woman. I have places to be."

"You are the shadow of his youth," Maura told him, steel in her eyes.

Vhogare pulled away at those words, his thumb catching her wavy brown curls in his clumsiness, and she winced but did not stop. "He could not love you when he hated himself," she said. "But while Milan may have been the son of his blood, you were the son of his soul, and he knew it. He said as much before he left our world for the next."

"Why do me this kindness?" he demanded. They'd never shared more than polite conversation.

"To thank you for what you did to my father." Maura gave him a cold smile. "And because Soleil is a smart woman. If she loves you, there is something to love."

THE RAIN

ELIAS

Vhogare had met with the celestial without him. They'd been given three days. Travel had eaten two, Joanna's labor another, and after the news the prince delivered, he prayed they would survive to see the next sunrise. Their sovereign had passed from their world into the Ark's arms, his fire within rejoining the eternal flame in the sky. But he'd picked a sorry time to do it. *Rest his soul.*

The deep-seated panic in Vhogare's eyes left an uneasy feeling in Elias's gut, but there was far more at stake than a coronation. Filling his lungs, he squared his shoulders and approached Einar with his request.

"Father." Elias knelt beside the man who had taught him all he knew. "I need you to summon our cleric."

Einar took Elias's face in his calloused hands. "Don't lose faith. All is not lost yet."

"Jesse delivered Vhogare. He can deliver my child."

His father's face grew stern. "You need rest. They cut Vhogare out of his mother because they had no choice."

"And what choice do I have?"

Einar set his jaw. "Queen Seonna——"

"I know what happened to her. I need you to trust me." And in turn, Vhogare.

His father searched his face. For sleep-deprived madness, no doubt. Joanna had been a fixture in their life for the last decade; his father had raised the three of them, and Einar would not give his gooddaughter up without a fight.

"You take a grave risk." Einar leaned forward in his chair. "Don't lose what you're fighting for trying to save it."

Elias steeled himself. What they were about to do was unthinkable, but he was out of options. If he had any opportunity to save Joanna, he would take it. Elias tapped his fist against Einar's knee, his decision made. "There will be no death today."

Whatever Einar found in his son's eyes made him stand. "Are you certain?"

"I am."

If anyone understood a powerful secret, it was the royal spymaster. Forty years at the kingdom's helm, and Einar never failed to play the odds. Elias's father set his jaw and rose to retrieve their house's cleric. "Then my prayers are with you. Both of you."

Alastair stood with Elias while they waited in the empty stone hall, listening to Joanna sob and curse through the wall. No midwife had left the room for some time, and Elias hoped with all his soul that it meant good news. After a rare stretch of silence, Gabriella, dressed as a nursemaid, brought a fresh armful of linens and brushed against Elias while opening the door. She transferred a thin strip of parchment from her hand to his before disappearing inside.

Elias did not open the note, opting instead to tuck it up his sleeve, but Alastair's sharp gaze understood his every move. "You don't need to explain yourself to me," the warrior whispered, checking with Aadriek stationed down the hall to ensure no one approached without warning. "But there is blood in the water tonight. And it's not Joanna's."

"I wish you had stayed at the inn," Elias confessed, mopping a hand over his face as he drank in a brief moment of stillness. Another pair of eyes, another scope of reason, another mind on the matter would've been invaluable against their unfathomable threat. "You have far more experience with the world than I."

"Then trust me when I say, whatever happened, happened to the wrong one."

Elias looked up to find himself pinned by the commander's sharp gaze. "It happened the way it was meant to," he deflected.

Alastair's voice was edged iron. "Do not mistake man's choice for the Ark's will."

The sinking stone in Elias's stomach turned to lead.

Aadriek shifted down the hall, the swornguard hearing every word. Alastair glanced from his brother back to Elias and shoved off the wall. "Whatever becomes of this, you have allies in this castle. Whether you need them or not."

Einar and Jesse returned an hour after leaving. The cleric's long gray robes were laden with instruments that turned Elias's blood into shards of ice. Jesse seemed no more at ease; the man's dark eyes were wary as he ran a hand over his receding hairline, a token of the stress of his years in the medicinal arts. "I've brought all I can think of," he told Elias by way of greeting. "Your father did not explain much."

Elias gripped their cleric's gentle hands. "I promise you will understand soon enough."

With a concerned dip of his chin, Jesse stepped past Elias into Joanna's suite.

"We all have our battles, son," Einar told Elias in comfort, laying a strong, steady hand on his shoulder before Elias entered the room. "War, birth . . . they are so much the same. Tell Joanna the fight is hard, but it is worth it. Worth it all."

THE FIRE

VHOGARE

"Ark above," Vhogare began as he made for the great hall, "hear me please before what I am about to do makes You hear me no longer." *Kinslayer*, they would call him after this. *Cursed.* "Your horseman has betrayed You. Send Your sword for Erembour," he prayed, "protect the weak from him. I thank You for this gift, and I am sorry for how I must use it. But I will do all I can to protect mine until You arrive."

The gift had frozen inside of him, its dancing fire shielding itself with solid ice, and that warm, bright tether to the Well of Creation grew taut. Sorrow surrounded him, fierce and damp as a father's tears.

But though his hands trembled, Vhogare had no time to cry. He could smell his brother's blood beating in Milan's veins as he crept through the hidden passage behind the throne. Scent the weakness in it.

Grateful as Vhogare was for the gift, Erembour would soon come to know just how sorely he had misjudged him. When the ruthless celestial returned, he'd find no sniveling king nor kingdom crawling at his feet. No, Vhogare would truly do what needed to be done.

He and Elias, his true brother — the one of his soul, not the one of his blood — would be ready, and they'd pry the rest of the bastard's chaos from his cold corpse before Erembour could finish his war.

But they would need every soldier on the continent if they hoped to withstand the horseman's onslaught, Vhogare's new gift included. He would not be swallowed, and he would not plead nor ply their politics. Vhogare was tired of being stolen from. Never again would he be left behind or betrayed.

Strength was not begged for; it was taken, and the dear elder prince lacked the spine for what was coming. Lacked every ounce of will it would take to protect them.

And it was now or never before the heir was crowned.

Milan's brows shot up when Vhogare entered his room. "Brother—"

"Why is Aadriek not with you?" Vhogare snapped. The heir's sworn sword was in the east wing, waiting with Elias and Alastair for news about Joanna.

Milan's face fell. "I gave him leave for the night." He waved, straightening the books on his nightstand.

Leave? On this *night?* Vhogare surveyed Milan's room for weapons, a knife, a sword, anything. All he found were piles of dusty books, a small, onyx raven figurine in a golden cage, musty carpets, and lit candles. The only glass available was a full pitcher and decanter, which would leave a noticeable mess.

Milan huffed a sad snort. "What would he do but sit here and watch me grieve?"

Vhogare scowled; their father was dead in his bed, and the crown prince still refused to think like a king. "Good," he muttered. He was glad Aadriek would not need to be included.

"Good?" Milan frowned.

"He doesn't need to hear this." Vhogare clenched his fists at his sides. He was not sure he wanted to know, but he needed to. "You lied to me. About what my father said when he died."

Milan froze. "I did no such thing. Father barely had the strength to breathe, let alone share last words—"

"Maura told me!" Vhogare shouted before Milan could finish his lie. "I wanted to be there with him. *For* him. Do you have any idea what I said to him the last time we spoke? I could have had a chance to make things right, and you took that from me. Why?"

Milan turned to face Vhogare, and for a moment, his brother only studied him, chewing his lip as if deciding which blade would be the sharpest. "Because you're a disaster, Vhogare," Milan said at last. "You always have been. I knew Father's death would shatter something in you. I did, and I'm sorry. But you do a poor job of hiding your ambition."

Vhogare stiffened. He drew in a sharp breath to retort, but Milan cut him off. "Never once have you attempted to show me so much as a modicum of respect," the crown prince hissed. "My standing amongst our court is tenuous as it is. Why would I give you anything you could use to press your own claim? I am not as oblivious as you may think, and I am not stupid enough to add wood to your fire."

Milan's eyes grew wide at his accidental confession, and he pressed his lips together into a thin, straight line, but he could not take the words back.

Vhogare had to clamp his mouth shut to keep from gaping at Milan. His brother, the golden son, was afraid of him. The realization cut through Vhogare like lightning. All those years they'd spent fighting, and they'd both vied in different ways to earn their father's smile. But they'd both drawn poor odds, and there was no healing what time had broken. Their entire lives, they'd labored under an impossible task, and with their father gone, the masks had come off, and the knives had come out.

"Well, then." Vhogare raised his chin and squared his feet. "Speaking of claims, I've come to ask you to abdicate."

It was a hollow gesture. Though he was pathetic, Milan would never relinquish the throne despite his grievances. It was a matter of familial pride, and loyalty to their father, not duty. But that was not enough. *You cannot serve a kingdom without loving it.*

Even so, Vhogare had to make this one last offer, for the sake of the mother who bore them, and their father who fought for the kingdom now laid at their feet.

"Abdicate?" the crown prince gasped.

Vhogare shook his head in confusion. "You have the nerve to be offended, even after that . . . tantrum you threw in Father's suite?" He threw up his hands, dizzy and unsteady from exertion and dehydration. "You don't want this. So leave."

"Father's ghost would haunt me until the day I died if I left this country to rot." Milan looked Vhogare over, scowling. "And all those dreams of mine, all that travel, takes gold, Vhogare, and time. I have spent *years* devoted to this office. What has my life, my work, been for if I am not king? What would I even do?"

Milan's voice grew frantic. "Do I look like I'm built for hard labor?" He waved a hand at his reedy frame and his fine clothes. "Could I buy my way across the world with service instead of a crown? Of course not. If I left this castle, I would be a failure. I would die as a pauper on the street. Is that what you want?"

"I would rather you live."

For a heartbeat, a flicker of understanding dashed across Milan's face. But for all his studies, the crown prince had stifled every instinct that might save his life. "You're as high-strung as your horse," Milan scowled, deflecting. "What's gotten into you?"

"You." Vhogare took a rickety step forward and jabbed his finger at Milan's chest. "You are a pathetic excuse for a crown prince. You are weak and spiteful, and you could read a thousand books and yet not have the knowledge of what must be done. So travel. Whore. Sail. I will give you the money." He waved an arm at the tower's open window. "I don't care what you do, but turn your crown over to me and agree to never press your claim, and the world is yours."

A torrent of emotion swelled behind Milan's eyes. Vhogare could see the choice dancing there, the freedom reaching out. A golden ladder dangled in front of the crown prince's soft, scarless hands. If his brother would just seize the opportunity while he still had it, Vhogare could take power without blood.

But Milan's jaw hardened, and his mouth set into a thin line. "And leave Anchora to you? After you neglected all our studies, fawning over that woman?"

"I promise I will take care of our kingdom." Vhogare clenched his fists. "With you gone, I can marry Soleil—"

"Soleil?" Milan scoffed. "You would exile your own brother over a harlot who couldn't keep her legs shut?"

"You speak one more word about Soleil, and it will be the last thing you do on the face of this earth."

Milan clamped his jaw shut.

"She is brighter and wiser than you could ever hope to be,"

Vhogare seethed, "and she will make a far better queen than any poor woman stupid enough to hitch herself to your weak will."

Milan's face reddened. He clenched and unclenched his hands, flustered like a small bird caught in a net that it flew straight into.

"*I* will do whatever it takes to protect this country," Vhogare continued, his heartbeat surging. "To rule is an honor, not some chore you can abandon when it doesn't suit you."

His brother's upper lip curled, long-suffering malice boiling over. "And how are you going to protect a country when you couldn't protect her?" Milan jabbed, abandoning all caution.

Vhogare flinched, but Milan plowed on, undeterred. "Mother. Joanna. You leave a string of corpses. Perhaps, soon enough, it'll be Soleil. One more dead queen left in your wake. Then we'll see if it was all worth it, won't we?"

"What did you say to me?" Vhogare felt himself growl, and there was nothing human in the sound.

"Really, Brother." Milan turned his back, feigning indifference as he faced the open window. But his hand shook as he poured himself a glass of water. "I admit to a moment of weakness, but you can't seriously think—"

"Say it again."

"You know very well what I said." Milan whirled to face Vhogare, a reckless dare in his ice-blue eyes. "I am tired of playing these games with you," he spat, trembling. "You think you are owed more than you are worth. Father knew it, I know it, and soon Soleil will know it, too. I will not abdicate, but you do not have to stay to see me crowned."

His brother drew himself up as their father so often had, ready to cause pain. "I am the ruler of Anchora," Milan snarled, "whether I like it or not. And I will not have a dog lying around waiting to bite my throat. You can live in exile, brother, or you can lose your head."

Milan quivered as he stood there, waiting for Vhogare to react. The man's eyes leaped across Vhogare's face, searching desperately for any sign, any indication, that Vhogare might obey.

But his brother looked so small standing there, armorless and weaponless. He was nothing but a studious boy cowering behind the steel shell of a kingdom, and all his books and dust and papers would not save him. Beads of perspiration clung to Milan's brow, and the fright in his eyes overshadowed any resemblance he may have borne to their father.

Vhogare couldn't help himself. He barked a laugh. A laugh that kept tumbling out of him like sickness. He bent over, bracing himself on his knees as tears spilled from his eyes.

Milan's brow furrowed as Vhogare kept laughing. He couldn't stop. The sound transformed into something low and terrifying, sinking deep into his throat.

"You think I am joking?" Milan shouted, fear cracking through the edges of his voice. "Every guard in this castle answers to me. They will execute you in a heartbeat if I ask."

"If you ask?" Vhogare angled his head. "You never ask. A king commands. But you're not a king, are you?" He advanced a step. "You live a life of comfort and shelter, and never concern yourself with the world outside your head, even if it's falling apart right in front of you."

"Falling apart in front of *me?*" Milan gaped, baffled. "You have worked for nothing in this life but one woman and she will sit on *my* Council, not yours. Hell, I may even make her my queen. You were the one who said I needed heirs, and she's already got your royal blood in her."

"Soleil loves me!" Vhogare thundered. Spit flew through his teeth, and his face grew red and hot in his ire. "She wouldn't choose you if you tore your heart out and laid it at her feet."

"*Loves* you?" Milan retorted. "No one loves you, Vhogare. We tolerate you."

The words fell out of his mouth with the slippery ease of truth—a long-kept family secret no one ever intended to see the light of day.

Vhogare went slack with shock, and Milan seized his opportunity. "Father may not have been able to say it, but I will. The first son wears the crown and the second wields the sword. That is the way it has always been and always will be." Milan lowered his shoulders and raised his chin. "You are simply a necessity we cannot outrun. A means to an end. Just as you are to Soleil," the golden prince spat with venom. "She will be no different. And she will not miss you when you send your poor bastard child letters from some country across the sea."

"You will die for that." Vhogare kicked the door shut behind him, rage giving him strength.

Milan's face fell as he realized he'd gone too far. "No. You will get out of my country, traitor, or I will have you killed and feed your bloody corpse to the hounds." The crown prince's words shook, fear melting into outright panic as dark scales came out of Vhogare's skin.

"I am your brother." Vhogare let the dragon show through his eyes, his pupils rotating to slits of dark in a sea of silver. "And you do not command me."

He was tired of bowing, of kneeling and scraping and begging. A groveling king won no victories.

Milan stumbled backward, knocking over the books he had just righted. "Vhogare, what have you done?"

"I warned you," he growled, crossing the room in long, powerful strides. "One more word about Soleil, and your life would be forfeit. Say it again."

But there was nothing left to be said. Some things, firstborn princes just knew.

Vhogare didn't need his dragon, talons, or the chaos churning and roiling beneath his skin. A sliver of his beast's strength was enough. Milan had excelled at his studies and built a calm and level head for politics all his life. He was smart, fair, and cold at times. But he had no strong sword arm and always failed to raise his shield. His poor brother had no coin to flip when he needed it most, and Vhogare's had always fallen to the weighted side.

The idiot did not even sleep with a blade next to his bed.

Milan did most of the work for him, backing away like prey before a blood-crazed panther. Summoning just a fraction of his newfound strength, Vhogare hooked a foot behind his brother's leg and slammed him down onto the mattress. There could be no sound, no scream, no struggle.

Terror bulged Milan's blue eyes in the half heartbeat that Vhogare yanked a fluffed pillow off the headboard. But it was erased by pale fabric as he crushed it against the heir's face. The sumptuous fur and down bedding, pleasantries of Milan's station, became the brick around his neck in his sea of placidity.

"You are too soft to execute anyone, brother," Vhogare ground out, exertion clamping his jaw. "Too soft to save this kingdom from him, and I would spare you the trouble."

The heir apparent would sail no more seas in this life and climb no more mountains. He would not abandon them in their time of need. Vhogare would not give him the chance.

Milan scratched and clawed at Vhogare's hands, ripping shreds in the thin skin covering his tendons, but Vhogare suffered through. Right before Milan's wits deserted him, his brother attempted to break his grip by slamming his elbows down on Vhogare's arms, but Vhogare climbed atop and doubled down.

Shoved down until all sound ceased.

As if the very wind outside the castle stilled.

Vhogare's gift shrieked in horror and agony at the life he took in cold rage. That beautiful, shining bright tether connecting him to the light snapped clean in half.

And then the curtains fluttered, and Milan's soul left his body.

THE LOVE

VHOGARE

Gulping down air, he stormed out the door only to slam into Soleil at the top of the stairs, panting and breathless from her climb. She stumbled backward, but Vhogare seized her wrist to save her from falling.

"Thank you," she gasped, leaning against the railing of the landing. "I left the Council meeting for a moment, just to see if you got his blessing before —"

Her brilliant blue eyes fell to Vhogare's slick hand on her bare arm. Blood darkened his broken skin, every scratch carved into his soul. Soleil's searching glance danced across Vhogare's shoulder to his brother's open door. The too-still body on the bed.

"What happened?" She seized Vhogare's hands and shoved his hair out of his face, searching him for injuries or wounds. "Has there been an assassin?" Soleil stood on her toes to peer over his shoulder again before turning back to him. "Are you hurt?"

Vhogare's heart crumbled to ash in his chest. His midnight sun, always there in his darkest hour, always looking for his light. "There is no assassin." Not one of flesh, anyhow.

Fear — a deep, heart-aching thing he could not stomach — crawled into her beautiful gaze. "My darling, what have you done?"

"You do not understand," he hissed. "I did this to save us."

Shock sucked all the blood from her skin. "You don't even deny it?"

"No." Had she not heard a word he said?

Soleil put a hand to her stomach. Steel uncovered in his chest at the sight; she hadn't even begun to show, and yet already she protected their child. With her other hand, she pressed against the banister to steady herself. "You cannot ask for my hand, but you can kill your brother? Did you not think to tell me before—"

"I did ask!" he thundered. "I did ask for your hand before we even left for the hunt, and the king said no. I asked for the kingdom, and Milan said no. But I am tired of asking. I love you, and I love this kingdom, and—" Words failed him. She was his everything, and something utterly inhuman was trying to take her away from him.

Soleil's features sharpened. Hurt and betrayal warred in her sapphire gaze. "Your father did heinous things to get this throne," she whispered. "He took it from a cruel man, yes, and Anchora has thrived under his rule. But though it may have saved this kingdom, it ate him alive, and he became what he feared most in the process." She splayed her palms out in front of her. "He did not want this for you."

"And what about what I wanted? What you wanted?" he said. "Soleil, you have spent your life tiptoeing around their rules and opinions, playing their games. You've petitioned relentlessly to expand and modernize the royal archives. All your ideas of reforming our legal system, and improving the city—you can do that now. We can do all of that together. I will give you free rein to do whatever you want! Ask, and you shall have it. The world at your feet."

Tears welled in the bottomless depths of her eyes. "At what cost?"

Vhogare took a step forward, but she held up a hand for him to stay back. "You asked me," Soleil snarled. "And I am telling you. What you have done"—she thrust her finger at Milan's corpse in the room at Vhogare's back—"is wrong. Your father turns in his grave just thinking—"

"Milan was different," Vhogare reasoned, grasping for anything to make her see. "He deserved this. He stood in our way."

"And what if one day I stand in our way?" Soleil demanded, shaking with anger. "We have a thousand differing opinions. What if, one day, we disagree? What's to stop you from killing me?"

Vhogare's jaw fell open. "I did this *for you.*"

Soleil's eyes flashed. "You can justify anything if you're desperate enough."

"You were not there," he snarled. "You do not know." He could still feel her ashes in his hands. Still hear their child crying. "I met a . . . a man in the woods. He gave me a vision like Joanna's. Something terrible is coming for us unless we stop it here and now."

Her brows knit together in concern. She'd always believed Joanna, even in the beginning. "What did you see?"

Vhogare shook his head. How could he tell Soleil she died, screaming, in his arms? That their child had burned to ash mere hours after being born? She had access to a kingdom's worth of information, but he didn't have the courage to burden her with such knowledge.

"Tell me." Soleil's tears spilled, running down her face.

He was losing her. Losing her, but if he told her, she would never again sleep soundly. He'd known women who miscarried from far less than the threat of their world burning down to its bones. If she hated him, at least she'd live. Their baby would live.

"I can't," he whispered. "I just need you to know that even if the whole world were on fire, I would die to keep you safe."

Soleil's gaze softened just a fraction. "Perhaps the man lied," she offered, grasping at wind.

"He did not lie!" Vhogare thundered, so loud it was a roar.

Soleil stepped back at his outburst.

"I know it," he insisted. There was no way to put the raw horror he'd experienced into words, but— "I know it was real, Soleil, and you will not stand there and tell me I did not see what I saw, feel what I felt."

Soleil's eyes widened as she fought to reconcile the man she knew with the one standing before her. Vhogare felt strange even to himself, foreign and volatile like he teetered on a razor's edge and the blade would cut him in half if he fell.

"How am I supposed to help if you will not tell me?" she demanded. "Milan is your brother, Vhogare. Your family!"

"*You* are my family."

"Do *not* blame me for this!" Soleil's shout ricocheted off the stone walls as she pinned him with a damning glare. "Do not *ever* blame me for something like this."

"I do blame you!" he thundered, seizing her arms. "If I loved you any less, I wouldn't have done it."

She struck him, full across the face with the flat of her palm, and Vhogare released her, stumbling backward to cup his throbbing jaw.

Soleil stood as still as a snow leopard, panting. There was not an ounce of surprise or regret in her gaze at what she'd done.

Vhogare gaped at her, shock freezing him to the spot. She'd slapped him half a hundred times in bed, but never in anger.

"My brother died alone in a ditch in the dark," she seethed. "I don't even know if Byn felt it when he fell or if the horse ran over him like he was nothing. You know I will never forgive myself for not being there."

"And you"—Soleil dropped her broken voice to a whisper and pointed a condemning finger at Milan's open door—"you did not do this for me." Tears sliced down her moon-silvered cheeks. "I loved my brother," she sobbed. "I loved him, and he was taken from me. Why would you so willingly give up what some of us would die to have again?"

Vhogare opened his mouth, but he had no words. No apology for how deeply he had wounded her.

"And this"—she swept her arms out, encompassing his sins—"this makes me nothing. The mistress of a kinslayer. Mother to a cursed child. *You* made us nothing."

Wrath crawled up into his throat, but he mastered it. "I have made you a queen."

"I did not love you for a crown," she gasped, appalled. "If I wanted to be queen, I'd have fucked Milan! I loved you for your heart, Vhogare, and you have smothered it."

"Soleil—" He stepped forward to tuck a strand of night-dark hair back into her braid.

Her soft cheek was cold as ice.

His calm seemed to scare her more than his anger. She flinched at his touch, and he drew his hand back as if he'd been scalded. "I swear to you," he whispered, clutching a hand to his chest, "on every drop of blood in my beating heart, that I love you. I did not do this to hurt you. But there is not a damn thing in this world that would stop me from protecting you. You are everything."

Soleil shook her head. "Vhogare—"

"Please." He hated it. How weak she made him. But he would kneel. Would get on his knees and crawl if that was what it took to keep her at his side. "One day, the world will know what I have done. Until then, I beg you to keep this between us. Joanna is dying, and she needs our help."

"*Our* help?" Soleil's features had softened with sympathy at the start of his plea, but by the end, ice had frozen over her gaze. She glared up at him. "I am not letting you anywhere near her in this state."

"But it was your idea," he pleaded. "Look." Taking a chance, he raised his right hand and showed her his gift. Tiny bundles of flame danced atop each fingertip. "We can save her. Soleil, I have to try."

Soleil's face drained of all color as if she recognized Chaos's silver fire from her archaic studies. "Vhogare. You have played with powers far beyond your control. Mortal man was not meant to hold that."

"It was the only way."

Her sharp eyes pinned him. "You must give it back."

A lead weight dropped into Vhogare's gut. "Without this, we lose Joanna. Elias needs her."

"*Give it back, Vhogare.*" Soleil was angrier than he'd ever seen her. Her sapphire eyes blazed with relentless determination.

There had been a time he would have done anything for her. But giving up his gift meant giving up Joanna, breaking his promise to Elias. Letting this go meant letting Soleil and his whole world burn to the ground. "I can't." It was the truth. The truth, but a lie.

The beautiful, dancing flame between them suffocated like a bonfire in a rainstorm, and tempered steel came out of Soleil's mouth. "I know you," she growled. "And I know you stop at nothing. But you begged me to save you from yourself. You are a danger to us all with that power, and for your soul, my love"—she pressed her hand flat across the planes of his chest—"I will do anything."

A storm of emotion warred across her face, and she seized his collar and slammed her lips to his.

Soleil kissed him as she did in the dark, brimming over with the wildfire of passion she kept leashed just beneath the surface, and Vhogare melted into her.

He ran his bloody hands up her back, exhaling.

She would stand by him.

She would hold him through this.

"I love you," he whispered against her lips.

But Soleil broke away, and something hardened behind her eyes.

Something no one else would have noticed but him. He, who had seen her at the heights of pleasure and the pits of pain. He, who witnessed all her love for him fall to pieces in the wake of one choice.

"You're right." A desperate, reckless laugh choked out of her throat as she rested her brow against his, sharing the same breath. "You love me beyond reason." Soleil pressed her bloodless lips into a thin line, her piercing gaze frosted glass. "And I must thank you for it."

Soleil stepped down a stair and turned her back to him, and Vhogare understood.

That kiss had been her last.

He reached for her, but she descended the spiral staircase, her hand on the carved banister until she rounded the bend in the wall blocking her from sight and raced down the tower stairs. Her footfalls echoed like thunder against the stone.

"Soleil!" Vhogare roared, chasing after her, but his lithe historian was far swifter, far lighter on her feet, and exhaustion weighed his every move.

"Soleil, you will lose everything!" he shouted, desperation cracking through his voice. *We will lose everything.*

If she told Elias about Milan. . . .

No, Elias would understand. He had been there with the bear and had seen Milan's weakness. His true brother had *sworn.*

But she could tell no one else.

Soleil reached the main floor with Vhogare on her heels. He reached out for her as her knees buckled, fatigue from the night slowing her down, but she wrung free of his grasp. His love threw a determined glance over her shoulder and righted herself before she crashed through the doors of the council room. Vhogare stumbled in behind her, skidding to a stop before he all but tackled her.

All his father's leal Council looked up at the intrusion, deep in their planning for Milan's expedited coronation. Firelight from the seven hearths lining the walls flickered over their confused faces.

Vhogare's heart sank. *Einar.* He scanned the small crowd huddled around the long, walnut council table, checking every carved supporting column, but Elias's father was nowhere to be seen, thank the Ark. Vhogare prayed he was still upstairs in the east wing with his son. At the sight of Soleil's tear-streaked face, every council head rose from their seats, even the eldest.

The kingmaker stood. A mighty, ancient man, he'd served on the previous king's council and aided Ulrich's ascent to the throne. Pressing his fists into the council table for support, he glanced from Vhogare to Soleil and demanded, "What is it, my dear?"

"The prince has slain his brother," Soleil sobbed. Sorrow, anger, and justice twisted her features as she pointed at Vhogare. "In Milan's very bed."

The room went silent. Maura's mother glared from Soleil to Vhogare, buried under parchments in her daughter's absence.

Soleil couldn't take her eyes off him, like she didn't know him. Like she'd *never* known him. He must've looked terrifying; her hand slid to shield her belly, protecting their baby from him.

Vhogare's soul crumbled.

She hadn't told them about his gift, no doubt concerned they would not believe her, but she'd said enough.

The betrayal—the *fear*—on her face cleaved his heart in two.

Vhogare did not dare breathe as they took in Soleil's distress, the blood on his hands. The sweat sliding down his neck. Prince or not, there would be no mercy for him.

The kingmaker summoned his page. "Go and see if this is true."

Pale as a ghost, the boy sneaked past Vhogare like a rat by a snake and sprinted up the stairs. Favoring their beloved caution, the Council did not wait for a verdict before taking action.

"Our apologies, Your Royal Highness," the youngest amongst them began, "but I'm sure you can understand our concern."

"Arrest this man," the kingmaker ordered, addressing their household guard. *His* household guard. "Until we ascertain the meaning of this."

Confused, the guards approached, and Vhogare's gaze snagged on the royal sigils on their breastplates—the same black and silver as his house banners draping the high, shadowy walls. Without the king, they deferred to the named heir. But in the absence of both, the Council ruled with absolute authority. Cold steel closing around his wrist snapped Vhogare to his senses.

"We do not have time for this," he thundered, yanking his other arm away before they could bind him.

"There is time enough for justice," the kingmaker said. "We will find the truth of it, and if there is none, you will be on your way."

"No!" Vhogare shouted. "No, Joanna is dying. Take me there, I order you."

The guards didn't move so much as an inch, glancing between him and the Council like every thought had vacated their helmeted heads. Where was Alastair? Aadriek? Someone, anyone he could trust.

"Take me to Elias," he tried again. "I will explain. I need to be there."

"Their house cleric is already speaking over Lady Joanna."

On his right, Soleil clamped a hand over her mouth.

Speaking over her.

The words fell through him like sand. "Is she dead?"

If he had failed. . . . Failed *again*. . . .

"No, but—"

There was no sound left. No fear left.

No heartbeat, no reason, no air, no breath left in the face of that *but.*

Only fire.

Joanna.

He had to save her.

Scalding flame flared to life in Vhogare's chest. The heat wound out in vicious tendrils, tearing and shredding as it clawed its way out of his soul. His gift wept, but he had no choice. What had he done this for if not to protect Soleil? To save Elias and Joanna? And the Council stood in his way.

Scales ripped through Vhogare's skin, and great dark wings folded out of his spine. The Council members stepped back, aghast with horror, as his knees buckled and bent, and both ankles broke and reshaped. Every muscle and fiber stretched to snap as Vhogare's chest bowed out and his heart engorged. His fire blazed to life like the bellows of a forging flame.

"What in the Ark's name have you done?" the kingmaker shouted, reaching for a sword that would do him no good.

Vhogare hardly heard him. The world seemed to roar in his ears as the prince took the dragon's form, thrashing as his beast came out of his bones. But the sprawling council room was too small to contain him as his wings flared wide. Vhogare grappled for space, for balance in such confinement, and found none. His massive frame broke through the back wall of the fortress, sending columns and crenelations tumbling. Rain sluiced down the open stones.

Growling, he dug his hind legs into the floor and felt the granite buckle beneath his weight.

Thunder shook the earth, rumbling the castle down to its foundation. Vhogare opened his maw, flame pooling deep in his chest, and Soleil ran in front of him as if to shield the Council with her presence.

No. Vhogare's heart seized. *No, not you.*

But the fire was already burning, and he could not stop its escape. Desperate not to burn her, Vhogare flared his wings for balance and swept out his scarred right forepaw to keep Soleil away from the fire so he would not consume her in his blaze.

He slid her across the room to safety, but he was too strong, and her scream was cut short as the ceiling came down.

Lost in his rage, Vhogare loosed the jet of white-hot flame trapped in his throat. It ate up the Council at their precious table, leaving black scars streaking across the stones. The silver fire burnt every banner draping the high stone walls, curled around the carved columns, and danced with the fires in each hearth.

He strained to control his blaze, targeting only those who prevented him from reaching Joanna. But the decorative pillars crumbled, crushing the guards in attendance. The boom of their collapse deafened him to the Council's dying screams. Every painting, sconce, torch, and tapestry depicting his father's long and lustrous reign was reduced to ash and cinders in a heartbeat.

Vhogare roared until his breath ended.

Until all that was left before him was ash.

On his right, racing down the grand staircase to discern the cause of the catastrophic noise, Einar stumbled to a stop at the sight of Vhogare and took in the dark dragon with fire pouring from its open maw.

And stumbled backward, clutching his chest. He turned, grabbing the wall, shouting for reinforcements, and fell into his son's arms.

Elias caught his father as Einar collapsed and died, his heart burst inside his barrel chest.

Vhogare heard it stop beating.

Heard the last breath escape Einar's lungs.

The man who had raised him while his father ruled a kingdom, the arms that always caught him when all he'd done for so long was rebel. The warmhearted spymaster who dared believe Vhogare could protect instead of hurt.

The last beat of Einar's heart pulled Vhogare free of it. Free from the rage, the fear, the fire.

He sank, gasping, back into his human skin and turned to find Soleil crushed beneath broken rafters. *No.* He had missed her—had aimed his fire in front, at the Council alone.

But she lay crumpled, battered by his strength in his change. He didn't know how he'd done it. One moment, he'd pushed her to safety. Next, his wings had broken the rafters. But it did not matter.

Vhogare staggered across the broken stones and crashed to his knees beside her. He did not care that he was naked, his clothes ripped apart at the seams. Did not care that the world now saw him for what he was. Soleil was gone, and a light had gone out in his soul.

A far too human roar tore out of Vhogare as he heaved the collapsed rafter off of her, too lost in his grief to know fear at his horrific strength.

"My darling," he whispered, cradling her broken body to him. "Come back to me, please."

Cuts seeped blood from where the ceiling tiles had struck and torn her soft skin. He shook her, aching, gut-wrenching sobs breaking through his teeth. "Soleil!"

But Soleil's sapphire eyes remained unseeing, piercing right through him as he knelt amidst the collapse. The flush was gone from her cheeks, her red lips parted in pain.

"You are my sun," he rasped, brushing dark hair out of her face. "This was for you. I have done all of this for you. . . ."

Vhogare rocked over to press his forehead to hers as lightning split the sky, her brow bone soft and broken beneath his own. The scent of singed lavender clung to her clothes, delicate and destroyed, and Vhogare's chest heaved at the horrific memory.

"He will not"—he groaned, spit sliding between his teeth—"he will not take you from me."

But Soleil did not blink. Did not breathe.

"Why didn't you trust me? Why didn't you wait?" He never meant to hurt her. He meant to protect her.

But she would never hear his apology, never know his heart.

"Don't leave me with this," he pleaded.

Vhogare's gaze drifted to the bloodied hand draped across her stomach, Soleil's lovely fingers lax and pale against the cloth of her ruined gown, protecting their unborn child.

His child, though she hadn't yet begun to show.

His very blood and bone that he'd failed to save.

The scream of agony that shredded out of Vhogare took his soul with it.

Only emptiness remained as he laid Soleil onto the stones, and promised her a grave fit for a queen. *My love,* he wept. *You should have waited.*

But she hadn't.

Hold both my hearts, he begged the Ark as he shut her gorgeous eyes and folded her slender hands across her stomach—and their child—in peace. *Hold them until I can come.*

He had done nothing to deserve such kindness, but Soleil—she and his child belonged in the light. The Ark's well of life, of strength and fire and never-ending warmth, would keep them safe when he could not.

Fighting for breath, he scooped Soleil's silver dragon up from where it had fallen out of his torn pocket and crawled to Elias. Einar lay in his heartbrother's arms, more his father than his own had been. Vhogare trailed a trembling hand over Einar's soft curls, his gray beard, the lines from all the joyful smiles of his years. *May You carry him in Your arms,* he prayed, closing the eyes he'd hoped to look into forever.

Elias just stared at him, empty with shock.

Vhogare could not stand the horror on his friend's face, the battered grief, denial, and *blame* in his eyes. There had been no choice, no other way.

Steeling his shuddering heart, Vhogare unfastened Einar's red cloak and yanked it free, wrapping it around his waist to cover himself. He reached for the sigil pinned to the spymaster's proud chest denoting Einar as the king's royal Right Hand, and Vhogare froze with his hand around the steel.

Erembour's voice drifted, haunting, through his head. *Remember what hangs in the balance.*

Setting his teeth, Vhogare ripped the sigil off, seized Elias by the collar, and dragged his heartbrother to his feet.

Vhogare shoved the cold steel into Elias's clammy fist. "Stand up," he growled, "and come with me. Or Joanna dies, too."

THE STAIRS

ELIAS

The summer storm broke above them as Elias staggered to his feet. His legs were water beneath him. Had that really been his father, dead in his arms? The man who'd taught him to pray, fight, sing, and spy? Given his whole heart and life to see him safe and loved?

No. No, it couldn't have been.

Elias looked behind them as Vhogare dragged him through the hall, daring one more glance to confirm that it was indeed Einar, still and empty on the stones.

He was not hallucinating. His father was dead.

"What are you doing down here?" Vhogare demanded as they moved. "You should be with Joanna."

"We couldn't find you!" Elias cast an arm out at their destroyed surroundings. "Aadriek and Alastair searched the whole castle, the king's quarters, your chambers, everywhere. Where have you been, Vhogare? Joanna needs us——"

"She's still alive, yes?" Vhogare wheeled around to search Elias's eyes for answers.

"Yes, but Jesse can't save her alone." It had torn Elias's heart out to leave her, but Vhogare was her only chance. He'd come to find the prince and his fire for Joanna and arrived just in time to witness

Vhogare's monster and hold Einar as he died. "Where were you?" he repeated, reeling at the carnage around them.

Vhogare didn't answer.

Numb, Elias bumped into Alastair, who'd thundered down the stairs from the west wing and stood, frozen, as he surveyed the destruction. All the blood drained from the swornguard's bronze face at the sight of the ruined council room.

The roof had caved in; four of its seven weight-bearing columns crumbled and broken. Banners still burned on the walls, and black scorch marks licked up the stone floor. Ash was all that remained of the council table, the Council members themselves. Any bodies that hadn't been burned to dust were crushed beneath the fallen rubble. Soleil's fresh corpse stared at them, empty-eyed, as Vhogare hauled Elias toward the grand staircase.

Elias vomited before he made it ten steps. It had been almost a day since he'd last eaten, and bile and water splattered on the silver carpet. He retched until he hit his knees on the stairs.

Below them, Alastair swore something vicious in his mother tongue, but Elias didn't know enough Marian to translate. Gathering himself, the commander shouted orders, and soldiers who'd been stationed in other parts of the castle and yard rushed into the destroyed council room. In their haste to respond, they stumbled over castle staff that hunkered in corners, their shaking arms wrapped around their heads in terror. Cooks and dishwashers gaped from the kitchen's doorway across the great hall as Maura raced down the stairs and wailed at the ashen pile of dust where her mother should've been.

Vhogare did not stop to console her.

He seized Elias by the shirt and pulled him up the grand staircase, panting as they reached the tower housing the second stair to the east wing.

Beneath Elias's feet, the tower's stone steps blurred, the walls a gray shroud pressing down. He clutched the pin of office Vhogare had shoved into his fist. It was cold and unforgiving, a stark reminder of the empty space in the world where his father should have been. Elias would never hear Einar's laugh again, never thank him for all he'd done.

He would never put his baby girl in his father's strong arms.

Elias choked on a sob, throwing his hand out to brace himself on the granite wall. Below him lay his father, and above him, his wife was dying. *Joanna.* How could he tell her the man who'd raised her, who'd stood by her side day and night since her parents died, would stand by her side no longer?

"What did you do?" Elias demanded, his voice hoarse as he gulped down air to keep the panic inside his chest. "What did you *do?*"

"What I had to," Vhogare snapped, pale as death ahead of him on the stairs. Sweat ran down the prince's chest in rivers, scales shifting and sliding beneath his skin as if he struggled to contain the beast.

"Saving my wife does not justify killing my father, you fucking bastard!" Elias put his elbow to Vhogare's throat and pinned him against the tower wall. "This is not what we—"

"I didn't kill him!" Vhogare shouted, shoving Elias back with far too much strength.

Elias hit the opposite wall so hard that he blacked out for a moment. When he could see again, he found himself slouched on the stairs. His head throbbed like a hammer had struck him. When he put a hand to the back of his hair, it came away bloody, the skin of his scalp busted from the impact.

"Stop it," Vhogare pleaded. He stared down at Elias with the raw terror of a man who could not believe what he'd just done. "I loved Einar. I didn't kill him. I swear it. He . . . saw me. And died running for help."

Elias grabbed his father's pin and rolled onto his hands and knees. The tower seemed to spin. "He died trying to save them from you."

Vhogare seemed to shrink at those words, but he recovered fast. "We can mourn later," he growled, standing on the stairs like a hound with its hackles raised. "Right now, we are wasting time."

Time. All this for more time. Elias forced himself to breathe around his overwhelming desire to strangle Vhogare. There was no fighting someone that strong. He'd get himself killed just trying. "Is that the gift?" he demanded as he struggled to his feet. "That . . . thing?"

"That *thing* will save us when Erembour comes back. And it will save Joanna. Come on."

Vhogare seized his arm, yanking him up the steps, but Elias dug in. "Where is Milan?" The whole council went up in flames, and they were planning the heir's coronation.

Thunder shook the tower. Vhogare went silent.

Elias smudged vicious tears from his vision and caught sight of the pale new scars on the back of Vhogare's hands. His stomach turned. "Is that where you went? Joanna has been lying there suffering while you left to secure your crown? Your father is not even cold in his bed—"

"You saw him with the bear," Vhogare cut in. "He didn't want our kingdom. And even if he did, my brother was too weak to see this through."

"You didn't tell me." Unstable and dizzy on the stairs, Elias seized Vhogare's collar for support. "We went into this together. I trusted you," he growled. "You didn't tell *me.*"

Vhogare pinned him with a dragon's glare. "You swore we would do whatever it took."

Elias did not back down. "*I* swore that I would *not* let this world burn, and you have put a torch to its pyre."

"I tried to reason with them, but they wouldn't listen." Vhogare pulled free of Elias's grip and brandished the healed scar on his wrist from the split cuff. "By will or by iron fist, we will fight that monster." Lightning struck, illuminating the razor-sharp terror in his gaze. "You did not see what I saw."

"Nothing in the world could justify this. Soleil's whole life was in front of her—"

"Soleil died because of the damn Council!" Vhogare stepped into Elias's face, torture and desperation raw in his voice. "They were wasting time," he snarled, sweat dripping down his brow. "As are you."

Cold fear sliced into Elias's gut. "Time is what we wanted."

Vhogare blinked, the sign of a hammer striking true. "Then you should not doubt my resolve." He struck a bloody finger against Elias's chest. "And you *swore.*"

Don't give it, Joanna had told him. *Don't give your life and leave us alone.* "I swore to save them," Elias amended with caution—far too much caution for a brother.

"Then save her."

Joanna. How could he subject her to Vhogare's gift? His fire? But what options did he have? "This is madness."

"It is survival!" Vhogare's outburst seemed to horrify him. Whatever he saw on Elias's face made him master himself. "I know this is not what you wanted. It is not what I wanted, either." He put a hand to his chest, the other against Elias's. "Your father was mine. But he loved Joanna like a daughter, and I did all of this to save her. What happened to my mother will not happen to her, this I swear to you. But right now, we must hurry."

THE LITTLE LIGHT

ELIAS

S tomaching his grief, Elias went ahead of Vhogare into the room to prepare Joanna. But he could not prepare himself. His wife lay, exhausted, on the bed, covered as modestly as possible in the circumstances, and two days of pain had left her frail but breathing. Jesse stood at her side, all the cleric's tools displayed on a desk pulled up next to the bed.

"Elias?" Joanna's voice was hoarse from screaming, so soft he almost missed it as she reached for him.

"Hello, my love," he whispered. The ground seemed to move beneath his feet, and he took great care sitting at her side so as not to hurt her. Struggling through the mental fog, he brushed soaked blonde strands free from her cheek. "Can you hear me?"

She nodded, blinking.

Elias took a steadying breath. They had no other options. "You know the babe is turned," he whispered, pressing his brow to hers, "and the midwives are at the extent of their arts."

As they spoke, Gabriella tried to calm the women. The fortress was large, but not so large that the destruction could not be heard from Joanna's quarters. All three of Joanna's midwives were demanding answers, concerned for their children and spouses who were working on the ground level during the collapse. At Elias's nod, Jesse dismissed them to see for themselves. They needed focus for Joanna's delivery and whatever peace they could find amid such devastation.

With forced calm, Elias explained their plan to Joanna.

When he finished, Joanna squeezed his hand in understanding and confirmation. "Anything," she whispered. "Anything to keep her alive."

"I'm right here with you." He forced his voice steady. For her sake, he would not break. "We will be brave together."

Tears traced down her face, but she met his eyes and nodded. "Brave."

Joanna's eyes were already pale. They grew steadily lighter as the pain became too much, and her visions threatened to resurface. Her rich summer gaze lightened to a dull, soft sage, like a rainstorm rolling over the forest.

Elias turned to Jesse. "Are your tools sterile?" he heard himself ask, remembering his studies.

The holy man nodded. Questions cycloned in Jesse's weathered gaze: the collapse, the noise, the roar, Einar's disappearance—but they would all be answered later. "Boiled, with fresh linen for binding, and I've given her what I can for the pain. How do you propose to close the incision?"

"Vhogare," Elias called, and the prince entered the room.

Joanna took one look at Vhogare's distraught state and whipped her head to face Elias. "He did it?" she whispered, her bloodshot eyes wide with concern.

"Aye." For all Joanna knew, Vhogare had accepted the gift from the celestial and come straight upstairs to save her. Elias would explain the true disaster later. "It was more than we bargained for. But we will see you through this, I promise."

The cleric whispered a prayer at the scales shifting beneath the prince's skin. Though it appeared to take all his might, Vhogare battled the fire in his blood and held his human form. Half-naked, he trembled like a rockslide but managed to stand up straight. "How do we begin?"

Confusion and concern warred on Jesse's face, but to his credit, he maintained his composure. "My prince, you have no training in these arts. How are you to assist us?"

"You are a learned man," Elias answered, cutting Vhogare off before he could say something he'd regret, "and Einar has taught you well."

Understanding dawned in the man's eyes at the mention of the royal spymaster.

Vhogare held up his hand, sensing the direction of Elias's thoughts. A small bundle of flame lit and burned in his palm. "I spent hours mastering this fire."

"There is nothing natural—"

"One of the Ark's horsemen has given me this gift," Vhogare interrupted. "I can use it to save Joanna and their daughter." The fire in his palm banked and guttered, going out. "She wants me here, so I will stay."

"Cauterization?"

"Soleil explained how it might work." Vhogare held Jesse's gaze. "Unless you have a better idea."

Elias's heart seized. *If only Soleil were here.*

Cutting Elias a wary glance, Jesse washed and dried his hands before passing the cloth to Vhogare. "See that you are as clean as possible, and follow my instructions without fail."

Vhogare nodded. After using the cloth to remove the rubble from his arms and face, he rifled through Elias's things until he found fresh clothes. Dressing himself, he ensured he was decent, tied back his hair, and washed his hands in the nearest basin of fresh water.

Elias said a prayer, too, and leaned against the head of the bed beside Joanna, both his hands bracing hers for support. She went rigid at the sight of Vhogare's gift but did not object.

Once clean, Anchora's new heir apparent went straight to the water pitcher and drank, gasping as he drained it dry. Steadier on his feet, Vhogare straightened, held up his right hand, and concentrated a tiny flame through the tips of his fingers, so much smaller than the river of fire that engulfed the entire council room.

Elias locked eyes with his friend. "Your hands cannot shake."

Vhogare met him with a steel stare. "They won't."

Jesse said a final blessing and began to work. In all their histories, such a delivery had only ever succeeded in saving the child, not the mother. Elias emptied every prayer in his heart, begging that day they would save both.

"If I . . . leave," Joanna panted, exhaustion and stress already sliding her beyond reality, "keep her alive."

Elias forced himself to nod. "I'll be right here when you come back."

Joanna bit down on the leather strap the cleric offered her and signaled she was ready.

She screamed through her teeth when Jesse made the first incision, and it took all his weight to keep her still. Panic, bottomless and empty, reared in Elias's gut at the blood that pooled on the sheets.

One moment, her hands were strong around his, every muscle straining with pain.

The next, the pain overcame her. Joanna's eyes went wide and vacant, her breath coming in short gasps as if she'd gone somewhere and seen something other than the stone ceiling. Another one of her visions, no doubt, though they had always been short glimpses. None had ever lasted so long.

"Joanna?" he called, but she couldn't hear him. "Joanna!"

He couldn't shake her. Could do nothing as her breath evened out, like she could feel nothing, hear nothing.

Jesse looked up from his work.

"Continue," Elias ordered. Whatever was happening, Joanna was not gone yet.

Vhogare did not move; the crown prince stood fixed to the floor with fear.

"She's still breathing," Elias assured them. He could not explain it, but perhaps it was some gift, some mercy, that her mind had gone elsewhere. Wherever she was, whatever she saw, it was far better than there.

Lightning split the sky, thunder shaking the windows close after. The cleric reached in and removed the child with care, handing the babe to Gabriella. "A girl," the spy said, smiling through tears.

Elias's heart soared even as his gut sank. Vhogare's eyes snapped to him from the foot of the bed, understanding barrelling through them. *Erembour spoke true.*

Was it all true? Did it even matter? His daughter was here, and she was everything.

Elias heard no cries, but he could not leave Joanna's side.

"We must move quickly," Jesse ordered, waving Vhogare over. "Start here, cauterizing this tissue together."

Vhogare went to work. He shook with strain and focus, every spare muscle shuddering. But his right hand remained steady, and that thin flame of fire at his fingertips never faltered. As Vhogare repaired the last layer of flesh, closing the final incision into a gnarled, burned scar sprawling across her belly, Joanna resurfaced, screaming, from wherever she had wandered.

Her broken wail tore her throat raw as she came back to consciousness only to withstand the final cauterization, and Elias could've sworn there was grief in the sound. He pressed his forehead to hers as she bit down on the leather, heaving for breath through her teeth, her skin cold and clammy as she endured the excruciating agony. Vhogare finished the work as efficiently as possible, stepping back when the cauterization was complete, and Joanna sagged against her pillows, gasping for breath.

Her gaze roved across the ceiling until it anchored on Elias. She swallowed, staring at him as if willing her sight to sharpen and clear. Joanna's brow furrowed as she fought to come back to him, to focus. "Promise me," she rasped. "Promise me that . . . if I don't survive . . . you will not be alone."

"No. If you go, tell Him to take me with you." A man's greatest dishonor was to remain when all he loved was gone.

Joanna shook her head, heaving for breath through clamped teeth. "Swear it to me," she growled, steel in her eyes. His wife reached up the smallest fraction, her fingertips shaking, to brush them across his cheek. "On all your love for me . . . for our daughter." Her voice was barely a whisper, barely a breath as the storm lit her face. "That you won't leave them with him. There is more left for you."

Perhaps she was dying right there in his arms as his father had. Elias could not bring himself to distress her, to deny her what might be her very last wish. "I swear."

The moment the words left his mouth, her eyes closed. Some strange, transcendent peace overtook her features as she lost consciousness and went limp from exhaustion in his arms. Elias rested his brow against hers, savoring her every breath that ghosted over his lips. Still fighting, still holding on. *My lionhearted woman.*

Across the room, the tiniest cry sounded. No louder than the smallest songbird.

Tears poured down Elias's face at that little voice, his chest cracking open with joy.

"Is she alive?" Vhogare breathed, as if he didn't dare utter the words.

"Aye. She made it," Elias whispered, pressing his fingers to Joanna's wrist to keep track of her heart. "She made it." It would take far more than this to keep her down.

At the foot of the bed, Vhogare stepped toward Gabriella, his arms out. "May I?" he rasped.

Elias's stomach sank. The spy had stayed behind when the midwives deserted. She glanced between him and the crown prince, weighing her odds. Elias didn't dare shake his head, and Gabriella had no choice but to hand his screaming daughter to Vhogare.

Vhogare nearly fell to his knees. "She has her father's eyes," he whispered, a shuddering laugh breaking out of his chest. "And her mother's spirit."

Elias kept his voice even as he held out an arm. "Bring her here."

Vhogare glanced up at him, surprised.

"You're not yet . . . in control." A single slip of resolve and Vhogare would be the dragon again. Joanna appeared unconscious, and they could not afford another disaster like the council room. His daughter had just come into the world, and Elias would not live to see her go out of it.

But after all his training and years as an apprentice under Einar's good name, Elias knew his mistake. Recognized the catastrophe that one slip of his tongue had caused. His head spun, nausea churning his gut, but it was no excuse. Spymaster's son or not, he had failed to maintain his facade.

Something shuttered in Vhogare's eyes as he handed Elias's daughter to him. "Of course. I will"—Vhogare searched for an urgent excuse to leave—"see to sending some food your way." He smiled, but it was a shattered, broken thing. "And water. Ark knows you need it."

When Vhogare left, the cleric stopped gathering his things to tend to the wound on Elias's scalp. "Watch yourself," Jesse whispered when he had finished, shooting a glance at the door Vhogare had exited through.

Elias met his gaze and kept his voice low. "I'm not going anywhere."

"Nor I." His father's friend bundled up his instruments and slipped out of the room.

Thank you. Elias lifted every inch of his aching heart to the Ark as if he could volley his soul past the stars. He cradled his daughter safely in his arms. Joanna was still breathing beside him. Relief flooded through Elias like a river. *Thank you for my daughter's life. For Joanna staying with me.*

"What will you name her?" Gabriella asked, shaken yet filled with a fierce, determined joy.

"I have an idea," Elias answered. He wept as he held his daughter. "If Joanna approves."

THE SILVER ASH

VHOGARE

In control. No, no, he was not.

Vhogare stumbled out of Elias and Joanna's suite. Soleil did not greet him, did not hold him, or support him as he leaned against the wall. Light had come into the world, but his midnight sun had gone dark.

In the hall, Aadriek's glare was cold stone, as unyielding and immovable as the iron axe at the warrior's back. Milan's sworn sword should've been grateful Vhogare had not dismissed his service, but in truth, Vhogare wished to thank him.

He had no wish to spill Marian blood and start the war before he was ready.

Vhogare glanced down at Einar's gilded, cushioned chair and choked on his grief. The seat stood empty, its vacancy howling at him. Their beloved spymaster would not hold his granddaughter or sing over her birth and Joanna's victory.

And Soleil? His love had left him, forsaking him in his darkest hour.

A bitter sob broke out of Vhogare's chest.

No, there would be no soft embrace to greet him, no fiery kisses to celebrate his success. The cauterization had been Soleil's idea, and he couldn't even thank her for her lifesaving wisdom. Not a single soul would congratulate her on the historical feat he'd just achieved in her name.

Vhogare's gut roiled. Everything was broken.

He'd almost killed Elias on the stairs from sheer strength. His heartbrother did not trust him, though Vhogare had given his humanity to save their family. He was no fool; he understood the monster that he was, but after the nightmare he'd endured, Vhogare wanted to feel life in his arms. Something to prove to him—remind him—that he'd done the right thing. That he'd not given all for naught, and this would be worth it, in the end.

He thought Elias would understand. But his heartbrother did not even want him holding the daughter he'd bought with his own blood. And there was no undoing it, no removing the gift that was now branded into his soul.

My brother, have I already fallen? Have I already failed?

After his heinous mistake, he would never hold his own child. Never stand at Soleil's bedside during birth. Vhogare would raise no son, shield no daughter.

Perhaps he had given that up for his gift.

Perhaps he had given everything up.

Dark spots swam in his vision, like a sea of sand crowding in until Vhogare could not see. Could not breathe. Gasping, he stumbled and caught himself on the cold granite floor, splinters of pain shooting up his wrists from the impact of his fall. Aadriek, stiff as steel, moved to help him out of pure duty, but Vhogare shoved him away.

"Do not touch me," he seethed, struggling to right himself. No one would ever touch him again.

He did not blame them.

They did not need to help him; he deserved no love after what he'd done.

Einar had been his father's staunchest supporter, the old soldier the pride of their castle. Their country. And Vhogare had ripped him from them, from Elias, orphaning his closest friend. He could not stomach to think of what he must've looked like, bathing the council room in flames. Some hideous, twisted beast with broken fire where his heart ought to be. So horrible and frightening, Einar had died where he stood just from the sight.

So unforgivable. So untrustworthy.

Vhogare knew it was true.

He was fire made flesh, and yet it was not the beautiful, dancing weapon he'd desired. No sword of precision and skill. He'd not been given the warmth and light of a campfire on a cold winter night, but the blazing roar of a house fire at the height of summer. And he would forever suffer the screams.

The dark spots in his vision cleared, the sand parting until he could see the stone, and Vhogare staggered to his feet. Off balance, he pushed past Aadriek and all but fell down the first flight of stairs.

At the middle landing, he turned and lurched through the corridor connecting the two sweeping wings of the castle, hauling open the heavy door to his royal apartments in the west wing to find his bedchamber dark and empty. The curtains leading to the balcony swayed and snapped in the storm winds, the gusts buffeting the fire flaring in the hearth.

Dragging down deep breaths, Vhogare crashed to his knees and opened Soleil's chest of robes with shaking hands. The ornate lid creaked open, revealing her lustrous midnight-blue and silver velvet regalia. Bracelets and jewels were draped across the gown and stole of her impending office, and he discovered a tiny dragon stitched into the inside of the robe's right arm. *You would've been the most beautiful historian.*

The air in his lungs evaporated, and he lifted the luxurious robe out of the chest and held it to his nose. But she'd been months away from her appointment and had never worn it. The rich fabric did not smell like her.

Panting, Vhogare stormed to his bed and stripped off the heavy sheets until he uncovered the soft linens below. He pressed them to his face, inhaling as if he could sear the last of Soleil's perfume into his chest.

Lavender and lilac, as beautiful and calming as her arms around him and her smile in the morning. Not five days ago, she'd sneaked away from the royal gathering, and he'd held her against him, laughed with her, as they bound their souls together.

Rocking back on his knees, Vhogare loosed the fear he'd been holding back for hours. Years. His howling scream broke free, leaving his throat raw and aching. His chest caved in as he let the pain out. He had paid a heavy price and gained a matchless weapon, but lost his love. Soleil would never hold him again, never run her hands through his hair.

"Our baby," he wept, cradling the sheets to his chest. He'd lost every year, every memory, every heartbeat before their life had even begun. In one breath, he'd sent up in smoke any chance of being a better father than his own.

The guilt was unbearable. He crumpled, imploding beneath its weight. Everything he should've done, every word he should have said, every choice he should have made differently welled up in his chest. It was too heavy. There was no carrying this—no living with it.

A sob broke out of Vhogare's chest, spit flying through his teeth. What would the world be without his family? Without Soleil's laughter, her touch? Without the defiance in her sapphire gaze, the fierce, vicious flame of her heart? All his love in the world, and Soleil had betrayed him.

Every muscle in his body shuddered, each sinew drawn tight as wire.

If this was what it meant to lose a family, what would it be to lose a kingdom?

Vhogare's gift was a drop in the ocean of Erembour's power; any destruction he had caused was not even an ounce of what was to come. Soleil had not survived him. But not a living soul would survive Erembour when the celestial returned.

Vhogare glanced down at his shaking hands in his lap. All he wanted was to help them. To do something.

He'd made a bloody mess of it, but against the end of everything they knew, there was no such thing as too much. Too far.

"Soleil. . . ." Vhogare's hoarse voice splintered. Soleil had been his north star. His midnight sun, burning in all his darkest hours. And she had forsaken him. Abandoned him. Chosen justice over his mighty cause. *Why?*

Fishing in his pocket, he dug out her beautiful silver dragon.

Vhogare slid off the bed onto his knees on the cold stone floor, hyperventilating into the sheets against his face. He held the fabric to his chest as he had held her ashes in Erembour's vision, as if he could push Soleil's spirit inside of him and make them one, even in death.

But there was no hope; an invisible veil separated the waking world from the resting one, and Soleil had slipped behind the curtain without him.

A roar of rage tore out of Vhogare, and he whirled, flinging the silver cups off his nightstand, hurling the wooden table into the wall with a strength he never should have had, never should have known.

When he'd broken every chair and armoire in the room, he stumbled through the open stone archway and collapsed on the balcony in the rain, staring out at the kingdom at his feet. The world Soleil had loved sprawled out before him, filled with all the history she'd spent her life cherishing and discovering.

"I can't have lost you," he whispered. He'd aimed for the Council, not her. Stone and rafters had killed Soleil, falling from the roof the way the sky would fall down on them all when Erembour returned. Salty tears ran down his nose, lost in the deluge pelting him as he wept there on his knees.

A sharp pain stabbed Vhogare's chest, his gift twisting his heart. He wasn't the only one bereft. The whole kingdom had lost Soleil, the whole world. Her father and mother would now bury their last child, their branch of House Corveau coming to a shuddering end. Raul and Myrline did not reside at the castle, but they would arrive soon once news spread. Soleil's parents already hated him. Accident or not, how could he tell them what he'd done?

He couldn't face them, couldn't admit to this.

Glancing behind him at the ruin of his apartments, he spotted Azrail propped against the wall by Soleil's chest of robes. For half a heartbeat, he considered following her and their child into the afterlife. But he was not ready to face the Ark after what he'd done. Someone with the gift had to live to stop Erembour. Elias and Joanna still needed him. Their kingdom needed him. And he'd need a lifetime to cover over all his sins.

He swore at the pools of rain darkening his borrowed trousers.

Water. He'd promised Joanna water. And food.

Shoving air into his lungs, Vhogare slicked his soaked hair back from his face and gathered himself. Forcing deeper, more measured breaths, he crossed the room and rummaged through the wreckage for another pair of dry clothes. The garments he'd stolen from Elias didn't fit him, and the rain had soaked the fabric through. Shivering and cold to the bone, he wanted to be in his own clothes. Clothes Soleil had touched him in.

Seizing a black shirt and trousers, Vhogare changed and strode for the door. He hissed as he crushed something underfoot. Bending, he found the silver dragon Soleil had gifted him for his nameday broken beyond repair. A wing had snapped free from the torso, a long abrasion running down its throat, and its ruby chest caved in.

Vhogare tried to grab the fractured wing, hoping to mend it somehow, but in his panic bent the pewter in his grip. "Why?" He scowled at the misshapen creature in his palm, all that was left of the beautiful gift Soleil had given him. "Why choose honor over life?"

In a fit of anger, he hurled the thing into the fireplace, sending up a cloud of silver ash. They danced down to litter the stone floor like bone dust, like the Council members as he'd torched them in their seats.

No. Vhogare shook his head, remembering himself. *No, Soleil did the right thing.* He would've wanted her to do the same if it had been him lying cold and dead on that bed instead of Milan. She'd upheld justice and fairness, as a queen should. He'd loved her for how she could split choices in a heartbeat.

Despite all his shortcomings and reckless choices, she believed there was good in him that could be saved. Soleil had turned her back on him *because* she loved him. She was willing to do anything to stop him from going down this road.

And he'd killed her for it.

"No, no, it was an accident." She and Einar's deaths had been accidents.

Vhogare began to shake.

Trembling, he snatched the broken dragon from the coals before it could melt. Cinders danced around his hand, and he hissed as the hot metal burned him, but he couldn't bring himself to let the gift go. Channeling his fire, he welded the twisted wing back onto the tiny dragon's bent torso. When it had cooled, he laid the silver statue on the pile of sheets with unsteady hands. His throat closed as the ash clung to his fists, grinding between his fingers.

"I'm so sorry," he whispered. "I did all this to save you."

But he'd killed her, instead. An apology did not put breath back into her lungs.

His chin quivered as he studied the ruined silver dragon, grief winding through the cracks in his resolve. Soleil had always given such lovely gifts. He would've poured all the blood from his body for one more second, one more heartbeat, of time in her arms. Her very presence had been precious; the picture of poised kindness at court and reckless abandon in his arms. And even she had chosen duty over love.

Straightening his shirt, Vhogare tucked the pewter dragon into his pocket and left his quarters, striding through the connecting corridor and down the stairs toward the kitchens.

There was no fresh air in the castle. No coolness to calm him, only thick, humid dampness that choked his lungs and plastered his clothes to his icy skin. Sand from the beach chafed his back and knees as he moved, a thousand reminders of his shame.

He descended the last step of the staircase, and his spent legs gave way, buckling so hard he fell again. On his knees on the cold stone of the grand hallway, he glanced to his right at the carnage he'd left in the council room. The destruction was complete, all done by his hands. His *gift*.

Columns had crumbled and fallen, collapsing across the burnt bodies of guards and attendants. Some of his father's most trusted minds had no form but ash. He retched at the smell of his fire—a singed metallic scent, like a sword held too long over a flame—and his vomit splattered his hands.

Soleil's body lay across the council room, crushed in the archway leading to the west wing and Milan's chambers. Soldiers had removed the rafters and roof tiles, leaving her small, battered form to the elements. His love's eyelids had drifted slightly opened, the muscles relaxing before she stiffened, and her soulless gaze pinned him across the stones. As if she saw what he'd become and now hated him for it.

Rain sluiced down the slope of the collapsed roof, pouring into pools on the floor where his dragon's feet had broken the stones. Servants picked their way, teeth chattering, through the devastation. They bent their backs and scraped their hands bloody toiling to remove smashed tiles and scraps of burnt banners and carpet. The shattered columns would require daylight and teams of draft horses to haul away. And the real work had not even begun.

"Out!" Vhogare thundered, staggering to his feet and shoving his way through the line of workers hauling rubble away. A few soldiers heard him over the storm and looked up, pausing their duties.

"OUT!" he bellowed again, and his voice became the dragon's. His rich timbre melded into a throaty roar, and every servant and soldier froze in place. They whipped to stare at Vhogare, pinned in place with terror as if he would eat them alive or bathe them in flame, as well.

Alastair had no such fear. The formidable commander of the guard strode to meet him from the far side of the ruined council room. Lightning flashed as he approached, illuminating the rain gleaming off his blue-and-silver armor. "You should not be down here."

"Leave me," Vhogare growled. Behind Alastair, the workers scattered like a flock of birds. They hastened out of the broken council room, taking cover anywhere they could find it.

Alastair did not move. Bits of stone dust and debris were stuck in the long waves of his tied-back hair, and water droplets collected in the man's thick black beard. Vhogare did not miss the split skin and bloody calluses of Alastair's tattooed hands. The swornguard had been working with the servants to remove the fallen stone.

"I will be in the hall," Alastair growled. "Should there be another *accident.*"

Alastair shouldered past him to wait in the grand hall, but Vhogare paid him no mind. He stumbled across the rain-slick floor to Soleil's corpse and lay down beside her on his back, staring up through the broken ceiling at the sky. The rain beat down on him, soaking him to the marrow, and he blinked the droplets away. Above them, purple and blue lightning struck as violent storm clouds rolled past, blocking out the moon. But even in the darkness, the faint silver light shone through.

Smudging the water from his face, Vhogare turned to Soleil. Her hair was wet; it splayed across the stones, blue-black in the darkness. Only the light of distant torches brightened her face, illuminating the cuts and breaks in her porcelain skin. Torrential rain had washed her blood off the stones, though Vhogare lay in an invisible pool of it all the same.

"My darling," Vhogare whispered, reaching across to brush her hair off of her still, slack face. "It worked. Your idea saved Joanna. Their daughter lives because of you." Guilt tightened his throat. She'd been the first person he wanted to tell when he held the little girl. But Soleil was gone.

You can't be dead. You can't. Had Soleil heard him where she had gone? He dragged in a breath, tears mingling with the rain on his skin. "It rained like this the day you first kissed me. Do you remember?"

Soleil's dead eyes stared at him, her pupils blown.

"We slipped away and raced down the sea stairs to the waterfall. I was such a coward." He heard himself laugh. The sound was half-crazed and cracked at the edges. "I hated those stairs, but I'd have followed you anywhere. You took my hand"—he reached for her palm and pressed a kiss to her cold, damp knuckles—"and led me behind the waterfall, and kissed me like I'd just come back from war. You were the best damn thing to ever happen to me on that beach."

Sobbing on his back in the rain, Vhogare slid his arms around Soleil's cold shoulders and held her to him. "Father named Milan his heir that day, and you still chose me."

She had been a miracle, and he'd broken her.

"You should not have." He pressed another kiss to her slick hair. "You could've had the world, Soleil. You loved me when I was nothing." He dragged in a breath, the bones of his chest heaving. "But you were everything—"

His voice failed him, but he needed her to know why.

"I should've told you sooner. You know every damn word that's been written," he grizzled. "You would've known what to do. But I couldn't put this in your hands and ask you to hold it." Vhogare shook his head, cauterizing the soft feel of her skin against his memory. "I meant to give you more time."

But time had ceased, and his world had gone eerily quiet. Boots scuffed softly across the stone as soldiers and servants lingered in the great hall, waiting for his permission to continue hauling away the utter destruction he had caused. Vhogare could feel their eyes on him, crawling over him like insects in the dark. He could live a thousand years, and they would never forgive him for this.

I will never forgive myself.

He would never have hurt Soleil, would never in his life endanger their unborn child.

Had he not done all of this for them? For her, as much as for Elias? Joanna?

"Erembour was going to take you from me. Both of you. All of you. What was I supposed to do?" Vhogare bent to press his brow against hers. He held the back of her head with tender care, rocking back and forth on the stones in an attempt to calm himself, but he could not breathe.

"How could you leave me with this?" he whimpered, whispering to her corpse. *Like this,* with all he had left to do.

There was nothing worse.

He lay there with her on the castle's broken stone floor, lightning glinting off the rain pouring down, and prayed the storm could wash his sins away.

"You were my wind," Vhogare swore, echoing the words he'd said to her beneath that waterfall all those years ago. "I will hold you, always, and my heart will belong to no other." He'd planned on making that sentiment his marriage vows, but that dream had burned.

Soleil could not answer him. Could not call him her fire.

"But my father was right. You deserved far better. I am sorry I took this from you."

She had been so fierce and relentless in life. A damn force of nature, as formidable and terrifying as a storm across the heart of the sea. But in death, she seemed so small and soft. Delicate, like a winter flower, and lonely. So unbearably lonely. Her fragile, stiff frame made him cry all the harder.

Elias was right; he was not in control.

He was empty.

And that must change.

Shivering, Vhogare pressed a searing kiss to Soleil's forehead. "I'll be back, soon, my darling," he whispered, "I promise."

Every muscle jumped with fatigue and bone-deep cold as he lurched to his feet, swaying from dehydration. Careful not to step on her hair, he picked his way across the rubble through the grand hall to the kitchen.

Inside was blazing hot, the large fireplace and wall of ovens and cauldrons all simmering with heat. The aroma of roasted meat and fresh bread greeted him, competing with the lingering scent of his dragonflame. The rich, herb-laden smell made his mouth water, and he wished he were ten years old again, chasing Elias through the kitchens for bait as they coaxed the fox out of the raven roost.

But he was a man grown—a monster—and those days were sand in the river of time. Cold with grief and soaked to the bone with rainwater, Vhogare sagged at the kitchen's warmth. He almost sank to the hearthstones, but Joanna needed him, so he kept his feet.

The cooks all looked up at him in shock, one man scalding himself while stirring a steaming cauldron of stew. All movement in the kitchen ceased as they took in their prince's ragged, haggard appearance. A stooped woman with red, puffy eyes halted her chopping at the long wooden table, and even the butter boy paused his churning in the far corner. Every soul in the room stared at Vhogare, still as a herd of deer in the presence of a panther.

"Water," he managed, waving a hand toward the stairs, struggling to explain where to send it. "Elias and Joanna. And food."

They flew into action, their urgency no doubt spurred on by his fearsome state, but Vhogare did not stay to see it through. He grabbed the nearest thing he could find—a loaf of warm bread—and sank to the floor outside the kitchen doors, his back pressed against the comfort of the heated stones.

The hearty loaf was ash on his tongue, but he forced it down. He would need his strength. If he were to manage this beast, carve this fire into a weapon he could use, he would need discipline. Precision.

Alastair glowered at him from his post in the grand hall. He stood at the foot of the sweeping staircase, not five yards from Vhogare, and folded his massive arms across his chest. The swornguard did not have to say a word. Vhogare knew disappointment when he saw it. He'd been raised beneath it, and it was going nowhere soon.

"No one is more horrified about this than I," he managed, glaring up at the Marian warrior. "I am sorry."

Alastair had been his comrade for years, a hearty and jovial man.

But anger and disapproval shone in the swornguard's dark gaze as he answered, "You should be." He left without a bow and ordered his soldiers to return to their work.

One by one, the dismissed soldiers and servants worked up their nerve to return to clear the council room. The gift had enhanced Vhogare's hearing, and he caught the smallfolk's muttered speculations as they carried rubble and debris.

The whispers had already begun. Soldiers that Vhogare had known all his life now cowered in his presence, slinking by to avoid his eye as he monitored their progress.

Vhogare ripped off a piece of the bread he'd crushed in his fist and chewed. It hardened beneath his jaw. Across the vast lower hall, moonlight fought through the storm, casting a silvered glow across the chaos he had wrought. Soleil held his stare from where she lay, unblinking, accusing, and frighteningly beautiful, even in death.

Never again. Never again would he lose control.

Never again choose love over duty.

Never again would he fail.

THE SUNRISE

ELIAS

Elias remained by Joanna's side until she woke to a steady rain beating against their window. Her gaze, always bright as a summer forest, was pale and weak, but one glance down at the small bundle in his arms. . . . There had never been a more beautiful smile—the pride of a warrior who'd survived battle, brighter than any Elias had seen before. His entire sun had come to Earth.

Her joy turned into tears, and she struggled to rise, her arms shaking as she attempted to push herself back against the headboard.

Elias put a light hand on her shoulder to ease her back down. "Not yet. You've made history, woman." He busied himself fluffing her pillows with his free hand—a difficult task to do while holding his daughter, only to find Joanna gazing at him with laughter in her eyes. "What? Should I send for more? Are these not firm enough?"

"I'm okay, my love." She patted his side of the mattress in invitation. "You don't have to fuss over me so much."

"I promised you coddling and I intend to deliver." Elias leaned in to kiss her brow. "And you've more than earned your rest." He sat on the mattress. "What should we name her?"

"I've thought about this moment a thousand times," she whispered, reaching out to pull the swaddling cloth aside to peer at their daughter's delicate face, "and every name I'd once considered now feels too small."

When it came time to name their sweet baby girl, his beautiful wife had been unconscious, so he waited and thought of one he hoped she'd adore. "What about Liora?" Elias offered, praying she'd like it. "So she will look at the night and only see the stars, just like her mother."

"Liora," Joanna whispered. She kissed him through her tears. "I love it. Our little light, she shall be."

Elias ran a thumb across his daughter's soft cheek. His first and final child. Whatever the future held, he would never, ever put Joanna through that again.

Brushing Joanna's tears away, he wrestled the seven bear claws from his pocket and held them out to her. "For both of you."

Conflicting emotions washed across her face. "You've come a long way from your squiring days."

"And yet I shall always ask for your favor."

She pressed a kiss to his knuckles, wincing as she reached to roll the claws around in his hand. All the midwives and nursemaids had left for the night to search for their own families. Below, soldiers were no doubt attempting to clear the rubble so they could access the council room.

But for now, Elias and Joanna were alone, and their world was blissfully quiet.

He was afraid to shatter it, but her words from the night still tugged at him. "Did you have another vision during the delivery?"

Joanna tensed beside him, and he was afraid he'd hurt her somehow, but she answered, "You know I don't always understand them. Sometimes they are just . . . a sense." Another tear slipped down her cheek, and her chin quivered even as her lips turned up in a brave, aching smile. "Perhaps I will make peace with it one day."

"Regardless," he said, laying his cheek against the crown of her head. "If you wish to speak of it, I am here. I'm not going anywhere, I promise."

"I know." Joanna sniffled. "Do you remember the Three Stars?" she whispered a moment later as he pressed a kiss to her hair.

Elias shook his head, his throat too tight. He leaned back against the pillows, inhaling the crisp cedar and pine scent of the fresh sheets. "Another Solan folktale?" he asked as he reached to stroke her hair, pulling it away from her face and tracing the outline of her ear.

Joanna tried to give him a cheerful nod, but exhaustion still tugged at her gaze. "About the same three stars that I showed you on the roof last year."

"The Great Fire in the Sky."

She huffed a soft laugh only to suck in a breath as pain lanced through her. "Aye. On the border, they tell the story of a soldier who wandered the desert for six winters—"

"Must've been hell."

Joanna gave him an exaggerated scowl. "Stop interrupting."

Elias held his hands up in teasing offense and kept quiet. His head ached, and his heart hammered against his chest, but the world would have to wait. For now, he would soak up whatever time with his woman he could get.

"On the seventh winter, he reached a mountain," Joanna continued, her strong voice still hoarse. "The rise was bare, the color of bloodstone, and no one could tell how tall it was by looking at it. It took him an entire year to reach the top, but when he set his feet on the summit and turned to the east . . . the sun broke over the horizon. And it rose above those three stars, like the biggest, brightest fire the world had ever seen." Her gaze glittered as if she were picturing it. "Bloodfyre was named after it, for the sun's reflection on the ocean from the mountain's crown."

"Who can see that far?" Solis's capital was across the country from the southern kingdom's mountain range.

Joanna shrugged as the rising sun broke, beaming through her window to bathe them in golden light. "Always questioning."

Elias smirked, and she reached over to trace Liora's tiny cheek. Their daughter cooed and fussed, closing her eyes at her mother's touch.

"The point is, my love, it gives a man hope. After all the time that soldier spent wading through desert sand, an entire city sprouted from that fire. Life grows from ash," Joanna promised. "And we must protect the green."

THE TRUTH

ELIAS

Morning dawned bright through the eastern window. The sun hit the clouds like wildfire, and Elias handed Liora to Gabriella so he could retrieve water for Joanna. Jesse had stitched his scalp wound the night before, and though he was still somewhat unsteady on his feet, he no longer bled. By now, the castle should've heard his wounds from the bear were not as bad as they had seemed. He half-hoped his mauling had been forgotten in the night's events so he could move around without pretense.

Outside, the loch glittered, and even the eastern mountains seemed refreshed after the rain. The storm had broken the heat, and a comfortable cool covered the castle, though it did little to relieve the stormy mood. He retrieved a glass of water from the pitcher and held it against his wife's parched lips so she wouldn't bear the weight.

After slaking her thirst, Joanna glanced around the room. "Where is Vhogare?"

"He slept in the hall." There was much to discuss, but the new crown prince collapsed once the cleric determined Joanna would live. Between the toll of managing his new gift and the concentration of the delivery, Aadriek reported that Vhogare had been so distraught and exhausted that it was all Vhogare could do to leave the room.

"Get him," she rasped, before whispering so only he could hear, "I wish to take the measure of him."

Elias opened the door and nodded to Aadriek, who stood ever-vigilant outside. The swornguard roused Vhogare from where he dozed against the stone wall of the upper hall, and the prince straightened his fresh clothes as best he could before entering their suite. Joanna could not rise, but she reached out to clasp his hand.

"Thank you," she told him with every ounce of steel in her soul. "For saving my daughter. And me."

Vhogare let out a teary laugh. "The procedure was Soleil's idea. She read about it in a book."

Joanna's gaze misted. "Then I'll have to thank her; she saved both our lives."

"I told her." Vhogare bit his lip and clapped Elias on the shoulder. "And I'd do anything for my brother. He'd be miserable in a world without his sun."

Elias glanced across at Vhogare, who let on not a breath of what he'd done. His stomach dropped at the ease with which the prince spoke. As if he had not taken down the entire Council and murdered his brother and lover in a fit of cold rage just the night before.

But Soleil, Milan, the Council—all would have to wait as long as it could. Elias was not so naive as to think he could spare Joanna the knowledge, but she deserved as much rest as they could afford after surviving such a near-death experience.

Even so, his wife gave Vhogare's hand a firm squeeze. "You must tell me the full story when we're both well."

"That . . . will be a long while," he answered, and Elias did not miss the crack in his voice.

Neither did Joanna. "And Einar?" she asked Elias, trying to peek through the open door. Joanna frowned when she couldn't find her goodfather, knowing full well he'd have been there.

Elias swore. He'd not yet told her. Could not accept it, himself.

"Where is he?" she demanded. "I want him to see his granddaughter."

VHOGARE

Elias's face collapsed. "He won't be joining us," Vhogare interrupted, putting a steadying hand on his shoulder.

He stared at the ground for a moment, searching for words that would not come. Einar may as well have been her father. How could he tell her the man was gone? That the world had broken apart and turned on its head in a matter of hours?

"Our . . . beloved spymaster died last night," Vhogare managed after several heartbeats. "Along with the king."

Joanna's breath caught, her eyes darting between Vhogare and her husband, and Elias tensed under his grip.

She opened her mouth to ask a question, but Vhogare cut her off. "I am so sorry you have to learn of it now, like this."

Tears welled in Joanna's eyes, and Vhogare dropped to a knee at her bedside, clasping her hand even as his eyes stung and his throat drew tight. "But I promise you, we will have a funeral, with all the honor befitting his service." He risked a small smile at Liora sleeping in Joanna's arms. "And I know he is looking down now with joy for this beautiful gift."

Her gaze shifted between Vhogare and Elias, who gripped his brow to hide his tears. Vhogare's heart twisted at the love in her eyes for her husband, the concern, but dread crawled into Joanna's summer gaze. "What happened?"

"There was an incident in the council room," Vhogare hedged, rocking back onto his heel.

Joanna's bottom lip began to tremble, but she bit it to keep it still. Sorrow choked her pain-ravaged voice. "I wanted him to be here."

"As did I." Guilt wrapped its scaled fingers around the back of Vhogare's neck. "I wish he had not—" Vhogare caught himself, but too late. He shifted his weight, and Joanna's brow furrowed.

"Regardless," he corrected. "I will see him buried with all the love he is owed, in the Crypt of Kings at my father's right hand."

"What of Milan?" she frowned, confused. "Is that not his place when his time comes?"

He stood. *To hell with this charade.* "Milan has not earned it."

A measure of caution crept into Joanna's voice. "Then I thank you, Your Majesty, for doing my goodfather that kindness."

Her formality stung. He longed to explain himself, to grieve, but it was too much to tell her so soon.

"And send Soleil up here," Joanna instructed. "I wish to give her my personal thanks for her help. She deserves the world for standing by me all those hours."

Agony wrenched free from Vhogare's chest. His nose closed up, burning, suffocating him as he fought for words. Despite himself, a tear tracked down his cheek, the salt thick on his lips. "The world, indeed. If I can steal your husband for a moment?"

Joanna's gaze shuttered, but she waved her permission, exhaustion and grief overtaking her. "Don't keep him long."

Bowing out of the room, Vhogare led Elias down the stairs toward the ruined council room. "I'm sorry," Vhogare began, his wretched voice breaking again. He paused on the landing above the grand stairs. "For all of it. For Einar. For holding Liora last night. I overstepped."

"You have overstepped a great deal." Elias stopped walking. Unflinching steel edged his gaze as he searched Vhogare's face. "The last few days have been a nightmare."

"That they have." Vhogare exhaled, dragging a hand over his brow. "But you are her father. It was not my place." He'd done so much wrong, but he was a monster to fight a monster, not to hurt his friends. "Einar and Soleil . . . deserved better. I do not wish to hurt you the same way."

"You saved Joanna." Elias extended his hand. "And Liora. For that, you will always have my thanks."

Vhogare clasped Elias's palm, scar to scar.

His stomach flipped as Elias yanked him closer.

"But we are not done, you and I," Elias snarled, holding firm with a grip that almost hurt. "And Soleil must be looked after. She was my friend." He held Vhogare's eye, and Vhogare noted the scar on Elias's brow that Soleil had helped stitch. "I do not care if it is difficult for you," his friend snarled. "You owe her peace, at the very least, after what you did."

Vhogare nodded, not trusting himself to speak.

"I will see to my father myself." Elias released him. "And you have much to explain."

Aye, he did. All Vhogare could do was dip his head to show his understanding. There were no words to make it right—five beloved dead in almost as many hours.

Gratitude was not forgiveness, and Vhogare did not delude himself. He would spend a lifetime atoning for his mistakes. But he had to buy that lifetime out of Erembour's fist first, and Vhogare did not have the strength for strategy at that hour. Determination alone kept him on his feet as they descended the grand staircase, and he caught sight of Soleil again. His love lay pale and lonely beneath the fallen stones as if the workers were afraid to move her. Her dried hair splayed around her head in a dark halo and the summer sun beat down on her bloodless face.

"It is not right for them to stay like this," Elias grumbled, leaving him at the threshold to join the soldiers recovering bodies from the ashen council room. Though Vhogare had reduced the council members to ash, the royal guards and servants in attendance—and Soleil—had died from the collapse rather than the flames, and their broken corpses necessitated care.

"You will not help?" Elias demanded, yanking up his sleeves before entering the destroyed chamber.

Vhogare tried, but his feet would not carry him. Across the room, Milan's ghost scowled at him, pinning him in place. Vhogare had seen spirits walk the castle halls before; there was no denying it—Milan looked as he had in life, down to the clothes he wore when Vhogare had murdered him. His brother's soul shimmered, translucent, and though Milan kicked at the rubble as if to say, *"See what you have done?"* not a stone moved.

The dead prince stood, glassy and weightless, and propped his shapeless shoulder against the crumbled archway.

A bitter snort cracked out of Vhogare's chest. He could see his brother's lingering spirit but not Soleil's. Instead of his love's beautiful visage, he was cursed with Milan's judgmental scowl. Vhogare hoped Soleil's absence meant she and their child were safe and at peace in the Ark's arms.

Perhaps Milan had stayed behind to torment him. The spectral prince watched him, smiling the same knowing leer he often wore. His dead brother's phantom did not move as royal servants carried Milan's lifeless body down the stairs and out the door. Without the Council alive to advocate for Milan, he had been forgotten in the night's destruction, and Vhogare had made no time to give him the usual honors.

Perhaps it was also for that reason that Milan remained, a soul amongst mortals, as men walked through him.

Ahead of Vhogare, Elias knelt in the archway leading to the council room. He attempted to take his father in his arms and carry him to the chapel, but the royal spymaster had been barrel-chested in life, strong as a castle wall, and he was too heavy. Far, far too heavy for the son he left behind.

Elias cried, collapsing from his father's weight before he broke, sobbing over Einar's too-still chest. "I cannot do this," his friend whispered to his father's corpse. A sharp, ragged breath hissed through Elias's teeth, and Vhogare heard it as clearly as a scream. "You always knew what to do."

Vhogare should've looked away, should've given Elias privacy in his grief, but all he could do was stare at his friend, at the father he'd ripped from Elias when his heartbrother needed his guidance most.

Einar had practically adopted Joanna. Aside from Soleil, the three of them were the only family Vhogare had truly known. If it had been he who died, they were the ones who would mourn. And he'd shattered them.

Liora would know no grandsire. Einar would never heave a thunderous laugh again, never share his wisdom, or save Vhogare from the king with a well-crafted lie. He was gone.

Snuffed out as if he'd never existed, and there was a gaping hole in the kingdom where he'd once stood.

Elias's face crumpled, twisting with grief as he fought to draw breath in his sorrow. Shame and guilt wrapped sinking claws around Vhogare's chest at the sight, squeezing until he was certain his ribs would cave in. He'd caused such misery, such desolation.

This was not what I wanted.

A silent scream built in the back of Vhogare's throat. He never wished to see Elias cry like that again. Vhogare made an oath to himself, digging his nails into the healed scar of his right palm.

Never again would he leave Elias so broken he could not rise from his knees.

And if they didn't stop Erembour, the whole world would weep. The celestial would wade in a sea of dead fathers, bleeding mothers, and lost children.

Drawing himself up, Vhogare smudged the tears from his eyes and straightened, setting his jaw. The only thing standing between Elias and death was his gift. His heartbrother would not die like Einar, heartbroken in a burning castle with no one to save him.

Vhogare would be a wall. Erembour would not get past him.

He remained there, standing guard over Elias's grief, until Alastair broke through the ranks of soldiers, removing rubble to stand at Elias's side. With a kind word, Alastair laid a hand on Elias's shoulder and helped him carry his father to the chapel.

When they had left, Vhogare glanced up to find Milan still watching him. The dead prince's spirit pinned Vhogare with a rending gaze that cleaved him down to his bones.

Defiance rose in Vhogare's chest at that look—the dare.

One more dead queen, Milan had warned him.

And now, even in death, his brother judged him. Held Vhogare down as if he were unworthy. But Soleil deserved someone who loved her to carry her to the chapel. Deserved to be laid to rest by hands that had held her in life. Vhogare had promised that he'd return for her and would not stand aside in fear and leave her alone. He had *sworn.*

And his midnight sun deserved the man he would become, not the man he had been.

Steeling himself, Vhogare rolled his sleeves and stalked across the carnage he'd wrought, stepping over the fallen stones.

Tears dripped down his chin as he knelt beside Soleil's pale form and took her in his arms. One last time, for all they had lost. All he had taken from her.

Almost a day had passed since the throne room's collapse, and her frame had gone soft again. "I have you, my darling."

Her head rolled to rest against his shoulder, her dark hair cascading down her lax shoulders as Vhogare lifted her. She didn't smell like her anymore; the rain had washed the lilac and lavender away. He'd never breathe her in again, never bury his face in her neck, or run his hands through her hair. Vhogare's chest wrenched as he stood and strode from the room.

Soldiers parted as Vhogare passed on his way to the door. His shoulders shook with restrained sobs as he marched, but Vhogare held Soleil against him. Kept her close to his heart as he crossed the castle yard.

As he turned onto the cobbled path to the chapel, Raul and Myrline thundered through the gates on their horses. All the blood drained from her father's strong, anguished face at the sight of his daughter, dead in Vhogare's arms. Raul dismounted and fell to his knees in the mud. A cry of horror and desolation ripped from his throat, full of a weighty torment that should never come from a man. Vhogare would never forget the sound of her mother's inconsolable wail. Soleil was their only surviving child and he'd taken her from them.

Coward.

Vhogare cursed himself. He didn't even have the strength to meet Raul's eyes. Couldn't even make himself stop walking. What could he ever say? What could he ever do to make this right?

There was nothing. A mere apology was not enough. No words, no blood, or death would buy back the light he'd snuffed out of the world. He would die, himself, if it brought Soleil back. But it would not, and Soleil's beloved world would burn if he gave her father the vengeance Raul sought.

As if he'd heard Vhogare's thought, Raul rose to his feet and made to charge him, murderous wrath bulging the veins in his neck as he reached to rip his daughter from Vhogare's arms. But several of House Maekyr's guards closed ranks and blocked him, more afraid of the dragon in their midst than House Corveau's rage. The unrestrained condemnation and betrayal, guilt, and loss in Raul's piercing, ice-gray gaze sawed Vhogare's soul in two.

"I will see you dead for this," Soleil's father snarled, teeth bared with violent, righteous hatred.

Vhogare had no energy to fight him. "There is nothing left to kill."

Whatever Raul saw in Vhogare's stare sent the man reeling back a step. Something empty and lost fell across Raul's features as his knees gave way, and he sank into the mud next to his keening wife. He wrapped his arms around Myrline as the woman dug her hands into the mud, howling and pleading as if she could call up all the cold of hell itself and send it to chase Vhogare down.

Vhogare's chest heaved, his throat aching. He tore his gaze away from Raul's and held Soleil tighter against his chest, pressing his cheek to her hair. She would never see how much they truly loved her. Even after Byn's death and all those years of her parent's aching, stinging silence, she had been their everything. And she would never know.

The realization destroyed him, but he did not stop walking. Did not turn and hand Soleil to her father. If he did, he was certain he would never get her back, and he meant to spend what time he could with his love before she was eternally gone. Vhogare did not look back as he strode to the black marble chapel where Harun and the royal clerics made their burial preparations.

Elias met him in the doorway. His heartbrother's eyes went wide at the sight of Raul and Myrline, flanked by their retinue as they mourned in the castle yard. Elias's lips parted, his arms going slack in shared misery before he remembered himself. A sharp glint of blame sparked in his eyes as he turned to face Vhogare. But Elias only nodded and set his jaw in grim understanding.

May he never carry this weight.

There was not enough strength in the world.

What courage existed to carry one's love to the grave?

Vhogare left Raul and Myrline's heartbroken cries behind him and stepped into the chapel. The worship hall's sweet, burning incense mingled with the scent of old, dried blood lingering on Soleil's clothes as Vhogare laid her on the table before the holy servants. "Bury her in her regalia and jewels," he commanded. "I will bring them shortly."

Leaving, he retrieved the lustrous blue and silver velvet robes and carried them down to the chapel. "As acting ruler of Anchora, I name her royal historian," he told Harun. He hated that the title was now only honorary when she had earned it. "Put her name in the royal archives and afford her every respect due to her title."

The head cleric nodded until Vhogare continued. "As for Einar, entomb him at my father's right in the Crypt of Kings. He served King Ulrich well in life and will stand by him in death."

"Your Highness, that place is for your brother."

"Your *Majesty*," Vhogare corrected sharply. "My father and brother are dead." He cast out an arm at the covered bodies closest to the altar. "Their corpses are right in front of you. *I* live, and I am your king. You will address me as such if you wish to retain your station."

Embers flashed in the holy man's gaze. *"Your Majesty,* our holy order does not answer to you. And the Crypt is for royal blood. It has always been so, ever since Pax Anchora was built on the bones of what came before—"

"No, you do not answer to me," Vhogare interrupted, "but all men answer to death." He took a step forward, letting some of the silver fire flicker down his scarred right arm. "And I know of no one more worthy of a crown than the man who built our kingdom at my father's side, and no one less worthy than my dear, *royal* brother. Bury Einar on the late king's right, or I will bury you and your order in the sea."

For the ocean-faring warriors of Maria, a burial in the Great Water was the highest honor. But for Anchora, and a holy man who served the Fire, it was worse than no burial at all.

Harun glanced at his fellow clerics frozen in fear of Vhogare's threat and set his jaw. Determination glinted in his dark eyes as he stepped closer to the ever-burning flame of the altar and folded his hands over his robes of office. "Very well," Harun said, scowling at Vhogare. "And what of your brother?"

Vhogare glanced past the holy man at Milan's ghost standing by his covered corpse. The dead prince looked on, his brows raised in exaggerated, mocking expectation as he waited for Vhogare's answer. "He can have my place at our father's left. He deserved that much, and I don't want to spend eternity with him leering at me."

If Harun was confused by Vhogare's statement, he did not show it. The head cleric nodded in agreement but did not bow before he returned to his work.

Stuffing down the cold heat rising in his chest, Vhogare bent to press a last kiss to Soleil's brow, inhaling deep to sear her every last memory into his soul.

"You chose right," he whispered to her. "You should not be here for this. But know that my happiness died with you."

Every ounce of his heart wished he could do more for Soleil, but he would need to speak to her parents to arrange her funeral, as without marriage, he had no right to her grave.

THE LINE

ELIAS

The summer storm had long since subsided, and a soft rain peppered the castle yard. Elias sat on a wrought iron bench outside the gilded chapel, staring at the sky. At his back, the stronghold's hall of worship was busier than it had been in a long time. Through the gold filigreed windows, Elias glimpsed Harun, Jesse, and the other holy souls milling about, struggling to prepare the number of dead. Many kind souls from the castle had volunteered to help the chapel's clerics with the sheer volume of corpses Vhogare had produced, and the main chamber seemed to expand to accommodate the solemn activity.

But even swarming with death, the chapel seemed to swell with light as if the Ark Himself had come to comfort those who had passed. None of the chapel's gold-inlaid spires had crumbled in the prince's wrath. Each of the seven spirals still stood, reaching skyward with all their might. The thousand candles still burned through the propped doorway, and the fire in the blazing hearth danced warmly, a kind welcome for all the souls passing into the Ark's eternal arms. Elias prayed his father was well on his way into the bright afterlife.

He, however, was stuck in the dirt.

Sodden, trampled mud and the sounds of soldiers hard at work surrounded Elias as he leaned against the chapel's outer wall, wishing the gold cracking through the black marble's veins could fill him with strength.

Pax Anchora's fortress rose into the gray clouds, inky-black granite shimmering after the rain washed all the summer dust off the keep's outer walls. Even the old, gnarled fruit trees planted along the walkway seemed to glisten, each one's new blooms laying a carpet of bright color across the cobbled path. Bees buzzed in the canopies, but Elias took no notice of the sunlit beauty.

Yigael lay over his knees, the sacred steel gleaming up at him despite the cloudy day. His father's sword, and all his fathers' before. Einar had only used the storied weapon thrice, but it had never been without purpose, and the gilded beauty never failed him.

Never in all his life had Elias imagined he'd come by the wondrous blade in such a way, and yet it was his to carry now. His guardian, his promise, and his oath.

He ran a thumb across the pearls and rubies inlaid on the grip, the ornate gold work of the crossguard, before sliding it into the blessed scabbard. Exhaling, Elias fished Gabriella's note from the pocket of his trousers, unrolled it, and squinted at the smudged ink.

The king is dead. He tossed the small scrap of paper into the flame of the nearest standing brazier and watched the smoke curl as it burned away. *And the prince ran to the stables.*

If she had gotten him that note any sooner, he might've been able to stop Vhogare from taking the gift. But as it stood, strength had made an enemy out of his friend. Desperation had cracked the crown, and there would be no mending it.

Behind Elias, House Corveau's cleric prepared Soleil for burial. Jesse prepared his father to go into the good earth. Ulrich would be buried in the ornate breastplate Elias had given the king at the hunt— a high honor, but Elias would've traded it for just one more hour with Einar, one more chance to ask his father what to do. But the spymaster had moved on, and all that was left in his place was an empty seat Elias had no choice but to fill.

According to ancient tradition, Anchora's sovereign and his firstborn son were meant to be embalmed and entombed beneath the castle in the Crypt of Kings. There had been an uproar when

Vhogare decreed Einar would take Milan's place on the old king's right side—the firstborn prince to be laid to rest at Ulrich's left—but the head cleric was a wise man. Harun had chosen to protect his fellow holy servants rather than bait the dragon, even if that meant bending to Vhogare's will.

"And what will become of you?" Elias had demanded as Vhogare exited the chapel. "When your time comes?" With Milan in Vhogare's place, he would have no choice but to take a lesser position in burial.

"Burn me." The new heir had left before Soleil was covered with the royal blue cloth of her house. "I died on the beach."

Perhaps he had.

Despite the rigorous proceedings, Elias was glad his father would not fall by the wayside in such heat.

Lifting his eyes to the sky, he allowed himself to mourn, his tears trickling into his beard. His sire had deserved far better; a soldier's death, as he had lived a soldier's life. *But I know He and Mother welcomed you home.*

The sun was high in the cloudy sky when Vhogare wrestled up the will to join him again. Crown prince and heir apparent, the man looked beat to hell. Humidity was heavy in the air, and Vhogare's clothes clung to his frame as he sank onto the bench beside Elias, but nothing could conceal his grief and exhaustion.

"You have to believe this was not what I wanted," Vhogare began, mopping a hand over his face.

There was no mending what had broken, but Joanna's words drove Elias to agree. *Do not leave them alone with him.*

"I know," Elias sighed. The fog over his mind had cleared somewhat, and he'd taken the rest of the morning to gather his strength and shore up his resolve. Vhogare may not have intended this outcome, but intentions did not rectify choices. Bracing himself, Elias summoned every ounce of his father's lessons, every shred of spymaster embedded in his soul, and prepared to play the game. If the man could not live on, his legacy would. "They gave you no choice."

"We have to stop him." Desperate determination blazed in

Vhogare's eyes. "What will happen if we face the Ark, having let this land slip through our fingers?" Elias opened his mouth to correct him, but Vhogare plowed on. "I will have proof that I fought. I meant it when I swore to protect you. To protect Liora." Vhogare's right hand shook as he raised it. "Is this not confirmation that we fight on the right side of this war? Confirmation of what this gift can do?"

Confirmation that they must weather this storm to reach the desired end.

Elias fought the urge to stand and walk away. Any good general knew the rule: the few for the many. It was plain warfare. *But at what cost?* He hoped Vhogare remembered it was all meant to be a trick. A subterfuge of the stars.

Shoving his grief down, Elias steeled himself to maneuver. "And what will we do when our sister kingdoms learn of what you've done?"

Joanna's tale had been bright and heartfelt, but Solis was the might of the South, the sun given a kingdom on earth. If the southern king turned his attention their way, nothing short of dragonfire could stop him. If he wasn't careful, Vhogare's fear would lose them the greatest army the continent had ever known.

Scowling, Vhogare scanned the castle yard for prying ears and eyes. The courtyards and walkways were still awash with servants and soldiers bustling back and forth, removing debris and bodies from the collapse. No one dared to pass nearby, and if any of them met the prince's eyes, they did not hold them for long. Word had spread.

A council chamber could be rebuilt, but a truth could not be unsaid.

Vhogare knew it, too. "I take the throne tomorrow, on my nameday, before anyone can stand in our way." He put a heavy hand on Elias's shoulder, his thumb digging in. "I need you to have faith, brother. We are part of something far bigger than ourselves. We must pull our weight."

Elias drew in a heavy breath. "And stand our line." He had vowed to protect innocence. It was why he had first taken up an apprenticeship to his father's craft and later sworn in as a knight. And though Erembour and Vhogare had changed everything, Elias's heart held firm—and his determination remained. He would work from within to keep a hand on the rudder and a shield against the sword.

"I saw the world fall apart," Vhogare confessed. Leaning his elbows on his knees, he cradled his face. "And mine has. The bastard saw right through me. Perhaps Erembour expects this gift to tear me apart. But he gave it to me anyway. I will not fail," he swore, straightening. "I *will* buy us time."

"It is easier to pit a man against himself than to pit foes against each other," Elias cautioned the man who would be king. The man he no longer knew.

"As I am well aware." Vhogare waved over a servant carrying water, filled two cups, and handed Elias the better of the set. "There are winners and losers, and we *cannot* lose. Erembour will devour this world whole. He will show no mercy to fathers or daughters, and all the grief we feel now will be nothing compared to the guilt we'll swim in if we fail. But to win, I need to know." Those ice-blue eyes bored into Elias, desperation now a permanent fixture behind them. "Where is your line?"

There it was. His opportunity. Elias's one wish—that he not go into his grave having done nothing at all. That he could *do* something. That dream had been twisted, contorted into something Elias no longer recognized, but his mission had not changed, nor had the goal, even if it was to be water poured over Vhogare's fire. A hand to temper the blaze.

Elias summoned all the steel in his soul. Every word was molten lead against his lips, in his heart. "My line is behind you."

Vhogare's shoulders sagged, relief washing over him. Confidence.

Nausea roiled Elias's gut at his lie. "But swear this to me," he asked, "on the oath you swore me in the forest."

Vhogare searched his gaze. "Anything." In some aching part of his soul, Elias knew the man meant it.

"No matter what happens to me in our war, you will protect my family. They are all that I have left of my soul." If he were to soil all his oaths to stop this madness, it would never be at the cost of them. "And that you—you, Vhogare, *your* fire within—will not be consumed. Guard what is left of your light, brother. Without it, we are lost."

Vhogare splayed a hand across his heart. The same hand he swore his blood oath with. "I swear, on my very life and all I stand on. On every second of our brotherhood." He moved that hand to Azrail's hilt. "On this very sword. No harm will befall them that I will not repay with blood."

THE NEW BLOOD

ELIAS

Leaving his father's cleric to prepare Einar for burial, Elias climbed the stairs once more to check on Joanna—and found her glaring at him as he walked in. "Where is he?" his wife demanded from where she lay abed.

He didn't need to ask who. "Vhogare is down in the yard." He nodded to Gabriella as the spy helped Joanna nurse Liora. His father had trusted the woman with his life, and she never failed him. "You can say what you wish."

Joanna wasted no time. "I understand what's at stake, but he cannot go on like this. It will crush him. It *has* crushed him."

Elias heaved a weighty sigh. "I was raised to see these things coming," he scowled, pacing to her window. *And failure gets a spymaster killed.* Had that been his father's warning in the tent? To not let his guard down around the bear?

The sun glittered on the waves of the loch below like the ocean itself had been set aflame. "How could I have missed something so world-changing?"

"He was our friend," Joanna whispered from behind him. "Reckless and volatile, yes, but I always believed he had a good heart. I was wrong."

She said it with such unforgiving fire that Elias turned to face her.

Joanna did not take back her words. His lionhearted woman doubled down. "He has been brittle from the start. Whatever the intentions of his heart may be, he is no longer the boy we grew up with."

"Aye." Years ago—hell, days ago—Elias would've been overjoyed for his closest comrade to hold his child. To celebrate new life with the brother of his heart and drink to the continuation of his house and name.

But when Vhogare had reached out for Liora, every ounce of Elias's soul had screamed for him to rip her from Vhogare's arms. Elias traced the healed scar slicing his brow and cheek. No, Vhogare was a man grown. And he had become dangerous. Nothing would stop Vhogare so long as he thought he was saving them all.

Joanna still could not sit up from the delivery, but she was far from weakened by it. Unflinching steel edged his wife's voice as she seized the bear claws he'd left on the nightstand. "Tell me. Tell me what you're willing to do, and I will help you."

Elias braced himself and turned to face her. "Soleil is dead, as well."

Joanna's jaw hardened. "I suspected. He would not let me see her." She met his eyes, and though her lip quivered and her eyes glistened with tears, there was nothing but fiery judgment on her fearless face. "By his own hand?"

Elias did not know what was worse: that Joanna had lost a father figure and a dear friend all in one night, or that she didn't even hesitate to believe Vhogare had killed his love.

"No," he answered. "Vhogare became a dragon in the middle of the council room." The story sounded ludicrous on his lips, but if anyone would believe him, Joanna would. "He broke through much of the structure, and the rafters crushed her."

Soleil. Elias's throat closed up, his chest seizing. He hated himself for not intervening when he'd had the chance. Perhaps if he had found some way to stop Vhogare's heedless courtship, Soleil would yet live. Guilt ate him, and he gripped his brow and leaned to sit against the windowsill. "Losing her broke him," he sighed. "Give me time to work."

"Time?" Joanna demanded, grief and shock fraying her words.

"He killed Einar. In deed, if not by hand. And Soleil—his very heart? He has loved her for years. She was so close, Elias, so close to everything she ever wanted." Her voice broke. "And now she is gone. They are gone. Forever. How much time do you need before he proves once more that he will stop at nothing to see this through?"

"I need to see what *can* be done," Elias offered. His fingers drifted to the stitches in his hair. "Bears and dragons are different beasts. Unless my eyes deceive me, he received wounds from Milan that healed when he became his dragon. There is no telling what else he could heal from if I were to make an attempt on his life, and then there would be no hiding my intent."

He was no coward, but he couldn't get himself killed and leave her and Liora alone against that monster.

Mopping a hand over his face, Elias crossed the room and knelt before the bed to fold Joanna's fingers in his. One of the bear claws remained hidden in her palm. "We will think of something. But promise me, you will wait. We must be careful and manage this threat without losing our advantage. Because what I saw in those woods was real. And Erembour will not go easy on us just because his puppet is dead."

Joanna leaned her forehead against his, breathing him in. "Very well. But he will never touch Liora again while he is that *thing*. Not so long as I live. And I will make sure he knows it."

A decade of Vhogare and Joanna's friendship had boiled down to this.

"Swear to me you will be careful." He pressed his brow to her knuckles before holding her gaze and laying a light hand on the crown of Liora's soft, downy hair. Her mother's hair, as golden as wheat in the summer sun. "You are all that's left for me."

Tears welled in Joanna's bright eyes.

—⋅— ❧❦ —⋅—

Elias couldn't bring himself to go back into the chapel yet. Standing vigil as Jesse prepared Einar for burial meant his father's death was real. Einar was gone. And Elias couldn't do that, yet. Could never do that.

Trusting Joanna would rest in his absence, he excused himself and made his way to the kitchens. Though the summer sun beat down outside, the heat of the kitchens was different—a welcoming warmth.

The scent of roast fallow deer reached Elias from the pit on the farthest side of the room, two men turning the meat on a spit. Bakers managed the wall of sweet-smelling ovens, and cooks bent over cauldrons in the blazing hearth. Sauciers, butchers, and scullions wove amongst each other along the spacious wooden tables in the center of the room as they tended their tasks. Elias's stomach stung as he peered at the vegetables they chopped. How long had it been since he last ate? He had no desire for food, but he needed his strength.

Navigating through the crowded space, he made his way to the right of the room, where Alastair sat at a smaller table pushed off to the side for staff meals. The commander hunkered over his food, working his way through a steaming trencher.

"Aadriek still stands guard," Elias told the commander by way of greeting.

Alastair gave a bitter smirk. "No one's getting through that door with their life."

"And for that, I'm grateful." Elias sat across the table from Alastair, a little more at ease knowing that his family was well looked after. "Another trencher, please." One of the cooks brought beef stew over and thunked it down in front of him, along with a tankard of ale.

Elias's association with Vhogare brought him quick service but not kind looks. Officers of their station ought to eat in the feasting hall, but all that cavernous, empty space had not seemed welcoming. Sighing, he raised his cup to Alastair. "Glad to see I won't be dining alone."

The commander shook his head and ran a hand over his beard, clearing the grease. "I tried to eat in the hall but couldn't stand the quiet. At least here it's loud and warm."

Loud, it was. Elias strained to hear his comrade over the commotion. Fewer mouths didn't mean the entire castle did not need to eat.

"The man in the inn that night," the warrior across from him began, careful to keep his voice low even with the ceaseless din.

Alastair leaned onto his elbows, taking up half the table. "The prince was just a prince before him."

Elias searched his eyes, trying to read his intentions. "Aye."

Alastair seemed to consider for a moment. "I'd wager, based on the coffins being crafted, you wish it had been you who'd become the beast in his stead."

A pit yawned open in Elias's stomach. The commander understood far more than he let on. But Elias could not agree. At least not aloud. Desperate for anything to keep his mouth shut, Elias downed the entire tankard. The ale was bitter and stale on his tongue, and he set it on the table with force. "Even if I did, it is too late now."

Alastair glanced over Elias's shoulder, then his own. And beneath the kitchen's cacophony and the castle yard's tumult, he whispered, "It will not be too late forever."

Treason. And far worse, betrayal of the only brother he'd ever known. But that was Elias's father preparing for the grave, Soleil crushed beneath Vhogare's choice.

"He swore to protect Joanna. Liora." And any good spymaster knew that where there was a promise, there was a threat.

Standing, Alastair swung his war axe over his shoulder and prepared to go. "If he ever breaks that promise, you know where I stand."

THE THRONE ROOM

VHOGARE

Food. After checking on Joanna, Elias had offered to bring Vhogare something from the kitchens, but the thought of eating turned Vhogare's stomach. The bread from that morning sat like an anchor in his stomach, weighing him down and churning his insides with nausea. How could he eat when there was so much to be done?

His heartbrother's words still lingered, uneasy, in Vhogare's chest. *Protect my family.* Was it not clear that he would go to his grave to defend Joanna and Liora? Must he swear an oath on it, as well?

He'd given up his humanity, his kin, his very love to protect them. Soleil had died because he fought to save Joanna. And now Elias, Joanna, and their daughter were all that Vhogare had left. He would bleed out in the dirt before he let Erembour have them.

Did Elias not see that?

Dread curled in Vhogare's gut. Their world, their very existence, was at stake, and his heartbrother did not trust him. But their salvation was worth any price he had to pay.

They did not need to love him.

They just had to live.

To make things easier, he should make amends.

Fear ate at Vhogare until he found himself in the royal gardens.

Wrought iron fences hemmed in lush bushes of blossoming orange, red, and yellow roses. Hibiscus and fire poppies lined the twisting cobbled paths. Verdant creepers and vines spun around obsidian lattices, the stone chiseled into the shape of winding fire.

Their fragrance floated around him like a sweet shroud. Gathering a bouquet of red and orange flameflowers, Vhogare snaked around the central wrought iron fountain. Making his way past the irises, tulips, and lilies beaming up at him, he crossed the path to stand before a rich, manicured collection of rose bushes.

The royal blooms had been his mother's pride, and King Ulrich often mused that she spent hours in the garden caring for them. All of Queen Seonna's flowers were beautiful in summer's high bloom, and beyond the tidy red, yellow, and white bushes spread a wild, untamed patch of inky blue roses.

The northern beauties were her favorite. Or so he had been told. Each dark rose was magnificent, climbing in lush, relentless vines across the intricate wrought iron trellises with a fierce, restless will. His throat tightened at the sight, and he turned away, bending his head to his task.

Trimming a few white and yellow roses, Vhogare bound the flowers together and climbed the sweeping castle stairs, his heartbeat rising with every step.

At Joanna's door, Aadriek stood guard.

"Step aside."

The Marian warrior may have worn Anchoran armor, but his eyes showed no love nor loyalty when he met Vhogare's gaze. "My lady is abed," Aadriek told him. "I have orders to allow her rest."

"I am the crown prince now, soon to be king. My orders supersede whoever gave yours."

Aadriek's iron bloodline bled through his scowl as he retrieved his axe from the wall. "Until the crown is on your head, I don't answer to you. Unless you'd like to ask your *Council.*"

Shifting the delicate flowers in his arms, Vhogare held up his right hand, displaying the scars from Milan's nails. Though his brother had cut deep, digging troughs in the thin skin, not a scab remained. Only scars. Pale new flesh ran in ribbons up his wrists, mingling with the vicious burn marks from Erembour's gift.

"These were fresh before I became my dragon," Vhogare whispered. "The second I took my wings, I healed. You may fight me well enough, but are you prepared to fight *that* beast and win?"

Aadriek's clean-shaven jaw ticked, but the mortal had no answer.

"Step. Aside." It was a bluff; he couldn't transform so close to Joanna's suite without hurting her and Liora. Even so, he hated threatening Aadriek. The warrior had been a loyal comrade for years. But Vhogare had no room for love any longer. He was a monster in a man's skin, and his man's skin grew thin.

Aadriek's arm shook as if he were restraining a blow, but he did as commanded. It hurt more than it should that Aadriek believed Vhogare would risk such a thing, but he was grateful for the man's caution, regardless.

Even so, defiance was defiance, and Vhogare made a note to keep a close eye on Alastair's brother as he swept into Joanna's room and shut the door behind him. The nursemaids and midwives had returned. Many of them sported eyes red from crying, grief from the night's casualties pulling at their features. Guilt wrapped its iron fist around Vhogare's throat at the baleful looks they cut his way.

He raised his chin beneath their silent accusations. There was no denying what he had done. But a show of such violence made even the strongest men targets, and the second a servant scented weakness was the day he would find an assassin at his back. So, Vhogare smiled at them with as much grace and benevolence as he could muster and turned to face Joanna.

Elias's wife was far from asleep. Though still pale and exhausted, she watched every nursemaid like a hawk as they cared for her little girl. Propped up on pillows, she wore a loose sage-green dressing gown fastened with a glittering sapphire pin.

Vhogare froze in his steps. Joanna owned sapphires, but she never wore them.

Long dubbed the 'queen's gem' in memory of Seonna, sapphire was his mother's favorite color, and Joanna was always considerate of how it affected him.

But the small pin she wore glittered with the jewel. A blatant, silent slap in his face.

His friend of ten long years met his eyes like she hadn't known him a day. "To what do I owe the pleasure, Your Majesty?"

Each word was sharp, clipped. Like he hadn't burned her back together just hours ago.

Vhogare straightened. "I brought these to sit in front of your window." Unable to hold her gaze, he busied himself preparing a vase and standing the flowers on the sill in the bright summer light, but Joanna's eyes burned his back all the same.

"Flameflowers," she mused, ignoring the white and yellow roses as if they did not exist. "Is this an apology?"

"They're your favorite, aren't they?" Finishing, he turned and cleared his throat. He could withstand the disdain of the castle staff, but Joanna was another matter. An entire decade she'd been the sister he never had, but all the love was gone out of her eyes, washed away in a sea of judgment.

Vhogare forced himself to swallow and folded his hands in front of him. Why did he always feel like a child when she looked at him like that? Like he'd been caught somewhere he didn't belong with something he shouldn't have. But Vhogare now bore his brother's blood on his hands. He was about to be king, and he'd saved her life. What else did he have to fear?

"After last night's . . . events," Vhogare began, steadying his voice, "I wanted to reassure you of the security of your place at the castle. Your husband will be my Right Hand and thus indispensable." Several of the women in Joanna's charge glanced up at that, but at a glare from him, they continued their work. "As are you. Please understand you are under my every protection, every hospitality. My father's death changes nothing. Should you need anything—anything at all—all you must do is call."

Perhaps it confirmed too much. Joanna read his guilt like an open page. But she smiled, albeit far too sweetly for the salty-mouthed stable maid he'd met from the Solan border all those years ago. "Enough with the formality," Joanna said, waving him over to her bedside. He sat, sinking into the mattress. The pine scent of her sheets clung to her as she wrapped her arms around him and squeezed.

"Elias loves you," she whispered in his ear so that none of her attendants might hear. "And I did, too. But it is for him alone that you leave this room today."

Vhogare started to sit back, but she held firm, and he dared not use force and harm her.

"Soleil was my friend; Einar the only father I have ever known. And I am no flower, dear little brother." They shared no blood, and yet the endearment pierced like a sword through the chest. "I am your thorn, and I see you for what you are." Her breath was hot on his neck, her nails digging in. "You are a vicious, broken man, and I will never forgive what you've done."

She released him, and Vhogare stood. He surveyed the room, searching for something to say, and his eye snagged on an ornate bronze letter opener atop her bedside table, sharp as any dagger. Vhogare's throat closed up, and he glanced from the frightening sweetness on her face to the scar that bled through the bandages on her stomach. Behind him, Liora began to cry, and Vhogare clamped his fists at his sides.

For her daughter, for Elias, she would live.

His nose prickled with unshed tears, but Vhogare straightened his shoulders, though his heart cracked in two. "My offer stands all the same. For Elias."

"For Elias." Her steel grin was less a smile and more a baring of teeth. "And I am grateful."

Shaking, Vhogare left, shutting the door behind him. Aadriek's gaze pierced his back, a thousand iron blades driving true, as he stumbled, numb, down the stairs to the throne room. When its doors were shut behind him, he let the tears stream down his face.

Joanna hated him.

He had damn near laid his life at her feet, and she had cursed him for it.

All he had given, and she did not trust him.

Alone, he crumpled to the stone stairs of the dais and let himself sink into the haunting silence.

Hours later, his father's throne room was dark around him. The vaulted ceiling's sharp arches and intricate ribbing crawled with shadows. They crept around the stone carvings in each corner, watching him.

Vhogare stood in the center of the hollow, cavernous room. Days ago, he would've marveled at the lofty architecture and wondered what mighty hands had built such a beautiful castle. Every column lining the massive hall was carved to match the Ark's three horsemen, faultless mirrors to the likenesses depicted in the chapel. But the stone statues of the celestials loomed larger than they should've, like they'd grown eyes and stared down at him.

Justice, Judgment, and Chaos.

There was no mercy in their cloaked, stone gazes. Each visage was indiscernible, wreathed in mystery. But Vhogare had seen Chaos's face, and there was no forgetting it.

Above the throne, the three stained-glass windows shimmered with moonlight. The pearl, amber, and gold-tinted glass depicted the Ark's great fire rising high, undefeatable, keeping the shadows at bay. On the brightest days, Anchora's morning sun shone through to bathe the throne and the stone in golden light. Vhogare wished such sun would shine again, so the warm light could stream through and cover him.

As it stood, the throne room was cold. No living soul visited him. He sat alone at the foot of the dais, and Elias did not even come to look where he had gone. But Milan had become one with the moonlight and the air he passed through. Vhogare would sit on the throne tomorrow, but for the night, he sat beside his brother again.

Milan's ghost took a seat on the step next to him, forever in the clothes he wore in death. The formal attire he'd donned when their father died had no wrinkles. Not a thread nor a hair on Milan's head was out of place as he put his elbows on his knees and gazed at the doors ahead.

The steel throne stood behind them, so vast and empty without the old king in its arms. Its solid frame was worked through with dancing petals of flame as if the steel chair was cast from columns of living fire. The seat itself remained uncushioned, for no king should rule in comfort. Below the throne, the metal flowed down as if molten to meld into the dais, a symbol of Anchora's immovable strength and history.

Strength Vhogare would have to wield if we wished for a better end than his brother's.

"You must forgive me for what I've done," Vhogare rasped to Milan's spirit. He wiped his face with the back of his hand; he'd been so exhausted and dehydrated that it had taken three pitchers of water and several meals to recover even a fraction of his vigor.

Vhogare ground his jaw. The gift was a monster under his skin. It writhed, ever begging to be let free. Chaos was meant to change, to grow, to bloom. But it could only burn and destroy in his hands, and the gift despised what he'd done. Each heartbeat struck a glowing anvil, the flame a relentless, white-hot heat in Vhogare's chest. His fire within seemed to war with the chaos, every ounce of his soul spent containing it, and Vhogare worried it was still not enough.

Milan must've sensed his struggle. His elder brother didn't answer. He just looked at Vhogare like he knew, like the bastard would forever know and never speak.

"If you had been stronger," Vhogare grizzled, gripping his brow. "Braver. We could've done this together. Why?" he demanded, voice breaking. "Why were you always such a *coward?*"

Now, Milan could never run. He was there yet not there, in some life between life. And Vhogare had cast him into it. Did he stay behind as punishment? Or for some piece of Vhogare's soul that had not yet broken? Some lingering part of him that could not break despite the darkness pressing down on him.

"Why didn't you just leave?" he half-shouted. "I begged you to go. Of all the times you have left me, you should've taken your chance while you had it and run."

Milan had always chosen caution and security over challenge. Vhogare loathed his brother's ease, but he already missed his laugh when they were boys, his sharp wit, and the teasing, tormenting way he always held Vhogare to account.

But Milan scowled at Vhogare, his mouth set in a hard, disapproving line. Though a thin man, his jaw was strong as an anvil, so like their father's. And he had Ulrich's cold, piercing gaze to match.

"Will you sit there forever?" Vhogare shouted, shoving to his feet and whirling to face the throne that was his life and death, his sword and shackle. "Will you never speak to me again?"

His brother stood and slipped his hands into his pockets.

That damning silence broke Vhogare. Tears would not bring his brother back to life. No amount of begging and pleading, of guilt or remorse, could put a body back onto his soul. But Vhogare wept all the same.

"Then tell Soleil. . . . Tell my midnight sun her knife was sharp, and I will carve it into my heart forever." His voice shattered. "For I loved them both."

Each precious memory of her pulled the lungs out of his body. "I will never forgive myself."

Milan's blond hair blew back from his forehead in an immortal breeze, and a sad smile graced his lips before he was gone, and ice took away the air at Vhogare's back.

"I see your work has begun."

Vhogare whirled to find Erembour standing in the middle of the throne room, staring up at the ceiling. Hoarfrost crept across the high windows, each tiny shard of ice reflecting the moonlight. The air grew so cold it seared his skin as frozen crystals raced down the stone walls like white blood.

A chill snaked along Vhogare's spine. He didn't bother wiping his tears. Summoning whatever fight was left in him, Vhogare held fast to their plan. "Only just. Tomorrow, the throne will officially be mine, and the kingdoms will come to heel."

The celestial studied him. His blazing silver gaze trailed the sweat bead trickling down Vhogare's temple.

"Your gift hates what you've done," Vhogare snarled. "I can feel it." He didn't know where his courage came from, but he could not take the words back.

In Erembour's presence, the chaos writhed. *Traitor,* it seemed to weep. *Oathbreaker.* Like a bird in a cage, it sang, but with sadness.

His throat ached. "It hates what I have done as well."

"I do it for love," Erembour argued. "You'll be surprised at the sacrifices you make when you have no choice." The celestial glanced down for a heartbeat as if he felt some semblance of shame. When he looked up, a shred of empathy had warmed his eyes. "For what it's worth, it was never meant for mortals."

Vhogare squared his shoulders. The weight was heavy, so heavy, but he had no choice. "I will make do."

The creature turned to go, his cloak whispering over his shoulder, but Vhogare couldn't stop himself.

"Tell me," he asked. Just in case this was the last time he could. "How many? How many have thrown themselves at your feet only to find bones?"

"Many," Erembour answered without hesitation, and his voice had no joy. No warmth or compassion. Nothing but iron will. "But the bones are at their feet, not mine. And you will buy us all time."

Keep your hands clean. Elias's father would've recognized such bloodless warfare. Vhogare cursed himself for paying so little attention to Einar's lessons.

Even so, he did not miss the threat in Erembour's obsidian eyes as the celestial whispered, "If it's any comfort, they always gave it back. In the end."

"You razed their worlds, anyway?" There were others, like his own, and the bastard had lied to them all.

Erembour's coal eyes hardened. "They tried to trick me. They stood between me and saving Invar's life. So I did it myself."

Vhogare straightened under that look. "My father, beloved king though he was, died in his bed of a wasting illness. I assure you, I will not do the same." He was the last of Ulrich's legacy, and he would not fail.

"And you will make a name for yourself, contending with the hearts of stars?"

Cold, mortal fear snaked like ice through Vhogare's soul. Even so, he was king. In oath, if not in name. His people depended on him to defend them against this monster. So, he did not back down. "Stars die."

Something deep inside his chest shriveled up as Erembour chuckled. "You're right," the celestial sighed. "They do."

Vhogare couldn't stop his flinch as Erembour's gift rallied, snaking the silver fire up his marble arms. The white-cold heat struck him in the face, and the smell, like a sword held too long over the forge.

Vhogare's gut hollowed out.

The horseman took a step toward him, and Vhogare summoned all his courage to hold his ground. "Invar spends his lifeblood protecting you. Saving *you.*" Erembour spat the last word as if humanity were filth. "The Ark bound Chaos up in me so it would be controlled. Did you think I would not know how you planned to use it?"

Vhogare's chin trembled, but he raised it all the same. Forced steel into his spine and stood tall. "I love my home. A life here is all I ever wanted, and you meant to take that from me. What did you expect me to do? Stand by and watch?"

Something vicious and cruel sawed through the creature's smile. "I did take it from you."

Vhogare blinked, and Erembour began to laugh. The sound was a hammer against his heart. It rose to a full, throaty roar that bellowed from deep in the celestial's armored chest. The windows of the throne room cracked, and Vhogare fell to his knees, clamping his hands over his ears at the deafening timbre. Every fiber of his being wanted to run and hide, to shrink and cower behind the throne until the storm had passed, but Erembour had tricked him. The creature had taken Soleil and his child from him, and Vhogare could not let that stand.

Trembling, Vhogare removed his hands from his ears. The world seemed to tilt and ring, a high-pitched wail piercing his mind, but Vhogare got to his feet. Cold, aching vengeance gave him strength. He stood and stared the celestial down, teeth set and fists clamped at his side until Erembour laughed himself dry.

"Oh, ho," Erembour chuckled at the raw hatred in Vhogare's eyes. The celestial's face twisted into a violent scowl. "You believe you are the only one who has paid a price?" he snarled, stepping into Vhogare's face. The creature towered over him by more than a foot. "You think you are the only one who has lost love? Who has lost his brothers' trust? There is no limit to what I will do for Invar's life. You *will* do this work for me, and when you do, and their blood is heavy on your soul, remember." His voice dropped to a low rumble, his breath colder than the frostbitten north. "You did not save the world. You saved a god."

The gift inside Vhogare's chest wept. The way Einar would have wept if Elias betrayed him. The way he had wept when his unborn child died.

"No." Unflinching, icy wrath bubbled up in Vhogare's chest. He spat at the celestial's feet and stepped to match the monster. "But I will bury his dog."

Erembour's lips peeled back to reveal canines far sharper than any mortal man's. "I am coming back for my gift. You cannot defeat me, but you can try. And when you fail, your sun will join your love."

Before Vhogare could respond, the ancient, heavy doors behind Erembour cracked open, and the celestial disappeared in a circle of swirling stars. Shadow ran back into the absence of light, and the doors finished opening, revealing Elias.

"We need to speak."

Vhogare sank to the floor and crossed his legs. His hands shook beyond control. Every muscle in his body jumped and trembled like a wire wound too tight. Heaving down air, Vhogare mopped a hand over his face and tried to breathe.

Elias's gaze drifted across the throne room. Though he remained oblivious to Erembour's visit, his steps faltered as he noticed the cracks in the windows. "Are you all right?" he asked, eyeing Vhogare as if he might erupt into a dragon again.

Vhogare didn't have the energy to correct him and explain what Erembour said. He cleared the tears slicing down his jaw and retrieved Soleil's silver dragon from his pocket. His pulse beat like a war drum in his ears, but he concentrated on filling his lungs with air and steadied his wild heart. "I will be."

Elias nodded, but doubt stalked behind his eyes. His heartbrother did not believe him, and rightly so. Vhogare was on the knife's edge. But at least Elias had the kindness not to pry when Vhogare could barely breathe, let alone speak.

Exhaling, Elias sat beside him, so small beneath the cavernous ceiling. How long would it be before it all came crashing down on him? On them?

"I am grateful for what you did for Liora," Elias began with care. "But desperation will win us no lives."

"This was the darkest hour," Vhogare promised. His muscles twitched and tightened with tension, but he forced his fists to release. Focusing, he drew a breath into his chest to calm himself. Perhaps if he could show control and moderation, he could ease his brother's fears. Joanna's fears. "Milan needed to be dealt with. The Council . . . was unfortunate collateral. They were attempting to arrest me before I could reach you and Joanna."

Understanding dawned on Elias's face. "You didn't think you'd save her in time."

A vice clamped around Vhogare's throat. "All that matters is that I did."

Elias's gaze softened just a fraction. "Thank you. For what you did for her."

"It does not make the rest of it right."

"No." Elias sighed. "It does not. But they are alive. And I am thankful for that."

Vhogare couldn't breathe under that crushing weight. All he could do was sniff and nod. "I'm sorry about Einar. He was a good man. As you are." His heart crumbled. "You didn't deserve any of this."

Elias was silent for a long moment. When he spoke, he did not accept Vhogare's apology. Only said, "None of us did. But it is our war all the same." He gestured to the silver dragon Vhogare twirled in his fingers. "And Soleil?"

"She did not believe me." Air shuddered across Vhogare's teeth. "But I was not wrong." He held his trembling palms out before him, the weight of the pewter dragon heavier than the world. "I can still feel her ash in my hands. Can still hear her scream." He turned to Elias, tears running down his face. "I held my child in my arms, and that bastard burned them alive."

Elias grimaced. "You did not tell her what you saw."

"How could I? How could I burden her with all that I cannot forget, can never let go? I close my eyes, and all I see is silver fire eating everything I love."

Vhogare fought for words to describe what he knew was coming. "All those lives at stake, Elias. The entire world." He pushed his hair back from his face. "The south, the border city where Joanna grew up. The west, where Alastair and Aadriek's sister and Aadriek's wife live. To hear my father tell it, the north is the only place on the face of this earth that my mother truly loved. And Erembour will burn it before he turns east unless we stop him here. Now."

"We will not let him take everything." Elias wrapped a strong arm around his shoulders, squeezing just as Einar had as they strolled through the hunting camp almost a week past. "If we play this right, we can save many lives, and Soleil can be proud of you again. But only if we keep our heads."

"I tried," Vhogare sobbed. "But I . . . broke her trust. She misunderstood my ambitions."

His friend heaved a weighty sigh. "I am sorry for your loss, Brother."

Vhogare shook his head. "She was right," he whispered, and even at that volume, his voice shattered. "And she will not be forgotten."

But the truth was the truth. Vhogare pulled away and attempted to compose himself. "Even so," he rasped, clearing the tears from his face, "she betrayed me. And now that Milan and the Council are removed, we can begin anew. Prepare for his return."

He could feel Elias's eyes on him, weighing, but Vhogare was not ready to confront the chasm forming between them. So he kept his gaze ahead and stared at the throne room doors. Behind his eyes burned nothing but fire. "Because Erembour will raze our world to the ground if we do not stop him."

Joanna could be his thorn all she liked. He would earn her trust back by weathering her barbs and blades. With her, Elias was whole, and Vhogare would keep all his promises as long as he could.

"Tell me true," Elias whispered. He studied the colossal carved columns, his voice still hoarse from the night's terrors. "Do we have a chance?"

"We will make one." How often had Vhogare seen those small pinpricks of light wink out in the night sky, so far above his west wing? Nothing was impossible if suns went dark. "I will not leave us at that monster's mercy. He will never see me on my knees again."

Elias fell quiet for so long that Vhogare pivoted to face him.

"Erembour is one soldier," Vhogare told him. *"One* life. And he is alone."

His heartbrother pinned him with a searching gaze. "How do you know that?"

Vhogare wiped his nose on the back of his hand. "I know loneliness when I see it." He took another steadying breath and tightened his grip on Soleil's dragon. "And when we kill him, we are free. Invar may even thank us for saving not just our world but every other one on Erembour's butcher block."

Elias crossed his legs, thinking. "And when Invar dies?"

Vhogare gripped his knuckles. "You were right." He huffed a sad laugh. "You always are. The Ark and Invar did not send that monster. Every time Erembour is near, my gift cries." He tilted his head back. "When Invar dies, we can all go in peace. Not in the torment and agony I have seen." Emptiness sank into his soul. "This cannot all be for nothing."

"Then I am with you." Elias rocked back, staring at a stone sky with no stars. "We will do this together."

Vhogare's chin trembled, and he hid his face in his scarred right hand to hide his searing tears.

"But tell me this," Elias asked. "Will my daughter hate me . . . when our work is done?"

There was no sugarcoating it. "Yes." Vhogare lifted his gaze and met Elias's eyes. "But she will live. Stay faithful, keep course, and I promise I will see us through."

His comrade pivoted to face him, propping an elbow on a knee. "I did not ask you where your line was."

Anywhere, anything that kept that ceiling together and Elias's shield intact. Vhogare had doomed them all and had no choice but to fix it. There would be no fear of holding this too tightly. When Erembour's schemes came to light, Vhogare would be ready. He met his heartbrother's gaze.

"My world."

Elias sat with him for a long while. When words had dried up between them and the torches burned low, Elias excused himself for the night. But Vhogare stayed behind in the dark throne room, surrounded by cold, cavernous, echoing stone.

Alone, he cradled his head in his hands and sobbed until there was no water left in him.

He'd become a king of wrath and rage, divesting himself of everything he loved, his very humanity. Everything that had been whole and right inside of him was wrong. Twisted. He was a monster in a man's skin, and there was nothing left of him to love. No end to the chain wrapped around his neck. "Nothing will ever be the same again," he mourned.

THE CROWN

ELIAS

Morning dawned gray and merciless as Elias stood in the great hall. His headache had abated, but exhaustion pulled at his muscles, weighing him down. Wan light filtered in through the windows, casting light on the carpeted stone floor and winding through the smoke drifting from the many hearths. The soot stung his eyes, and he blinked the dampness away.

The hearth fires illuminated the banners of House Maekyr streaming from the vaulted roof. Anchora's royal sigil stood out on the heavy, limp fabric. Vhogare's new colors were stark in the dim hall. Originally silver, each banner now sported a black field with a white fire burning in its center in honor of the Ark's eternal flame. A sword pierced through the flame's heart, and dark tassels dangled from the bottom fringes like tiny hands clinging to life.

Behind Elias, peasants crowded inside the great hall. Though tradition deemed the small folk to be informed of coronations in the city squares, Vhogare had ordered that anyone who could attend would be allowed entrance. The more eyes confirming his rulership, the tighter his grip on the throne. Elias scowled. *Honor does not matter when you have numbers on your side.*

He drank down a drowning breath and wished his father were still alive. Einar would know what to do and say to make this stop. But before he could finish inhaling, the throne room's heavy carved doors split open before him.

Beyond them, all of Anchora's nobility turned to face Elias. The absence of representatives from their sister countries stood out like a gaping hole in the crowd. In their vacancy, only Anchoran blood attended. A poor sign for international relations, and Vhogare's reign had just begun.

No musicians played. There was not a single horn or shout to announce his entrance. The smoke from the fires combined with the nobles' overdone fragrances until the room smelled like a garden burning.

When Elias stepped through the doors, Alastair fell into step at his side as a silent show of support. The swornguard wore shining Marian blue armor over Anchoran silver mail, his long, wavy black hair tied back, and his dark beard oiled. A cutting, imposing figure, indeed. Alastair cast him a sidelong glance as they walked and laid his gloved hand on the pommel of his sword. Elias's chest ached with gratitude for his brother-in-arms.

The guards who'd opened the doors stood aside, flanking the path to the dais. The royal hall yawned open like the mouth of a beast ready to devour him whole. Elias swallowed at the cracks running through the myriad stained-glass windows high above their heads—cracks that had not been there the day before. *What have we done?*

Vhogare waited for him at the end of the ceremonial aisle runner. The prince stood before the throne, hands folded in front of him, jaw set like stone. Harun scowled, cold as steel, at his side, the royal cleric ready to crown the prince king.

Better the enemy that I know. Elias's father was at home in the Ark's arms, but his voice had never rung louder.

Squaring his shoulders, Elias strode down the center aisle, Yigael a steadying weight at his side. All the remaining heads of the high houses regarded him as if it were a funeral march. Perhaps it was.

Soleil's parents had been given seats of honor in the front. The lovely historian's family wore dark, muted blues in mourning, though no tears could buy back the brilliant future Vhogare had stripped from her. House Corveau was the greatest in the kingdom, and the prince had dealt them a grave insult with Soleil's death. Her mother would not meet Elias's gaze as he passed. Her father, however, stared him down.

As if Raul held Elias accountable for what Vhogare had become.

A knife twisted in Elias's chest.

He *was* accountable. Responsible. And there was no turning back from this, no backing down now. Liora was in the world, and it was his job to save it.

Elias counted every step to the foot of the throne. He wished Joanna were at his side. The woman could chop Vhogare in half with a glance. But his wife needed her rest, especially if they were to prepare for the days to come.

When he reached the dais, Alastair broke to stand opposite Aadriek, both brothers facing the crowd. Alone, Elias tucked his silver cloak behind him and climbed the stairs to stand at Vhogare's right. Dressed in full regalia, Harun approached with Anchora's steel crown in hand. Jesse, Elias's own house cleric, waited below in the crowd of honored guests, watching Elias the way one might a beast marked for slaughter. A small bird flying just beneath a hawk.

"Take your oath to your people," Harun prompted. His gaze was sharp with reproach as he beckoned Vhogare to kneel.

Elias recited the royal vow in his head. *I swear to rule with justice, to judge soundly, and to cherish the life of my kingdom and all those in it. I will serve you with strength and honor, striving for peace and not shying from war. My blood belongs to Anchora, and I will guard you all the days of my life. May the Ark have mercy and carry our kingdom in His arms.* Einar had hammered every syllable into his head since he was old enough to read because though it was the king's oath, it was a soldier's as well.

Vhogare glanced sidelong at Elias, as though he heard his thoughts, and went to a knee.

And though no noise, no visible crack could be seen, that knee shattered the foundation of their kingdom. Bowing his head, Vhogare pressed his scarred right hand against his chest in a solemn vow. "I swear to rule with strength and courage," the prince rumbled, the rich timbre of his voice filling the room. "To cherish this title entrusted to me, and protect my people at all costs."

In the crowd below, Soleil's father shifted on his feet at Vhogare's deviation from Anchora's ancient vow of kingship. It took all of Elias's control not to do the same. Gone was the oath of justice, judgment, and the sanctity of life. Honor and loyalty. The king mentioned nothing regarding good faith and kinship with their sister kingdoms. No, Vhogare had taken the crown and throne and made them a sword.

"My heart belongs to my country," the king continued. "I kneel for no one but this kingdom and I will defend you until I draw no breath and bleed no blood." Vhogare raised his gaze to the ceiling. "With fire and steel, I will guard you all the days of my life. May the Ark have mercy and carry our kingdom in His arms."

When Vhogare had finished, the royal cleric held the crown up for all to see. "May the Ark have mercy on your soul, son," Harun whispered in confidence. "And protect our kingdom."

And may He protect us from you.

When Harun had finished the ceremonial words, he raised his voice to address both Vhogare and the crowd. "Rise, Vhogare of House Maekyr, Anchor King."

Vhogare stiffened as the holy man set the steel crown on his head, but he rose under it, standing from one knee to take his place in front of the throne.

No cheer went up.

It was Vhogare's nameday—Harun himself had officiated the birth ceremony a quarter-century ago—and now the cleric pinned him with a grim gaze edged with fire. There was no Soleil to kiss the king, no father or brother to congratulate Vhogare on his accession. Nothing but the paltry assembly of scrambled surviving nobles, clerics, and castle servants. Witnesses, nothing more. The throne room might as well have been a mausoleum for all the sound the shattered gathering made.

"In my first act as king, I name Elias of House Aldernari as spymaster in his father, Einar's, place," Vhogare announced, his resonant voice thunderous in the quiet. He beckoned Elias forward, and though it took everything in him, Elias bent the knee and accepted the sigil the king had taken from his father's dead chest. "And I name you Right Hand, on this day, and for all the days to come."

Someone might as well have poured a barrel of blood over Elias's head. Every body they laid in the ground thereafter had his name etched on their deaths. His soul screamed to defy, to be free.

But he set his jaw and shouldered the new weight, standing. For Joanna. For Liora, he would do this. Suffer this burden. Whatever it took to save them. So he had sworn, and so he would do.

"And I entrust you with Castle Dawn, our strongest and most profitable keep. A beautiful place where your family can be safe and at peace."

Elias almost staggered back a step. That castle had been meant for Vhogare, his inheritance after Milan became king.

"For the blood on our blades," Vhogare whispered, extending Elias his hand.

"For all the blood in our hearts," Elias answered and clasped his king's arm, wrist to wrist. Vhogare pulled him to the top of the dais, and Elias drew Yigael from its scabbard. His father's sword, and all his fathers' before.

He raised the ornate, gilded weapon, the bright steel catching the wan sunlight and flashing. Majestic though it was, no one cheered. Even Gabriella remained stiff and silent at the far end of the great hall. His most trusted spy hunkered with the castle staff, each royal servant drawn with terror at the new reign. At least she stood with him in her own way—he would need all his allies to see this through.

Elias tightened his grip on Yigael. He prayed he would do well by the sacred blade and all the stories it carried inside, that somehow he would carve light out of the shadow spilled over their kingdom.

"Alastair," the king called, "son of Iedemir."

Elias stiffened as the commander stepped forward, every ounce of the salt and iron of his homeland. Dark fury and concern for the days to come shadowed Alastair's bronze visage.

"I name you his Second," Vhogare intoned, "for your leal service and compassion in our time of need."

To his credit, the Marian warrior nodded. But he did not kneel.

Vhogare did not seem to mind. He was too busy staring over the man's head at the ceiling as if he were waiting for it to come crumbling down. With a grim scowl, the king sat. The throne loomed over him, steel fire swallowing him in its embrace.

"Aadriek, son of Iedemir, you remain in my Swornguard."

Elias's stomach tightened with concern for his comrades. Though Vhogare had not been as studious as Milan, he retained enough crucial knowledge to keep his enemies close, and Alastair and Aadriek had been blatant in their disapproval of the destruction Vhogare caused.

Aadriek did not so much as incline his head at the king's words. Instead, he glared at Vhogare with a gaze as harsh and unforgiving as the sea.

"Banan," Vhogare continued, resolute. The landed knight in the first row of attendants stepped forward. "I name you Commander of the Swornguard, Captain of the Castle Guard, and Head of the City Watch in Alastair's place.

"Wyle." Vhogare gestured, and the old man stood from the row opposite Banan. "You served Einar well. I name you to my Council. Bring all your resources with you."

Waving to the far right of the gathering, Vhogare beckoned Maura forward. Gone was the quiet shyness Elias had come to expect from the young woman. He'd assumed she would be exhausted or grieving, but Maura had seen her fair share of darkness and appeared determined not to share her parents' fates. Her tumultuous brown hair was swept up, and she wore a gown of stunning purple with a dark cape clasped about her shoulders. A terrifying, quiet violence ruled her features. If she blamed the king for her mother's death, she did not show it. Only bottomless, hell-bent resolve glimmered in her russet eyes.

"You trained many years under your mother's tutelage. I name you to my Council as well, Lady Maura, as mistress of gold in Zarine's place. Make a new name for House Khodove in your father's absence."

Vhogare raised his voice to address his newly appointed Council. "There will be no master of laws. The Council as a whole shall perform that sacred duty. Serve well, and none of you will lack a seat at my side."

And with that, the king dismissed his coronation party.

The room emptied like a breath going out of the world.

Elias's heart surged as a foreign dignitary in strange armor disappeared into the crowd at the far end of the great hall, and did not return.

THE GRAVE

VHOGARE

The world hummed with lethal silence as Vhogare stepped from the dais and strode down the center aisle. Elias did not get in his way.

Eyes followed him like daggers as he pushed the heavy doors open with far too much force. They boomed against the walls as he took his leave from the throne room. He did not stop until he reached the garden.

Forsaking the pristine, manicured flower beds, Vhogare made straight for the rose bushes. Past the vibrant red, yellow, and white blooms, he found the twisting, climbing swathe of magnificent northern blue roses. Of all Queen Seonna's flowers, the dark sapphire beauties were her favorite. No one ever cut them. They wound around wrought iron trellises in fierce vines, with blood-red thorns sharper than daggers.

"I'm sorry, Mother," he whispered, wondering if the woman he'd never known would recognize his voice. "But I think you would understand."

How many times had he imagined he'd felt Seonna's presence in the garden, tending her roses? Vhogare wondered if his father was with her again, sitting somewhere watching her float between the blooming, picturesque rows. Were they happy together?

For a heartbeat, Vhogare squinted, trying to peer through the veil separating the waking world from the resting one, attempting to see his parents the way he could see Milan. But the verdant space was empty around him. Silent, save the bees buzzing around the flowers.

Vhogare ran a thumb across a velvety indigo petal. He'd thought about it every day, how like Soleil the flowers were. Bold and restless, searching out any crack, any purchase where they might bloom and grow. But no blade ever cut them down.

Steeling himself, Vhogare picked an armful of the magnificent blue blooms. He didn't feel it when the thorns pierced his skin. Didn't wipe away the blood that ran down his fingers and wrists. Their lilac and clove scent drifted up to him, borne by a summer wind, and Vhogare's chest caved in. Fighting back scalding tears, he cradled the roses and marched to the chapel.

Harun and the attending holy servants looked up as he stormed into the room, but he was not too late. Soleil's silver coffin sat atop one of the many work tables cluttering the sanctuary. Jesse returned to his work; the cleric kept a sharp eye on Vhogare as he finished clasping armor around Einar's dead chest.

Vhogare's throat caught, but he did not bother asking the clerics to leave; they were busy preparing others to go into the good earth, and all the dead deserved their peace. Einar and Soleil, most of all.

Heaving a shuddering sigh, he turned away from Harun and Einar and placed the roses atop Soleil's ornate coffin. "I'd planned to give you these when we were married"—his voice cracked—"but this will have to do."

Drops of his blood speckled the dark petals. It wasn't good enough, would never be good enough. But he had nothing to honor her with but pain.

The rich scent of incense clung to Vhogare's nose as he pulled up a wooden work chair to sit with Soleil one last time. He rested his head against the cold silver of her coffin, wishing the smiths had the time to cast her likeness into the sarcophagus so he could see her face. As it stood, he only had her memory to cling to.

"We would've been wed here, you know," he whispered, glancing up at the beautiful sanctuary, the bright flames and shimmering gold work arching across the black marble ceiling like living fire. "Assuming we didn't elope, of course."

For a heartbeat, he found himself waiting for her answer. Listening for the sound of her laugh as if she could reply.

But the chapel was silent aside from the clerics working, and Vhogare huffed a trembling sigh. "Your time as our royal historian would've been the stuff of legends. All those dreams." Vhogare shook his head. "I cannot accept that they are gone—that you are gone."

He would never marry her, never throw the elaborate festivals she'd pestered him about. Never hold her in his arms again, celebrate their child's first sparring lesson, or go for long summer rides through the rolling wheat fields to the north. He would never again make love to Soleil beneath the stars. She was so excited to be a mother, but their lives had gone up in smoke before they could even begin.

They'd had everything, had been so, so close, and he'd given her nothing but death.

He lifted his head, inhaling the sweet smoke of the candles. The chapel had always brought him such peace; the Ark's eternal flame lit up the night, a blaze of warmth that carried all life—the Fire that burned against the nothing, against the dark.

But Vhogare had gone from lying in bed with his love to sitting alone on a throne, and there was no light left in the world for him.

Vhogare leaned back in his chair and stared at the lovely blue roses.

"I will tear Erembour's heart out of his chest for what he did to you," he promised her, "and then I will give the gift back to the Ark and Invar as you asked. They can find a new horseman, and I will see you again when my work is done."

It would be enough if he were allowed so much as one more glance of his love in the afterlife. One more heartbeat spent in her arms. She was an ever-present ache in his chest, and he missed her the way the moon missed the sun when the whole world stood between them.

Vhogare rose to his feet. Placing a hand over the thorned roses, he pressed a kiss to the cold silver where Soleil's brow should have been and took his leave. His heart shattered as he walked away that final time and left her alone on the cold stone table of death. Tears cut down his face, his jaw quivering, as he strode through the castle yard, stepping over stones he'd thrown outward into the mud during his transformation.

Her loss tore the life out of his chest, but Soleil and their child rested in the Ark's arms, held tight in the vast warmth of the light above them. And they were far safer than he could ever keep them while he waged war.

THE SHIELD

ELIAS

S pymaster. Two days ago, his father held the title, and now it had been forced prematurely into his hands. And not only that, but he was a royal advisor as well. Commander of all the king's armies, all the Crown's forces. *Right Hand of the Dragon.*

That's how the world would know him when this madness was done. Einar had built a good name for their house, and now it would swim in blood. Every choice Elias had ever made paled in comparison to what he'd done when he suggested Vhogare take the gift from Erembour and use it as a sword. It could not have fallen into worse hands.

Elias summoned every ounce of his restraint to sit at the first council meeting while waiting for Vhogare to speak. The king sat at the head of the cobbled-together table in a room covered in burn scars. Elias's friend was gone; not a spark remained of the boy he'd grown up with. Only a hollow shell with Vhogare's face remained. There was nothing beneath the man's grieving facade that Elias knew or recognized.

Elias's stomach turned, and he closed his hand into a fist on the table. Desolation lay ahead of them, and he'd sent them blazing toward it.

Vhogare spun Soleil's silver dragon in his fingers as he waited for them to assemble and settle. Above them, the broken roof stood open to the elements, and stars burned bright in the dark canvas of the sky. Elias wondered if those stars had seen what happened in this room. If they'd borne witness as Vhogare turned lives to ash and dust.

As he sat in his high-backed chair, taking stock of the king's new councilors, even the stones seemed to shriek up at Elias that this was wrong. But he held his breath. Tried not to look at the threshold where his father had died. Just that morning, Elias buried the man, and already he sat his first council in Einar's place. Castle staff still wept in the hallways. Pages, squires, and serving girls were all exhausted and burdened with sorrow.

Soleil's parents, Raul and Myrline, had abandoned all their wealth and holdings and fled to the north in the night. Elias had no doubt they carried word of the dragon king to the Nivalian queen. Gelida was from an old branch of House Corveau, and would not take kindly to the news of Soleil's murder. Raul and Myrline had carried their daughter's coffin with them, denying Vhogare even her grave, and their strongest vassal house was now well out of reach of the dragon's retribution.

But a dying world allowed no time to mourn. Vhogare made no move to give House Corveau's castle to another family name. Their new king had spent the entire night in the library drawing up war plans.

Beside Elias, Alastair shifted, uncomfortable in the narrow, stiff chair. Banan was absent; Vhogare had sent him to number the castle's remaining soldiers. Maura, however, had seated herself across from Elias on the king's left. The smile she gave him had all the sweetness of poisoned fruit.

A small Council, indeed.

Vhogare met each of their eyes in turn. "These last three days have been far from easy," he began with gravity, "and we have suffered many losses. I am not ignorant of my hand in them."

Down the table, gray-haired Wyle straightened in his chair.

"You know my guilt," the king continued. "There is no hiding my dragon. Thus, it is only right that you understand why I am doing this. What we will all face, together, and why we must be strong."

Elias reigned in his shock. Alastair, Wyle, and Maura were tight-lipped, even if the latter two were not trustworthy. No wonder Banan was uninvited. The vile bastard followed orders without question, but he was a braggart on his best days, a whoremonger on his worst. Elias had no doubt that Vhogare sent him on his fool's errand due to such a lack of morals. The king wanted the landed knight close, yet uninformed.

"We are part of a celestial game," Vhogare told them. "You have heard of the Ark. And Invar, His heart. One of Invar's horsemen has betrayed him. Erembour, the rogue celestial, gave me this beast and vowed to return with a reaping blade in hand."

Maura gaped at the king, her eyes wide as saucers, all her vicious pretense melted away.

"I took this gift to use as a weapon against him," Vhogare said, no doubt hoping they would understand the depth of what had happened. "There is no surety about when Erembour will strike, but he makes ready as we speak. It is my life's work to prepare for that war and protect the garden of our kingdom from his fire."

Vhogare spread his hands on the bare council table. "In the presence of each of you, my royal Council, I vow to be fair during my reign. I will strengthen our defenses, shore up our weaknesses, and protect our land. I will be open-handed with you and our faithful people, so long as they side with me to protect our beloved world. But my enemies will know only fire."

Vhogare met Elias's eye as if searching for confirmation he'd said the right words. Elias managed a terse nod, but it seemed enough.

"Elias," the king rumbled, "send word to each of our sister countries, explaining our circumstances and asking them to rally to our cause."

They will never believe us. Vhogare had insulted them by not inviting them to his hasty coronation. Asking for immediate martial aid would make matters far worse. "And if they refuse?"

"Then we will assemble them under our banners nonetheless."

Behind Elias, Aadriek shifted, standing guard by the door.

"My father was a man of relative peace," Vhogare plowed on, failing to notice the silent dissent in his focused state. "But it is a king's job to protect. Our standing army has withered over the years, and our armory leaves much to be desired. Instruct Banan to put out a call: All the high families must assemble their soldiers. He answers to you, Elias, and don't let him forget it."

At Elias's side, Alastair flashed a bitter smirk.

"Wyle and Maura, speak with the builders."

The new mistress of gold snapped her jaw shut and straightened, recovering with impressive poise.

Vhogare did not so much as offer her a kind look to ease her nerves. "You have a fortnight to assemble the most skilled amongst them in my royal hall. I have a need for certain . . . machinery . . . for the castle walls."

"What sort of machinery, Your Majesty?" Maura inquired, curiosity curling through her smoky voice.

"Dragonbolts."

Elias slid his gaze to the king.

"They have not been built in many years," Wyle cautioned.

"They are the only long-range weaponry we have against a creature like Erembour." Vhogare retrieved a parchment from the inside pocket of his doublet and unfurled it on the table, revealing diagrams of an ancient design. "I had hoped Soleil would be here to oversee their development and planning—"

The king's voice broke, but he cleared his throat and soldiered on. "But I have stripped the kingdom of one of its greatest minds, a woman set to make history. Soleil would have been our head historian and mistress of laws, looking over the city and so much more. Without her, the task now falls to me. We will line our battlements with machines of war. It is my hope that the celestial bleeds."

Perhaps the piercing shafts would strike clean through Erembour on his return. Perhaps they would not. The king did not seem satisfied, regardless. Vhogare stood and laid his hands on the table. "There is much work to be done. This kingdom is not merely worth saving—it is worth giving our all, and I will stop at nothing until I see this war won."

A pit hollowed out in Elias's stomach. The second the council meeting ended, Alastair's brother disappeared. Spymaster or not, Elias did not follow him. There was no doubt in his mind that Aadriek meant to send word to his wife and his and Alastair's sister in Maria. The western country's royal court needed to be aware of Vhogare's immediate threat of war. Perhaps an early word could spare some lives.

Give Maria whatever chance they can get. But if Aadriek's letters of warning to his home country failed, Elias could not defend him, no matter how much he may wish. *A hand on the rudder,* he reminded himself, *is worth a hand on the sword.*

With the council emptied and Vhogare retired alone to his apartments in the west wing, Elias took the opportunity to search out his house cleric. With Einar's burial preparations complete, he found Jesse in his study, surrounded by scrolls and instruments. Dust and old parchment lent the royal library a calm, pleasant atmosphere, and Elias wished he had spent more time amongst its shelves.

"Congratulations on your new station," Jesse offered, clasping Elias's hand in his leathery palms, the gesture heavy with sorrow and support. Shutting the door behind Elias, he waved at the nearest chair. "Your father would be proud."

"He would not."

The holy man stopped sorting through his work to glance up at that. Red rimmed his brown eyes, and his lined face was weary from mourning.

"I came to thank you for what you did for my wife and for delivering my child."

"We all took risks that day."

"Some brought forth life."

"Ah." Jesse stood and leaned against his desk. "New life is an honor. But looking after it, safeguarding it, that is a tricky business. And it is treacherous ground you walk, now, Right Hand."

"That it is. And I require guidance." He explained their encounter with Erembour, and the man's eyes widened with every detail.

"So we are not alone, after all. . . ."

"I would have asked Soleil for her insight as well, had she lived." Anger rose in Elias's chest, and he forced himself to focus. "Tell me, are Erembour's tales of the horsemen true? Is any of this with Invar referenced in your holy scrolls?" Their world was old. Perhaps somewhere in its history was something that could help.

Jesse's gaze misted over. "Soleil is deeply missed. Perhaps I can find something in the books she left on her desk." The old man held up a finger and disappeared amidst his dusty shelves, returning with an ancient scroll that looked fit to crumble in his hands. "It is vague, but this references similar star-walkers. The original work is written in a dead language, but she translated that there were three of them. And they all warned we were bought with a price. I am not sure that is enough."

Invar's price. "It is more than enough. Do they mention any others? A court of these celestials?"

"No, only that a sun-eyed man came sometime later searching for gold. Some say there was a woman with him." The cleric peered at the weathered runes. "With skin like amethyst and hair the color of blood. But no celestial has given a human a gift before our king's, at least not as our histories have recorded."

Depthless dread laced through Elias as he studied the accompanying illustration. "What have we done. . . ."

"From what I understand, this Invar is a shield for our world," his father's friend gathered, peering up at Elias. "And Erembour wishes to remove us from the board. Lighten his burden."

"Vhogare is the only one strong enough to prevent that, now. Without him, we have no hope of contending against that creature."

"You are wrong. Strength has no discernment, no measure of morality. No requirement of virtue." Jesse rolled the parchment with the utmost care. "It is the minimum requirement to overcome, in order to do good or do evil. The question is not who is strong enough, but who is wise enough to consider what comes after."

After. With Erembour defeated and Invar still bleeding.

"Royal spymaster is a bloody office, yes. But your father was a shield to this realm. To the known world." The cleric straightened, his gaze falling on the steel sigil pinned against Elias's chest. "You carry that shield now, in his absence. For our kingdom, I trust you will do well with it."

"And it is your opinion I should raise it?" Einar may have been the king's most trusted advisor, but this man had been the spymaster's north star.

Jesse heaved a weathered sigh. "If you do, it is everything and nothing. The first step and the last stand." He raised his whiskered chin. "All you can do is take it."

"My father's house cannot fall." Elias straightened under that crushing weight. "I was born into this office."

"Perhaps, for such a time as this." The holy man laid a heartening hand on his shoulder. "Invar would not bleed for us in vain. Whom shall you fear, with the Fire at your back?"

Elias recognized the words from battle, a call to arms for when clerics locked wrists with soldiers marching to war. "Whom shall we fear."

His advisor's charge clung to him long after he left the man's study, digging deep and sinking steel teeth into his soul. Still reeling, Elias found his Second speaking with Banan, gathering details about the state of the king's standing army.

"Commander," he interrupted, addressing Banan in a tone that brooked no argument. "Speak with the smiths regarding our armory. All the men on the continent will make no difference without swords."

Banan opened his mouth to object, but Elias laid a hand on his sword, angling himself so the steel pin denoting him the king's Right Hand caught the light. "Maura will dispense your coin."

With a glare, the lickspittle dismissed himself and left Elias and Alastair to confer in private.

"I am honored to have you as my Second," Elias began. "There is no one else I'd rather have at my side."

Alastair patted the axe slung across his back. "On my iron, I will not fail you."

"I know." And he had never been more grateful for it. "But your brother needs to be careful. If Aadriek's warnings to Maria fail, I cannot save him."

"Why do you think I was here distracting that bastard?" his Second smirked.

Elias smiled at his friend's wisdom. "The smiths have logistical concerns. Simple math should keep him busy for a while." Alastair chuckled, and Elias carried on. "About what you said in the kitchens—"

"I meant every word."

Elias gestured for the commander to follow and wound his way up the east wing to Einar's solar. Sitting behind his father's desk felt like a dream.

A dream that had boiled into a nightmare.

Einar's solar still smelled like cedar and pipe smoke. Old leather books littered the desk, and ink had long dried on several letters. Shoving down his grief, Elias took his father's dark steel dagger from the drawer. The inlaid grip was worn and smooth against his skin as he held the pearl-inlaid hilt in his fist. Alastair sat down in the chair across from him. The warrior did not so much as flinch at the sight of the blade.

"You have served the royal house for five good years. And in that time, you have been there for every battle, every trial. You never failed the old king, nor my father. I trust you with my life." Elias took a bracing breath. "What I am about to ask, I ask with every ounce of solemnity and sincerity I can offer. But I need you to swear that you will never speak a word of our conversation to anyone but me."

Alastair unslung his war axe and stood it before him. With the end of the weapon braced on the stone floor, the Marian warrior laid both tattooed hands overtop the iron blade. "I swear on the salt in my blood and the iron of my soul. I will keep your confidence, Right Hand."

"You and I are alone in this." Elias leaned forward, his elbows creaking on the cedar desk. "I cannot promise safety."

"I do not wish for safety. I wish for sanity and the survival of my people."

"As do I." He sank his father's dagger into the wood. "Every word Vhogare said in the council room is true. We play a celestial game, and it is us for the world. Us against the stars."

"So it is the monster that we know?"

"Aye." Guilt and dread coiled their icy fists around Elias's throat. "Until a better option comes into play."

Alastair nodded. Their odds only tempered the unshakeable hope in his eyes.

"Stand by me," Elias asked, "as I will stand by you. Whatever we must do, we will not be alone against them both."

Yanking the dagger free, he drew his father's blade across the old scar on his right palm and held his bloody hand out to Alastair. Somehow, every drop felt heavier. Far more real.

Alastair took the blade with a solemn oath and drew it across his palm as well. "Blood of my blood in death and in life," the warrior swore. "Brothers, in this and after."

"Blood of my blood in death and in life." Elias clasped Alastair's bleeding hand. "Brothers, in this and after."

———— ✴ ————

Joanna started when Elias entered their suite. Liora rested, sleeping against her chest. He shook his head, and her fist eased around the letter opener in her white-knuckled grip. "Here," he said and offered her Einar's ornate heirloom dagger. "It will serve you far better."

Though if Vhogare's healed scars were any indication, not well enough. As the blade transferred hands, the engraved steel caught the light of her bedside candle, and the inscription flashed. *Shields before swords.* Elias's throat burned as he pressed a kiss to her hair. "Something for you to remember him by."

Tears welled in Joanna's eyes as she accepted his gift. "Thank you. I will use it well."

Once, Elias had dreamed of succeeding his father and receiving Yigael and the dagger to thunderous applause. How many nights had he dreamt of proudly bearing that steel pin on his chest? Taking his esteemed place on the old king's Council, or Milan's. In his wildest aspirations, Einar had cheered for him and clasped his shoulders as he descended the dais. Put Yigael in his hand and charged him to carry on the legacy of their great house. Joanna had kissed and held him; he had given her children and a castle and the world.

But there was no joy on his wife's face as he sat down on their bed. No congratulations on her lips as he lay Yigael across his knees. Instead, his lionhearted woman gifted him a soft smile and patted her free hand on the sheets in invitation. Elias laid down at her side and pressed his bloody, bandaged palm against the sword on his chest.

Together, they gazed at the ceiling, and for a while, he was content just to listen to her breathe—to hear the life flowing in and out of her chest. The last few days weighed like an anchor around his soul, but Joanna and Liora were alive, and that was enough.

"You can rest for now," Joanna whispered, reaching over to brush the hair off his brow. "Sometimes we must be carried so we can carry." Unyielding determination cut through her words. "I can take the first watch."

He was exhausted, but the sun had gone down, and the moon silhouetted Vhogare's dragon against the night sky, already on patrol. "Absolutely not."

Leaning onto an elbow, Elias held Liora's tiny fist, cherishing the whistle of her breath. His watch had just begun.

"She's a fighter already," he managed, but the crack in his voice gave him away.

Joanna's piercing green eyes seared into him, fierce and indomitable as a forest in the face of a storm. "No matter what happens, I know why you did this," she whispered, bracing her palm against his cheek. "Even if the world does not."

He took her hand and pressed a kiss to her scarred knuckles.

Joanna held his gaze, unafraid. "And our daughter will know you are a hero."

Tears stung his eyes. *Liora.* His little light.

Sitting up against the headboard, Elias settled in and turned his heart to stone.

―――✦――――

TZADDIK

Three days after Erembour's visit, Liora was born, and Vhogare ascended the throne. And the world bled.

The Fire of Judgment set down his pen and stood from his desk in Invar's Hall of Time, sword arm aching for a fight.

"Get ready, Brother," Tzaddik whispered into the bleeding cosmos, praying the bastard would hear it, wherever he'd gone. "The sand in your hourglass has begun."

Elias and Vhogare's Story Continues in
The Chaos Queen

MEET THE NEXT GIFT BEARER

ANDRA

An Excerpt From
The Chaos Queen

Book Two In
The Anchor Kingdom Trilogy

Part Of
The Phoenix Universe
By Lizabeth Phoenix

"Would you stop Vhogare, if you could?" her rescuer asked as he turned to face her, caution in his rough voice.

"I would give anything." Anything to get Marina back. . . .

The stranger's brows knit together. "You're willing to face such odds? Even injured?"

She cupped her bleeding side and felt the thick, slick heat running through her fingers, but it would heal. Three years she'd spent commanding the underground rebellion against the ruthless dragon king, desperate enough to believe that with enough strength behind her, she could take down the beast. Such risk did not come *without pain. How many wounds had her brother survived in battles before she buried him?*

Andra snarled at the throbbing ache, biting back her tears, and looked up at the stranger. "I will live."

"I—" the man rasped, glancing around. There was no one to hear but the dead. He raised a hand, and bright lights danced up his arm, baubles of fire flowing beneath his skin and armor. "If you are willing, I can help you."

"You're a celestial," Andra breathed. She began to shake. "Are you the one who made the king the dragon?"

Vhogare had no shame spreading the news of the rogue celestial returning to reap the earth; the king must've hoped his gift would be a weapon against Erembour, but he'd become such a monster that no kingdom would come to his aid.

The creature in front of her shook his head. "My brother. Erembour and I are at war. I wish to keep you alive."

"Why me?"

"Because your fire is tempered with justice, his with fear."

She held the celestial's gaze. Compassion met her, edged by sharpest steel. What was she willing to risk to bring Marina home? How much would she give to honor her brother's memory, and save what was left of her family? Was it worth it to become the thing she hated if it meant she could rid their world of Vhogare's scourge?

But she'd waged a war for this kingdom, and nothing short of the king's death would end it. Only fire could fight fire, and she'd named herself the Red Wing years ago just to spit in his face. Made herself the antithesis of the dragon's dark reign.

"Make me what Vhogare is, so I can end him for this."

*PLEASE NOTE THIS EXCERPT IS FROM AN UNEDITED DRAFT AND IS SUBJECT TO CHANGE.

JOIN THE PHOENIX UNIVERSE AT

www.lizabethphoenix.com

TO FOLLOW ANDRA'S JOURNEY

DRAGON SCALE

VHOGARE

 ELIAS & KANE

HOUSE MAEKYR

Ulrich, *Anchora's Sword* & Seonna Maekyr

|

Milan Maekyr — Vhogare Maekyr, *The Dragon King*

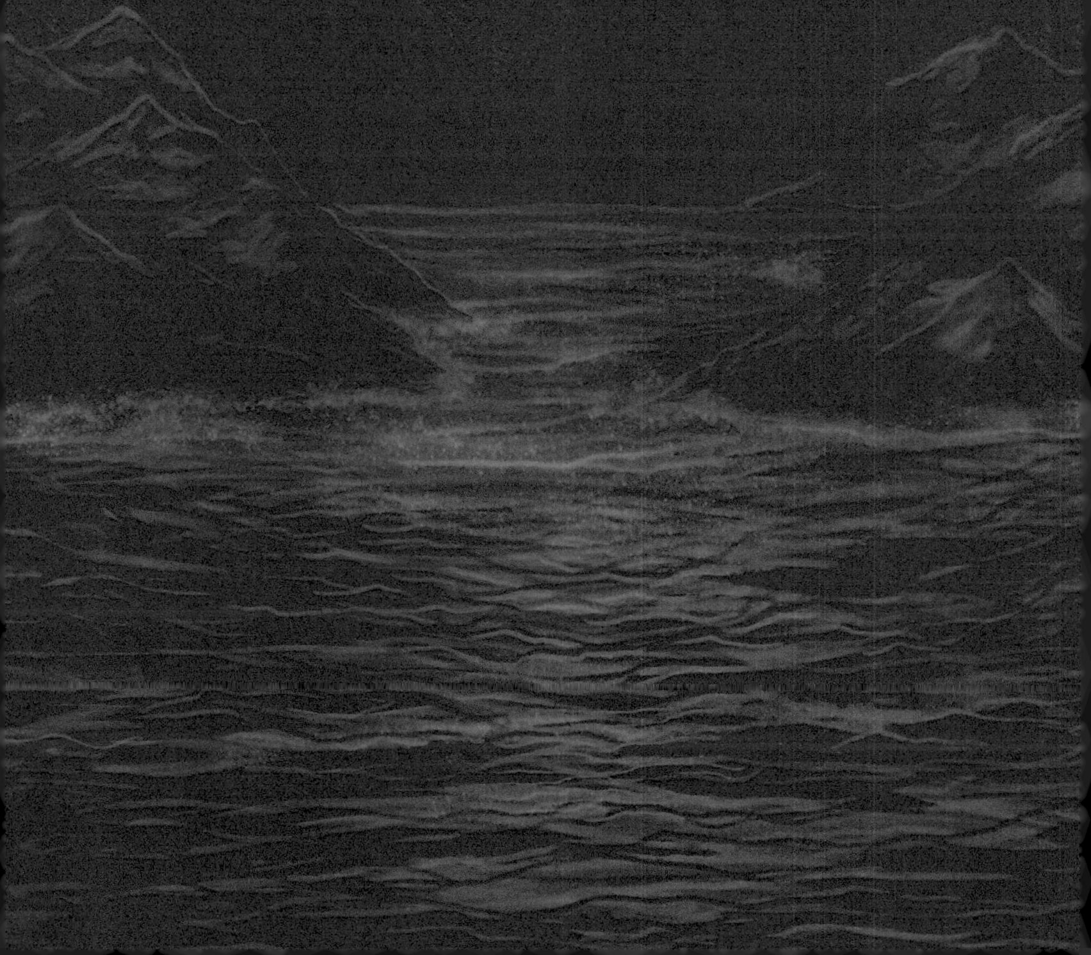

House Aldernari

Einar, *Right Hand of the Sword* & Aethena Aldernari

|

Elias Aldernari, *Right Hand of the Dragon*

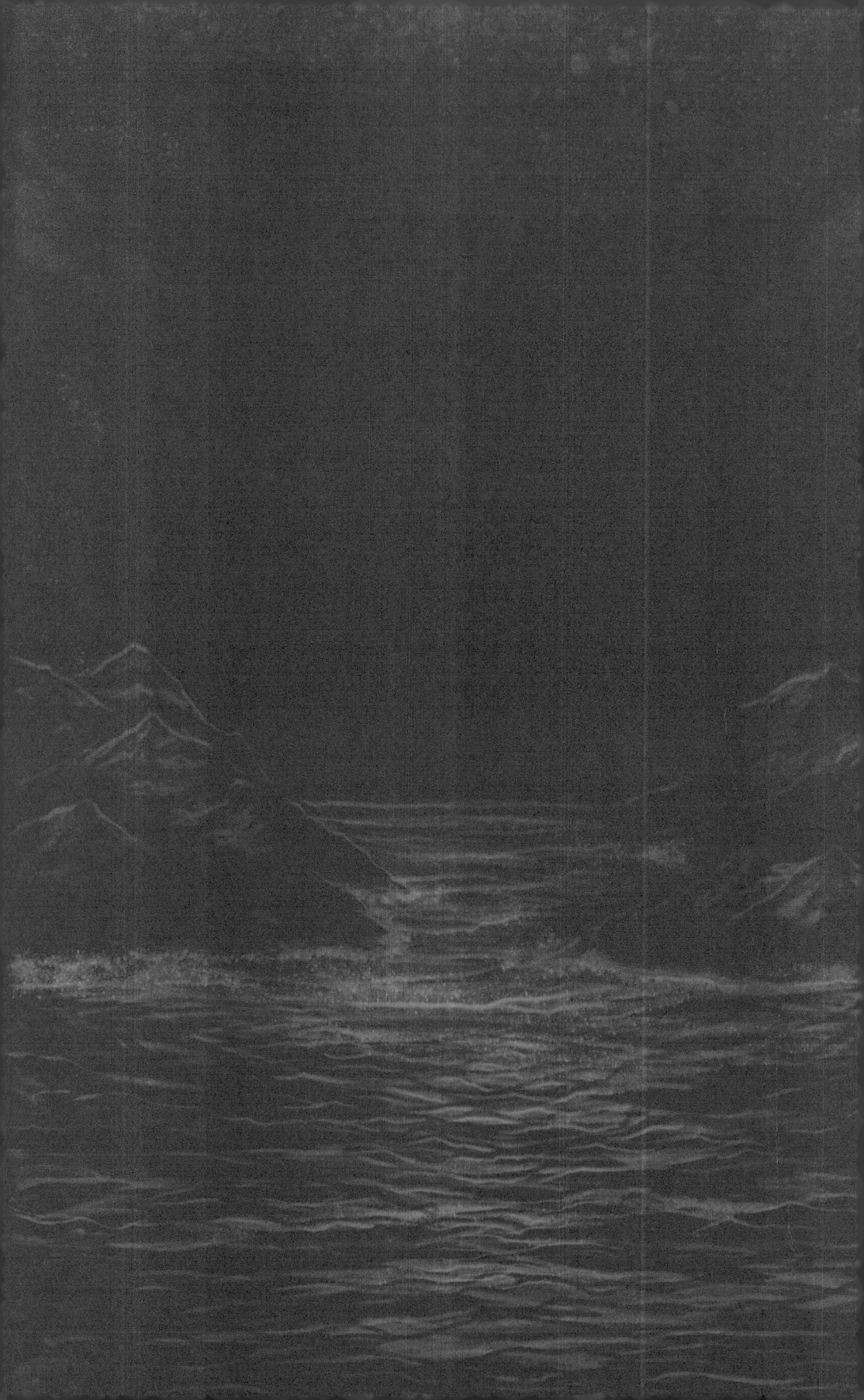

HOUSE CORVEAU

Raul & Myrline Corveau

|

Corbyn Corveau — Soleil Corveau, *Royal Historian*

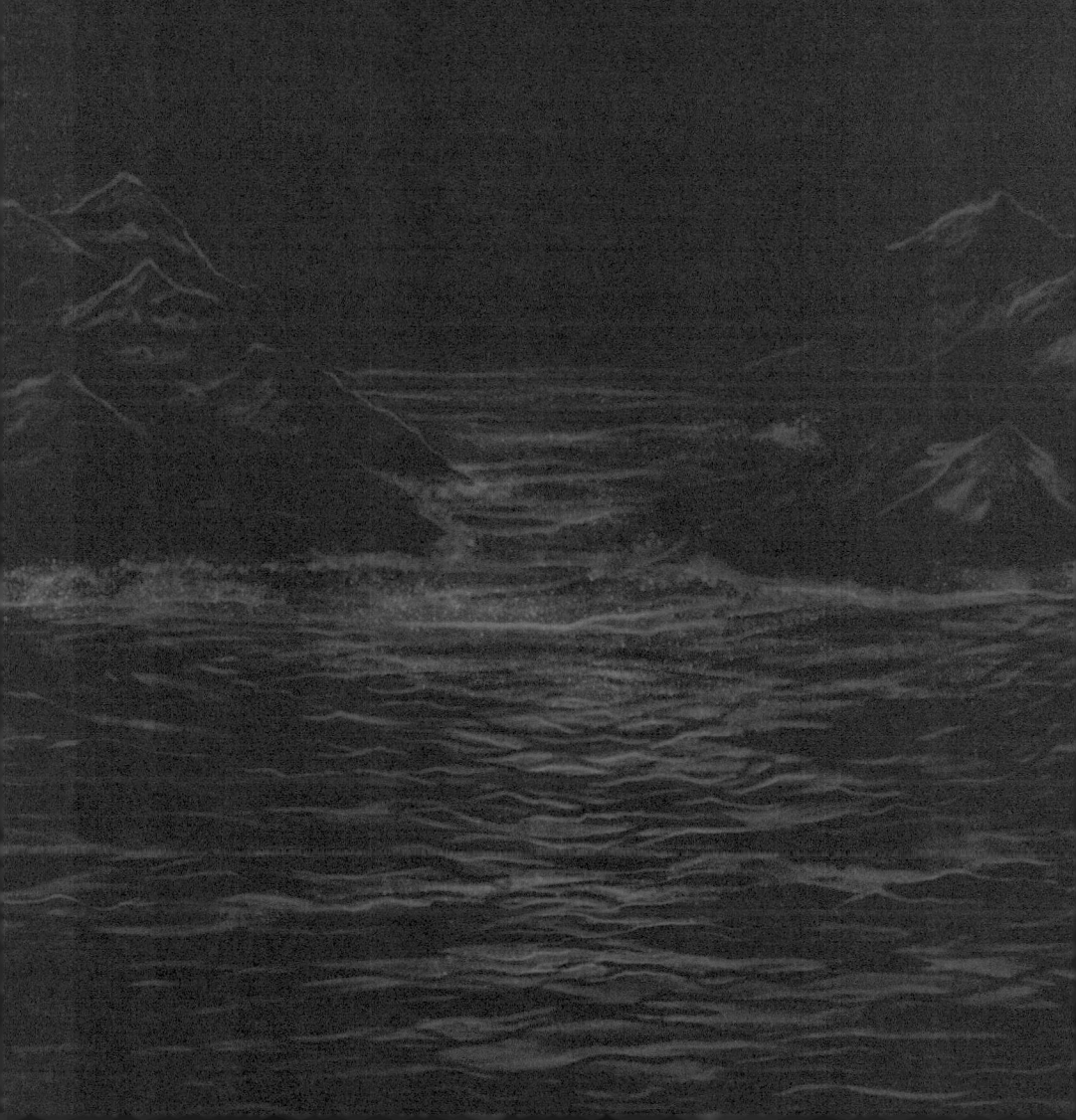

MORE FOR YOU

Need more of The Phoenix Universe? While the next book cooks, a whole world awaits you at www.lizabethphoenix.com.

On the website, you'll find:

- **An exclusive Q&A with the author**
- ***The Gifted King* merchandise**
- **Playlists & ambiences**
- **World lore**
- **A fan wiki**
- **And more!**

If you want to help others discover this saga, consider leaving a review wherever you purchased this book. As a self-published author, Lizabeth appreciates every single review her readers leave to help others know if they'll love this chaotic world.

Want first notice of new publications? Lizabeth sends out regular publishing and lore news. Visit www.lizabethphoenix.com to join the email list and never miss an update.

AUTHOR'S NOTE

ON VHOGARE

Vhogare is not an easy character to read, and he is not an easy character to write. As I crafted his story, I spent countless hours researching corruption arcs, consulting sensitivity readers, and educating myself to write this narrative properly. It may not be perfect, but my goal for Vhogare was to write a true villain origin story. Not a "shadow daddy" (no shade to the trope, I enjoy it), not an anti-hero, not an excusable, forgivable "meh" morally gray bad guy, but a *villain*. You have my word this trilogy—and this saga—will not romanticize him, but instead, the characters and the world around him and outside of his POV will treat him like the monster he is. This saga is complex, but one thing will always be true: Vhogare chose wrong, and he is held accountable.

ACKNOWLEDGMENTS

To the Fire that burns against the dark, thank You for stories that push our experience of existence to the limits, and for everything out there that we don't know about. If I ever meet a real celestial, I know exactly what to say. And *not* say.

Sends Vhogare a SEVERE side-eye

An eternity of gratitude to my glorious, patient, sweet family, for helping me hone these ideas into the sharpest blade, and for listening to my never-ending rambles and info dumps and mending all the holes in my plot. Thank you for believing in me and supporting me as I work on this dream. You introduced me to fandoms. You make my life rich with inspiration. You are the reason I write. You also deal with me shamelessly plugging my characters into every little conversation. And for all of that, I am eternally grateful.

To George R. R. Martin, Hidetaka Miyazaki and the team at FromSoftware, Inc., and Amy Hennig, thank you. Thank you for *A Song of Ice and Fire, Elden Ring,* and *Uncharted.* Emilia Clarke and Nolan North, thank you for bringing my favorite characters to life. Fandoms are everything, and I am honored to be a part of these. *Bloodborne* gets a special mention, as well.

"Dracarys." "We fight, sword and fang." "Sic Parvis Magna." And may we find our worth in the waking world.

Special thanks to Jenna Moreci and Angela J. Ford for taking the time to explain all the twists and turns of the publishing process. It's a minefield out here, and I appreciate you sharing the map.

To my phenomenal alpha readers, you saved my life with this book and helped me fix so many early story issues, thank you.

My critique partners, Kaelin, Tia, Hannah, and Samantha, your feedback in the earliest stages helped this book grow from a teeny tiny novella into a full-blown novel, thank you for your time and for helping me iron out Vhogare's earliest issues. He's a nightmare, but at least he makes (plot) sense.

To my fantastic beta readers, Thea, Zarah, Alba, Michelle, Valentina, Samantha K. and Samantha W., Elizabeth, M., Mireya, Justin, Rose, Kate, Caitlyn, Gabby, and Caroline, you are fantastic—the most wonderful beta readers I could have asked for—and thank you so much for taking the time to read this story. Your thoughts helped me polish it until it shone.

My editors, Jean McConnell and Aliyah Golden, and my sensitivity readers Kaelin Britt and Samantha Kassé, I'll never be able to thank you enough for not only improving this story beyond measure but also helping me improve my craft. You are shining stars in this industry and I appreciate you!

Thank you to the incredible artists who teamed up with me to bring Vhogare (and his dragon), Elias, and Soleil to life! Vishap.art and T. L. Combs did such a wonderful job and I am absolutely blown away by their creativity.

To all the parents who read this story early and gave me specific feedback on Joanna, Elias, and Soleil, *thank you.* I am the proud mother of one very fluffy and lovable feline fur baby named Sassy, and I do not have the depth of experience to do their story justice without you.

On that note, this story would not be what it is without any of you.

And to my readers, everyone who reads this tale of ruthless desperation, thank you! You make storytelling what it is, and I look forward to starting this saga with you. There's so much more in store for you.

ABOUT THE AUTHOR

 Lizabeth Phoenix is the woman in the corner of the room, neck-deep in coffee, face buried in her beloved MacBook. She's also hatching wild plots, dreaming up dragon names, and charting time-traveler visits. Her life's goal is to write morally midnight characters and battle-cry-worthy victories because light shines brightest in darkness.

When not writing or fighting the South Carolina heat, she spends hours immersed in the worlds of *A Song of Ice and Fire* and *Elden Ring.* One might say she's a little obsessed. . . .

Find out more about Lizabeth Phoenix and The Phoenix Universe by visiting her website and registering for the free newsletter at www.lizabethphoenix.com

Follow her @lizabethphoenix

VISIT WEBSITE | LEAVE A REVIEW | NEWSLETTER

ALSO BY LIZABETH PHOENIX

The Devourer's Oath

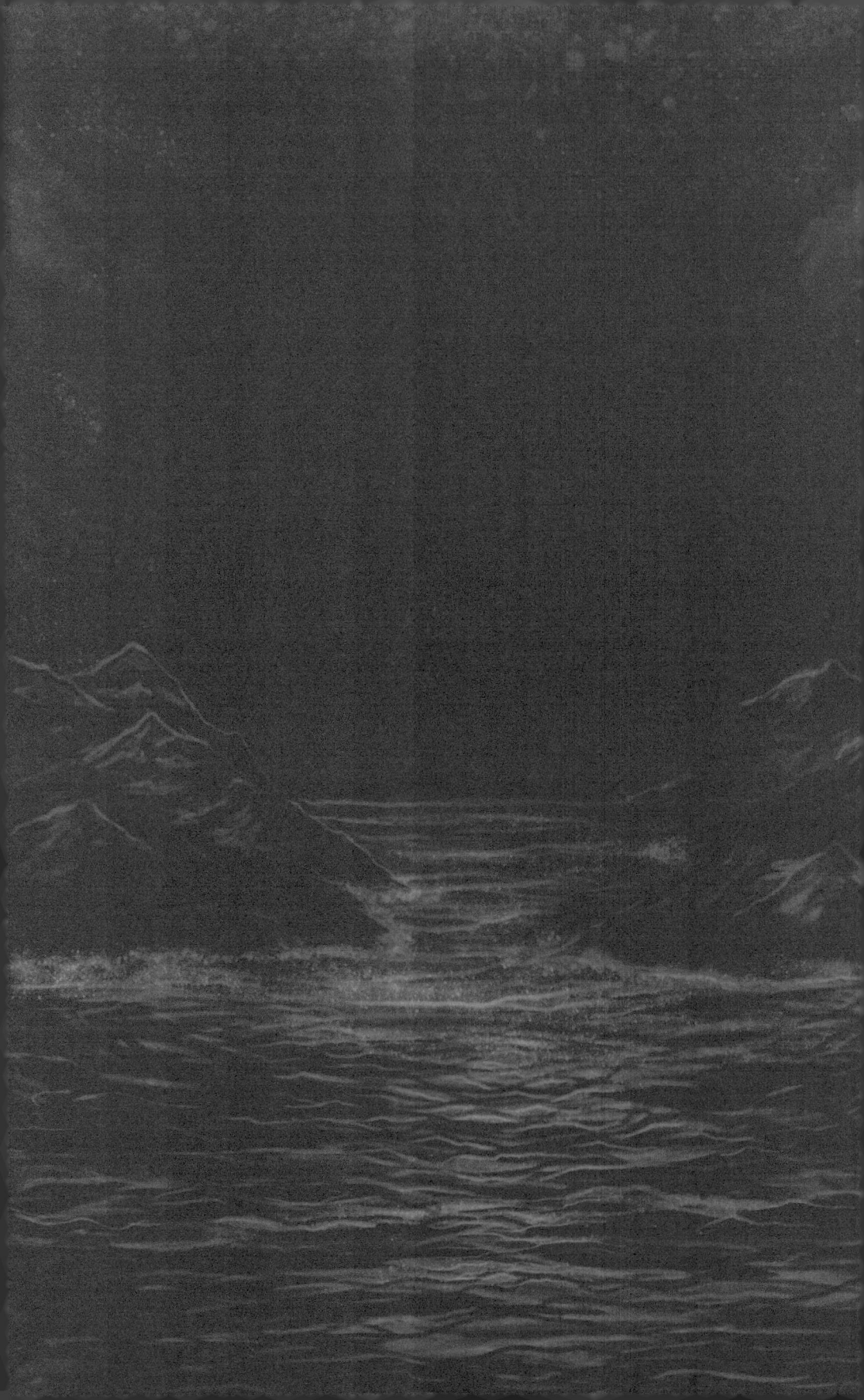

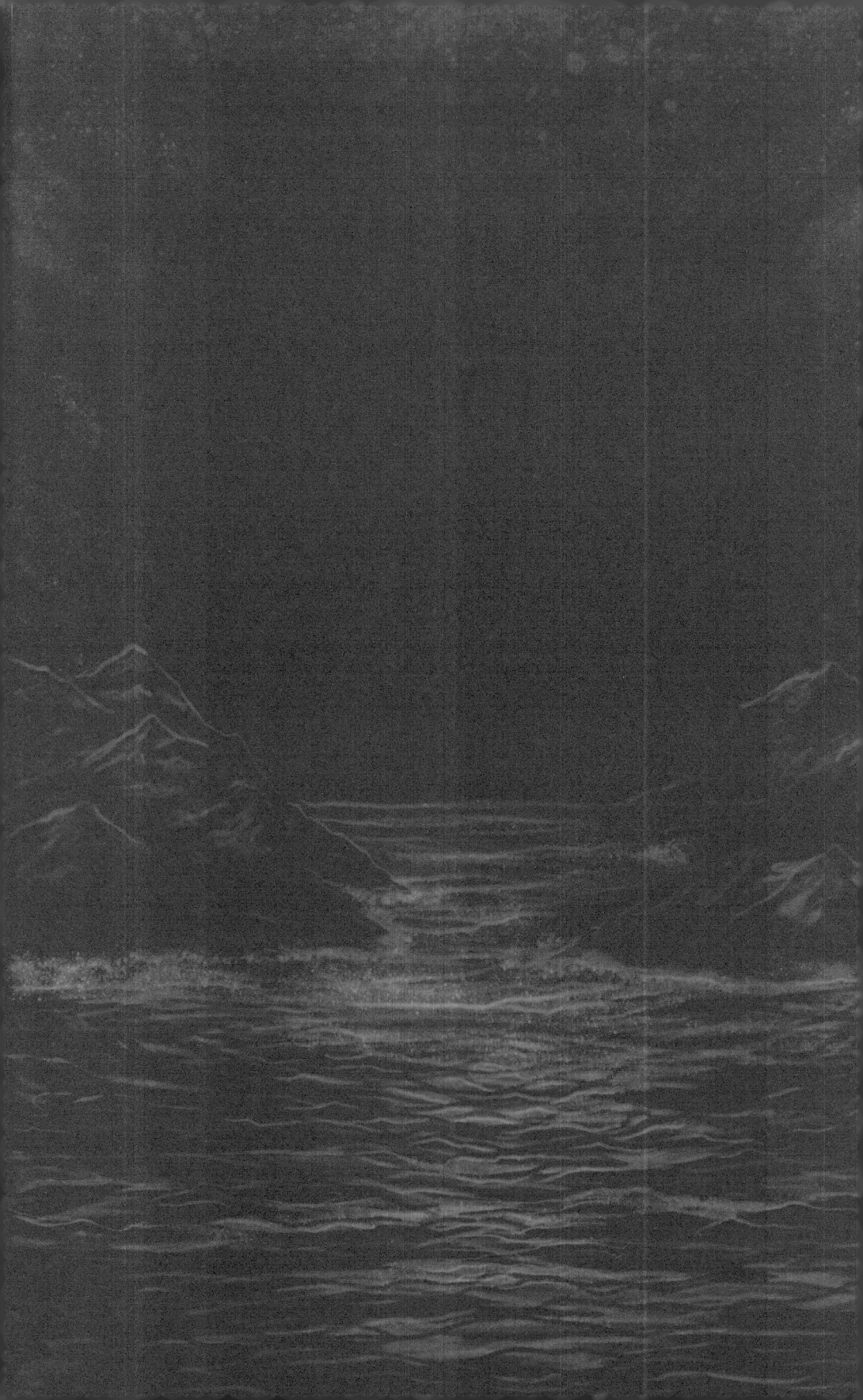

www.ingramcontent.com/pod-product-compliance
Lightning Source LLC
Chambersburg PA
CBHW050154120726
47903CB00002B/616